The Art of the Hustle

The Art of the Hustle

This book is a work of fiction. Any names, characters, places, and events are a product of the author's imagination. Any resemblance to any person (alive or dead) or event is purely coincidental.

Published by Imperium Publishing

Vancouver, BC, Canada

ISBN PAPERBACK: 978-0-9880487-0-6

Printed in Canada

Hustle

To make strenuous efforts to succeed, especially in obtaining money and business.

Characterized by a particular energetic drive, passion, or determination.

To use energetic and aggressive means to promote or sell.

To use force and other tactics to advance to a better position.

Also by Edward Mullen

The Art of the Hustle 2

Destiny and Free Will

The Secret Manuscript

Prodigy

Prodigy Eternal

Prodigy Returns

Eden

I am Rome

Zero

The Rider

Africa

Prologue

If someone had told me when I was seventeen that I would be where I am today, I would not have believed them. I'm not sure how long this feeling will last, but right now, I feel like I'm on top of the world. This is the culmination of a long and arduous journey. Everything I am and everything I have achieved seemed so impossible at one point in my life. I didn't have a trust fund, I'm not from a prestigious part of town, and my family didn't have any connections. I made it to where I am purely based on hustle.

***

"They're ready for you, Mr. Morrison."

"Thank you," I said, as I peeled myself off the plush leather couch.

I followed a production assistant down a long corridor and into the studio. When I entered the studio, I was instructed to take a seat. One perky assistant clipped a microphone on me while another one touched up my makeup.

"Are you ready?" the hostess asked.

"Yes," I said, then I took a deep breath.

"Roll cameras in three, two..."

The hostess looked into the camera, which was just beyond my right shoulder, and began to speak. "Hi, I'm Mikayla Martens for In the World of Finance. Thank you for tuning in with us this week.

You can find our next guest gracing the cover of this month's issue of Force Magazine. He is a self-made billionaire and is the President, CEO, and founder of Unity Inc. Remarkably, Mr. Morrison accomplished all this before his 30th birthday.

Mr. Morrison, thank you so much for being with us today."

"It's my pleasure, thank you for having me."

"Congratulations on all your success and making the cover of this month's Force Magazine."

"I appreciate that, thank you."

"I found this article about you fascinating. Is it true you were nearly homeless at one point in your life?"

"Yes, that's right. It was a very precarious time in my life. That was just over ten years ago."

"That must have been a trying ordeal to go through at such a young age."

"It was. I remember feeling as if I were teetering over the edge of a cliff, holding onto a small branch for survival and unable to get a foothold. I was physically drained and all alone. Left to the physical laws of the universe, I would have inevitably fallen - either the branch would have given way or I would have fatigued. I was at that point... I mean down to the last second, where I was facing imminent defeat... then something amazing happened. I reached out my hand in a desperate act of blind faith and somebody grabbed onto it and pulled me out of that situation. I was still not out of the woods so-to-speak, but I was lucky to have at least avoided an early demise."

"That's incredible. So from that point, you turned your life around and now you are a multi-billionaire."

"Yes, but it wasn't easy."

"I'm sure it wasn't. You mentioned the term luck. How much of a role has luck played in your life?"

"That's a great question. I don't think too many people would deny luck plays an important part in the lives of successful people, but I like to think people can create their own luck. I also think I have a unique ability to see the value in something. What may appear to be junk to some, may actually be something of great value."

"Can you give an example of that?"

"Okay, I can give you a trivial example. One time I was playing poker with some friends. It was down to three players at the table and I was the current chip leader. The cards were dealt and I ended up getting 10/6 off-suit. Now, if you don't know anything about poker, 10/6 off-suit is typically a junky hand, most people would fold it immediately. For a moment, I contemplated folding as well, but I decided to play the hand just to see what opportunities may come from it. As it turned out, I got lucky and took out all the remaining players at the table to win the game. Some may say I just got lucky, but I say I created that luck. After all, I was the one who played the hand, right? So, sometimes life is like that. We need to play those junky hands we are dealt once in a while, and they may create an opportunity that would otherwise not exist."

"That's interesting. I like your example because you are not saying 10/6 is always a good hand, but if the timing is right and you have the courage to play it, sometimes you can get lucky."

"Exactly. I put myself into the situation giving luck an opportunity to affect me. Had I just played it safe on the sidelines, the luck may not have entered my life. Even the most mundane moments can provide you with a life altering lesson, it's up to you to recognize those moments and apply them appropriately."

"So I gather there have been many situations in your life that were like this card game?"

"Yes, a lot. In fact, there have been too many to count."

"Can you give us another example?"

"Actually, my investing strategy is based largely on a concept that I learned while I was waiting for the bus one morning when I was in college."

"Really? Most people waiting for the bus in the morning are trying desperately to stay awake, or they're kicking rocks to occupy their time. However, you are coming up with investment strategies."

"To be honest, that wasn't my intent. I was presented with a scenario that on the surface didn't appear to have much value, but I recognized its potential in a broader scope. I knew if I applied it in the right way, it could be a tremendous lesson."

"I can't wait to hear it."

"It's actually kind of a funny story. One morning, I was waiting for the bus to take me to school and I noticed this gorgeous girl heading in my direction. When she got about fifteen feet away, she noticed I was checking her out, which in turn affected her behaviour. It was like the spotlight was on her and she was trying to ramp up her sexiness. She puckered her lips, flipped her hair, and batted her eyes a few times. She was trying to be subtle, but her actions were actually quite transparent. However, since she was doing all that fancy stuff, she wasn't paying attention to where she was walking and she stepped in this huge pile of dog crap. It was hilarious to me, but obviously she was completely humiliated. She hobbled away quickly with her head down, dragging her shoe, trying to scrape it off. It was great. So the lesson I took from that was - no matter how hot you are, you can always step in some crap if you are not focused."

"Those are some very important words to live by, presented to you by the financial prodigy himself, Mr. Trevor Morrison. We are going to take a quick break, but when we return, we will find out when all of his success began...."

PART I

Rags

Chapter One

I checked the time on my phone; I still had to wait another fifteen minutes until lunch. I had been sitting through this stupid ceremony for the better part of an hour and my stomach was growling. There was one more kid they had yet to announce, but everyone knew who it was.

"Finally, but certainly not least," Ms. Bennett, the school principal, said into the microphone. "This next student has continually demonstrated an outstanding level of achievement. Not only has he maintained a perfect 4.0 grade point average, but also he is the captain of the basketball team, and is actively involved with the community. I think we can all agree this young man has a bright future ahead of him. It is my distinct honour to present the Duke Elingberg Award and a one hundred thousand dollar scholarship from Harvard University to the student who needs no introduction. Please put your hands together for..."

I clapped like everyone else, but all I could think about was what I was going to have for lunch. I decided on a pastrami sandwich stacked high with lettuce tomatoes and pickles. By now, Kal-High's poster boy had taken the stage gleaming with pride. Ms. Bennett congratulated him on his achievement - a truly remarkable achievement at that. I had heard Harvard was a really prestigious school, but I had no idea where it was.

Academics were not my thing. I wasn't really sure what my thing was, but I also wasn't too concerned about it, I figured some kind of opportunity would surely present itself.

***

After I ate lunch, I stood outside with some friends. High overhead something caught the group's attention. It was a lone snowball soaring through the air. We all watched with great interest since based on the trajectory we could guess who the intended target was - Ms. Abraham. The snowball hit the ground right by her feet and disintegrated upon impact. Ms. Abraham did not look too pleased. She looked toward the group and stormed over.

"Come with me," Ms. Abraham said.

"Who, me?" I asked in disbelief. "What did I do?"

"You know what you did, don't play dumb with me."

"I have no idea what you're talking about," I pleaded with her as she led me back inside the building. "I didn't do anything, Ms. Abraham." It was no use; my defense was ignored. "This is bull—!" I belted out in frustration.

One of the greatest tragedies in life is the unjust incarceration of a man. I was about to find out firsthand what that would be like.

"Take a seat and wait here," I was instructed, as Ms. Abraham entered the principal's office.

Muffled through the wall, I heard the accusations of a smug Social Studies teacher proudly showing off her catch to the leader of the tribe. "I caught Trevor throwing snowballs outside."

A few moments later, I was called in. I stood at the edge of the principal's desk and waited for instructions to sit.

"Have a seat," Ms. Bennett said. "Ms. Abraham, thank you for bringing this matter to my attention. I'll take it from here."

Ms. Abraham exited the office, not before giving me one last dirty look.

"So…" Ms. Bennett began her interrogation. "Ms. Abraham said she saw you throwing snowballs, what do you have to say for yourself?"

"With all due respect, I think Ms. Abraham is very much mistaken. I saw the whole thing and there is no way she saw who threw the snowball. All I can tell you is that I'm innocent."

"Is that so?"

"Yes, Ms. Abraham was more than a hundred yards away and looking in the opposite direction, how then could she have made out my face in the crowd?"

"She must have seen something since she picked you out of the crowd. How do you explain that?"

"I don't know, perhaps she saw someone who matched my general description throwing snowballs, or maybe she saw me with my hands in my pockets and erroneously deduced they were cold from throwing snowballs, I can only speculate. Regardless, I contest these horrendous allegations."

"So it's a case of mistaken identity, is it?"

"Precisely."

Ms. Bennett looked at me for a moment, almost as if she had the ability to tell if someone was lying.

"Trevor, I have to say, I'm very impressed by how you defended yourself just now. You were calm, collected, and articulate with your words," she said with a slight smile. "You are obviously a very bright young man, but you wouldn't know that based on your grades. You are a few months away from your projected graduation date and you are failing, or nearly failing, most of your courses, with the exception of a few classes," she said, as she continued to study my file.

"I see you are currently getting an 'A' in Philosophy, which tells me you are a very patient and careful thinker. The comments from your teacher support that. Your teacher writes, 'Trevor attends every class and participates actively.' So it's not that you're not capable of good grades, perhaps you just lack the motivation."

Ms. Bennett paused and there was a brief moment of silence. I just stared back at her, waiting for her conclusion.

"As I'm going over your record, it looks like you're missing a lot of classes and you've been suspended twice this year, once for breaking into the games room, and once for fighting. I could suspend you a third time for this incident today, but I don't think that would be in your best interest. To tell you the truth Mr. Morrison, I'm not really sure what to do with you at this point."

Again, I didn't say anything. I just bowed my head in shame.

"Mr. Morrison, assuming you can graduate on time, what are your plans after June?"

"I'm not really too sure, probably just find a job somewhere, try to save up some money."

"Trevor, I'm going to be blunt with you. I see a lot of potential in you, but it seems like you're just throwing it away. I hope you realize the choices you make and the people you surround yourself with will determine how your life will turn out. Now, you have to ask yourself, are the choices you're making and the people you're hanging around with leading you down the path of success…or failure?"

As I was thinking about what she had asked me, the bell rang, signaling the end of the lunch break.

"I'll let you think about that. You're dismissed."

I left her office and sauntered down the hall towards my locker to grab my math books. I didn't mind math, it was one of the few courses I was actually doing well. I enjoyed the instant gratification of solving complex equations. Plus, I liked the teacher. He always wore these really nice three-piece suits and drove a brand new Mercedes. He seemed to be much more successful than a typical high school math teacher, and for that reason, I tended to listen to what he had to say.

About twenty minutes into class, the phone in our room rang and our dapper teacher answered.

"Yes, he's here," Mr. Stirling said softly into the receiver as he swiveled around looking in my direction. "Okay, I'll send him down right away."

"Trevor, Ms. Bennett would like a word with you," he said. The whole class chuckled as if they were in the third grade. I packed up my Superman comic with the rest of my things. Something told me I wouldn't be coming back.

I walked down to Ms. Bennett's office – the long way. I arrived a few minutes later and poked my head into her door. "You wanted to see me again?" I said.

"Mr. Morrison, please come in and have a seat," she said, as she gestured for me to sit. "The reason I called you back to my office is to apologize to you. A witness has come forward to advocate for your innocence."

"I appreciate that, but I was trying to tell you that I didn't do it."

"Yes, but given the situation, this person's testimony is more credible than yours. Do you know what that means?"

"Yes."

"What does it mean?"

"It means the person does not have anything to gain from the situation, but since I do, their word can be trusted more than mine," I answered. It was obvious she was testing me, but it was not clear why she was doing it.

"Good," she smiled proudly. "Trevor, I'm glad to hear you were not the one throwing snowballs today; however, I would be perfectly within my right to suspend you over the coarse language you used with Ms. Abraham."

"But I didn't even swear, I just said that this was 'bull...'."

"Yes, but the swear was implied. Mr. Morrison, that kind of conduct is unacceptable and I could suspend you on that alone. But I won't do that, provided that you meet one condition."

"Which is?" I asked.

You cannot miss a single class from now until graduation. In addition to that, for your two free blocks, you will come to my office and do your homework."

"Come here?" I asked in disbelief.

"Yes, I expect you here every day. You will sit in that corner and do your work."

I sat there in silence pondering this strange proposal. When I realized this was not open for discussion, I left.

On my way out I saw my friend Darrell sitting outside the principal's office. Darrell and his sister were raised by their single mother and were not afforded many of the same opportunities most kids had growing up. Without a proper male role model and supervision, Darrell got into all types of trouble. His activities included smoking a lot of pot, selling pot, writing graffiti, and...well, that was about it. He was probably one of the least ambitious people I had ever met, but for some reason, we were friends.

"Hey, Darrell, what did you do?" I asked.

"I didn't do nothin'. How bout you?" he replied.

"I didn't do anything either."

Chapter Two

The sound of my dad mowing the lawn at 7:00 a.m. was enough to wake me up. The fact he was up so early doing yard work meant there was a good chance he would come inside and put me and my brother to work as well. I peered out my window to see how much longer he would be. He was about halfway done, so by my estimation that gave me about thirty minutes before he came inside and started barking orders at me. Somewhere along the way in his life, he had not reached his goals. So ever since I could remember, he had been pushing me to make something of myself. That was fine, except that nothing I ever did was good enough for him. Since the bar was set so high, after a while, I had just stopped trying. A saying that summed up my life perfectly was, 'Don't reach for what you can't grab'.

As hard as I tried to think about it, it wasn't obvious which direction my life would go. It wasn't as if I was standing at a fork in the road with several paths laid out in front of me; I was standing at the edge of a jungle. I knew I had to enter it, eventually, and there was no better time than the present.

Still in bed, I leaned over and grabbed my phone. I spoke with a friend of mine who had recently moved out of his parents' place. He had forged ahead into the so-called jungle and was encouraging me to join him. During our short conversation, I made the decision to follow in his footsteps and walk the path he had already carved out. It was a hasty decision, but not a completely irrational one. It had been about a week since graduation and I still had nothing going on. My dad kept bugging me to get a job and move out, so that was what I decided to do.

I got out of bed and went into my closet. I grabbed a small backpack and began filling it with everything I thought I needed to survive in the real world. I packed a week's supply of socks and underwear, my favourite t-shirts, a pair of pants, a small knife, some Band-Aids, a toothbrush, and some food.

After my bag was packed, I secured the zippers with a small lock. I stood up, tossed my bag over my shoulder, and took one last look around my room. I wondered if I would ever see it again.

I made my way downstairs and saw my dad eating breakfast. I poured some cereal into a bowl and sat down at the kitchen table across from him.

"Going somewhere?" he asked, taking notice of my backpack.

"Uh, yeah, I'm going to stay with Will for a little while," I responded. That was somewhat true; I just didn't know how long 'a little while' was going to be.

"Do you need any money?"

"No," I responded coldly. I rejected the money to prove a point. I wanted to show him I did not need his help. Or maybe I was just too proud to admit that I did, especially since he had such little faith in me. I had less than a hundred dollars to my name, the last bit of money that I had left from selling bootleg mix tapes around school, but I was determined to make it work.

My brother, Brian, was really smart; he was already halfway through a university degree and was an all around good son. I, on the other hand, had poor grades and no direction. With all the trouble I had at school and home, I felt like my dad had pretty much given up on me. However, when it was time for me to leave, I was surprised at how little he fought with me to stay. I guess he didn't disagree with my decision. Or maybe he thought Will still lived down the street. Either way, I was happy for the freedom.

My dad finished his breakfast and started to clean his dishes. Not another word was spoken between us. I didn't even bother to say 'goodbye'.

Before I left, I knocked on my brother's door. Seeing as it was early in the morning and I had a large backpack slung over my shoulder, he made the logical deduction as well. "Where you going?" he asked.

"I'm moving to Banff."

"Banff? Why Banff?"

"I just need to get out of K-town."

"Alright, man. Call me if you need anything."

"I will, thanks."

After saying goodbye, I left the house and set out on foot like a man on a quest. It was a beautiful day, perfect for traveling. It was early in the morning, so the sun wasn't that hot yet, but I still managed to work up a sweat. After walking for over an hour and a half, I finally reached the bus station.

I walked inside and went straight to the bathroom. I cranked the knob on the faucet and waited for the water to get cold. I cupped my hand under the running water and then brought it up to my mouth to slurp up the cold liquid. I could feel it go all the way down. I splashed some water on my face then turned off the faucet.

"You ready to do this?" I mumbled to myself, staring back at my reflection in the mirror. I stood there a moment then wiped my face and left.

I exited the bathroom and stood in line. When it was my turn, I counted out over fifty dollars to purchase a one-way ticket, and then waited for the boarding announcement. I couldn't believe I was actually leaving this place. Next stop – Banff, Alberta.

Chapter Three

The bus pulled out of the station and drove toward the highway. I sat in the uncomfortable seat staring out the window, watching the town that I grew up in pass by. It was almost like a seminar on my life. We drove by the grocery store where I had been caught shoplifting when I was eight. Down the road from that was my old high school and the park where I encountered my first fight. We drove passed the video store where I rented movies, my old dojo where I trained martial arts, and the set of ten stairs that I kick-flipped last summer. When the bus finally merged onto the highway, I put my headphones on and shut my eyes.

A few hours into the trip, I woke up with a slight cramp in my lower back. I took out a sweatshirt from my bag and wedged it between my back and the seat. I made a few adjustments then looked out the window. We were driving through the Rocky Mountains. The massive jagged mountains made me feel small. It wasn't exactly a jungle, but I was entering the real world. Now that I was wide-awake, I had a lot of time to think. The first thought that occurred to me was, this is the first day of the rest of my life. I had no idea how my life would unfold, but I was eager to find out. The combination of excitement and nervousness sent my mind into a tailspin as I analyzed all the potential opportunities and dangers that lay before me.

After driving for six hours, the bus finally arrived in Banff a little after dinnertime. The bus maneuvered into the station and I continued to stare out the window, taking in as much of my new surroundings as possible. My eyes cascaded from the snowy mountain peaks down to two familiar faces that were outside waiting for me. I couldn't help but smile as I waved at them.

I stepped off the bus to see Will and his girlfriend Bailey standing there with matching smiles. It was if they hadn't seen me in years. In actuality, it had only been a couple of weeks.

My first impression of Banff was good; in fact, it was absolutely breathtaking. The entire town was nestled in between a bunch of snow-peaked mountains in the middle of nowhere. I immediately noticed the air was a lot cleaner, but it was also colder than I expected. Even though it was the start of summer I had to put on a jacket as we walked to Will and Bailey's place.

"Well, this is it," Will said, as we approached a small brown one-level house. Will led us around the side of the house to their entrance.

As we entered the house, I looked up at the top of the staircase and saw an old lady sneering at us.

"Who was that?" I asked when we arrived downstairs.

"That's the owner of the house," Bailey replied.

"She didn't look too pleased to see us."

"She's usually okay, but she's a crotchy old bag," Will said. "She made it very clear when we moved in that there was not to be any visitors staying with us."

"I'm glad to see you're still defying authority, Will," I joked.

I was not aware there would be an angry tyrant living upstairs. I sure hoped she wouldn't cause me any problems while I was staying there.

I set my bag down and Will took me on a tour of their basement suite. It had a log cabin feel to it, complete with a large sofa and a wood burning fireplace. So far, so good, I thought.

Will and Bailey had a way of making me feel warm and welcome, but this was not a summer vacation. I needed to start looking for work immediately. I estimated my money would run out by the end of the week. I had also packed enough macaroni and cheese to last me a week. So that was my time frame - one week to get my life on track.

The next morning I woke up and sat down at the computer. Will and Bailey had left for work so I used the quiet time to create my résumé. I didn't have any actual work experience to put on it so I used my imagination. I started out by putting Seasonal Labourer as my primary occupation. This covered all of my lawn mowing and snow shoveling experience. I also put on there that I did some landscaping and gutter installation. It was a small fabrication, but I didn't think an employer would care if I could install gutters; I just needed to pad my list and convey I was a hard worker.

My second 'occupation' was a Mechanical Assistant. This was another fabrication, I think I handed my dad a wrench one time when he was working on his car. As a general rule, I don't like to lie, but I was in survival mode, so all bets were off.

Nearly all the places I applied to wanted references or some sort of real work experience. I was starting to realize how difficult it was for someone fresh out of high school to get a job. Nobody wanted to take a gamble on a young kid like me, but I was not going to let this hurdle deter me and get me down. I was on my own and needed to become a man. That involved getting a job and taking care of myself. Being rejected was not an option.

I walked into the main snowboard shop in town and asked to speak with the manager.

"I'm the manager, how can I help you?"

I extended my left hand and he reciprocated. The manager looked at me a bit strangely, but then dismissed the left-handed handshake.

I proceeded to introduce myself, explained the reason for my visit, and then handed him my résumé. When he looked at it, he had the same look on his face that everyone else had. I knew I had to take action to impress him, so I began to speak. "Sir, I understand I don't have a lot of work experience, but my passion and hard work is second to none. Let me show you what I can do for you," I said confidently.

He looked at me for a moment, then asked. "Do you snowboard?"

"Yes, sir, I've been riding for ten years," I said enthusiastically.

"Do you know about bikes?"

"Yes, sir," I replied. It was another small lie; I didn't know anything about bikes. I figured since it was the middle of the summer, bike season would only last a few more months anyway. I didn't think it was all that important for me to know about bikes.

"I'm curious, why did you shake my left hand when you came in?" he asked.

"I did it out of respect, sir… you know, because you're left-handed."

"How did you know I was left-handed?"

"Well, when I came in you were crouching down, which allowed me to see the top of your head. I noticed your hair unconventionally swirled in a counterclockwise direction. This is a common genetic trait of left-handed people. Then, when you stood up I noticed you were wearing a chain wallet on the left side. Finally, I noticed you had ink on your middle and index finger on your left hand, an obvious sign you use that hand to write with."

"Wow, that's incredible. You're very perceptive," he said with a slight laugh, like someone who just witnessed a really good magic trick. "I like your style," he looked at me for a moment, still with a smirk on his face. "I'll tell you what, can you be here tomorrow at eight?"

"Yes, sir, I can," I replied excitingly. "Thank you so much, you won't regret it." I shook his hand again and left right away before he changed his mind.

Chapter Four

Now that I had a job secured, I could relax a bit, but I still couldn't afford to do anything. Even though the legal age in Alberta is eighteen, we were still too young to get into any of the bars or clubs, so at night, Will and I would go skateboarding.

"You know what's weird to think about, man?" Will said to me as we were walking back home after a long night of skating.

"What's that?" I replied.

"At this very moment, we're forming memories. One day, maybe twenty years from now, we will remember this moment. It will be just a memory from our past, but it is our life now."

"Unless, of course, we forget," I retorted.

We crossed the street and a group of loud and obnoxious partygoers captured our attention. There were four of them, they had obviously been drinking, and were acting a little rowdy. Something told me this would be an evening we would not soon forget. "Hey, bro, let me try your skateboard!" one of them said as he stumbled toward me.

My street smarts told me to ignore him in hopes of diffusing the situation before it escalated. So that's what I did. I placed my skateboard on the street and started skating away from them. Will did the same.

"Hey, I'm talking to you!" he shouted aggressively at me.

My heart began to pound as I realized I might have made an error in judgment.

My fight or flight mechanism kicked in and I chose wisely to flee. I began pushing my skateboard faster and faster down the dimly lit street. This incited the primal instinct in the predator as he began to hunt me down. The chase was on. I wish I could have zigzagged like a gazelle, but my best course of action was to continue in a straight line and hope he tired before I did.

The drunk lunatic was still in pursuit, grunting and screaming behind me. Will was following me at a modest speed while the other three drunken guys were walking casually, watching the entertainment unfold. So far, they were not posing any threat. I looked back to see how far away the crazy man was. That was when my wheel hit a small rock and I lost my balance. I was thrown from my board and my legs immediately hit the ground running to maintain my speed so I didn't face plant on the pavement.

I was about fifteen feet away from my board by the time I was able to reduce my speed. I cautiously observed from a distance and waited to see what the drunkard would do next. He eventually caught up to where my skateboard was, and was breathing heavily. It became clear he was no longer interested in riding it, and fortunately, he was no longer interested in me either. He picked up my board and began to walk back to his posse.

I determined my safety was no longer in jeopardy so I toughened up. I ran back to the much larger man who looked like he outweighed me by more than a hundred pounds. In a futile attempt at winning a tug of war battle with him, I grabbed the skateboard and tried to reclaim what was rightfully mine. The huge gorilla swung me around and jerked the board free from my grip with ease. He snarled and lunged toward me. Grabbing me by my shirt, he pinned me up against a parked car.

Will arrived on the scene and was yelling at him to let me go, but it was no use. He looked back at the other drunken guys and quickly calculated the distance between them and us. They were still casually walking toward us, but were about fifty yards down the street. In an instant, Will picked up his board from the ground, raised it high in the air, and swiftly whipped it down on the back of the drunkard's head. The sound of the low-pitched thud was disturbing.

The drunkard immediately let go of me and dropped to the ground in a haze of confusion; he had no clue what had just hit him. Blood poured from the back of his head and soaked his blonde hair.

"Go, dude, go!" Will screamed out.

He did not have to tell me twice, I quickly grabbed my skateboard and took off. We raced back to Will's house. I arrived first. Will showed up a moment later and did not show any fear. He seemed more exhilarated than scared.

"Dude, are you okay?" he asked, as he gasped for breath.

"Yeah," I responded quickly.

Will started laughing and instructed me to go around to the front of the house. "Come on let's go over here, we're making too much noise."

I would have been much happier to be safely inside because we were only about four blocks away from where the incident took place. It was doubtful they would ever find us, but I still remained cautious, looking over my shoulder every ten seconds.

We took a seat on the curb in front of Will's place. I gazed up at the stars as Will reached into his pocket and took out a pack of cigarettes.

"Dude, that was awesome!" Will said. "I kicked him too, did you see that?"

"You kicked him?"

"Yeah, buddy was down on all fours and I kicked him in the head as hard as I could." Will mumbled proudly with an unlit cigarette dangling from his mouth. He patted his jean pockets then his shirt pockets. He eventually found what he was looking for. He took out his lighter, lit up his cigarette, and took a huge drag. "Forget those guys!" he said, as he exhaled a huge cloud of smoke.

We waited until Will finished his cigarette before we went inside. Bailey had already gone to bed by the time we got home and would not get to hear our story. I doubted if she would ever hear it; there didn't seem to be much point in telling her.

It was a little past midnight and we were both hungry. We each filled up a big glass of juice and grabbed some chips before heading into the living room. Will threw another log in the fireplace as we prepared to stay up for the next while and watch some TV.

"Hey, have you ever done shrooms?" Will asked, not even trying to conceal his excitement. I looked over at him, but didn't say anything. I didn't have to; it was obvious I had not. Will had the same expression on his face that a kid gets when they have just come up with a really brilliant idea that will most likely get them hurt or into trouble. Before I could even reply, Will jumped out of his chair and went to his little stash spot he had in one of his movie cases. I stayed put, but I stretched out comfortably on the large sofa.

"Dude, where'd you get those?" I asked the first question that came to my mind, exposing my lack of experience in these types of situations.

"I got them from Rasta Mark - a buddy from work," he said, dismissing the seemingly irrelevant question. "Okay, here's what you do," Will said, as he was intently focused and clearly enjoying himself. "Take this," he handed me a small dried up flattened mushroom.

"What do you want me to do with this?" I asked.

"Cut it up into small pieces, then eat it."

I was not much into doing drugs, and I didn't even eat normal mushrooms, but I was willing to let go of some of my inhibitions. I looked down at the pile of dried up mushroom bits in my hand and thought to myself, a man's gotta do what a man's gotta do. I quickly swallowed them and chased them down with a big gulp of juice. Will did the same.

"Okay, now what?" I asked naively.

"Now we wait."

I didn't really feel much at first. We both just sat there staring at the fire. Neither one of us said anything for a while.

"I don't think mine are working," I said, finally breaking the silence.

"Shhhh, just wait," Will said softly.

The room went back to being quiet. The only noise was from the crackling fire in the fireplace. As I stared at the flames I became increasingly more fascinated with them. The drug amplified my natural inquisitiveness and I began to trip out. All the ordinary daily distractions were gone; the drug nullified anything that would even remotely interrupt my thought process. I was in the zone. At that moment, I was an uninhibited and purely inquisitive mind. The amount of focus I had was incredible. It was a philosopher's drug.

"Dude, you know what's weird?" I asked. "What is fire?" I paused for a moment to let the question marinate. Will did not say anything. "If you think about it," I began again "fire can never be analyzed under a microscope. It never sits still, it's always changing, so how do we really know what it is?"

I stayed intently focused on the flames. "You know what I think?" I asked rhetorically. "I think fire is the true reality. The normal everyday stuff we perceive is all an illusion, a veil that covers the true reality. When we strike a match or ignite a flame, that spark creates a force so hot it tears the artificial fabric, and reveals the real reality, the 'flame-reality'. Wherever there is fire, for that moment, at that time, the veil is lifted. Each dance of a flame forces out the fake reality in the same precise spot as the flame so it looks seamless, and when the flame goes out, the veil is restored, once again concealing the truth. I can see it now, it all makes sense."

I looked over at Will as if I had just unraveled the biggest mystery of the universe and I wanted to make sure he witnessed it. Will was completely passed out.

I finished my juice, peeled myself off the couch, and went to bed.

Chapter Five

It had been over a month since I moved in with Will and Bailey. The landlady made it very clear that I was not supposed to be staying there so I had to be a ghost for the next little while until I could get my own place.

My job was going well, but leaving for work was always a challenge. The only door to go outside was located in between two sets of stairs, one leading downstairs to Will and Bailey's place and one leading upstairs to the grumpy landlady's place. At the top of her set of stairs was a door, which was always left open. She sat there at her command post and kept guard. It was nearly impossible to leave at any time during the day and avoid detection. If she was not sitting in her old kitchen chair at the top of the stairs, she kept watch out her front window.

In order to slip under her radar, there were a series of steps that I needed to take. First I had to leave through the window in my room. Then I had to crouch low next to the house and walk underneath the large window in the front of the house. After that, I would continue around the back of the house and dart behind a stack of firewood piled near the edge of the small property. If I could pull all that off successfully, I had to run quickly to the street and then I was home free. The same tactics were needed to regain entry, although it was a little easier since I usually came home at night. Needless to say, I had to get my own place.

As it turned out, the snowboard shop offered staff accommodation. I later learned this was unheard of anywhere else, but with so many transient workers, it was the norm in Banff. I applied for the last empty room in a house with four other guys and was approved to move in right away.

The place was still a basement suite, but it was not nearly as nice as the one Will and Bailey were renting. There was no couch, no TV, no computer, no fireplace, no nice rugs, and it certainly did not have that cozy log cabin feel to it. The owners of the snowboard shop also owned a ski shop down the street on Banff Ave. I was the only guy from the snowboard shop living there, the rest of my new roommates worked at the ski shop.

My roommates were a mixed bag of guys. McKay was a twenty-six year old happy-go-lucky type. Dave was twenty-two and was an all-around nice guy with very little real world experience. Rob was twenty-four and was the quintessential heavy-drinker party-animal type. Then there was Brendan, a twenty-eight year old avid outdoorsman.

A few weeks after I moved in with these guys, Will found out his mother was ill. Almost instantly, Will and Bailey packed up all their things, and left.

Without the support of Will and Bailey, I was completely on my own. Like riding a bike for the first time without the training wheels, I was apprehensive at first because I wasn't sure if I could continue to ride smoothly. Even though I was making it on my own, I never removed the thought that I could always move back in with my parents if things didn't work out. I counted the days, weeks, and then months from the time I moved away from home. Each month that passed represented one more month that I was 'making it' on my own. I was determined to show my parents I was independent and did not need their help. Most importantly, I needed to prove to myself I had what it took to survive in the real world, even if it was just in a small town.

Chapter Six

When I turned eighteen, I started going to the bars with my roommates nearly every night. I was so used to approaching people and trying to sell them things at my job that meeting girls came naturally to me. I would walk up to a group of girls by myself and within minutes, I would have them completely engaged. The next step was to introduce them to my friends and hope everyone could find one they liked. If everything flowed smoothly, we would all leave together and party back at our place. This sequence happened routinely, which immediately increased my popularity with my roommates - my only friends. At this point in my life, hooking up with girls was everything to me. It was my only focus.

One morning, after a late night of partying, I strolled into work hung-over. I submerged myself in a stack of clothes and folded them for the first few hours to avoid contact with any other life forms.

"Excuse me," a sweet and innocent looking girl approached me. By my estimation, she was about seventeen. "Do you have any more of these in the back?" she asked. As girls remained my only known weakness, I happily obliged.

"I can check for you, what size are you looking for?"

"A small please," she said with a flirtatious smile.

A few moments later, I appeared from the back. "You're in luck, last one left," I said, as I proudly presented the size small shirt to her.

As she continued to browse, I continued to check her out. I couldn't help it, she was so beautiful. She was about five foot five with light brown hair. It was slightly wavy and a little past shoulder length.

"So are you from out of town?" I asked.

"Yeah. I'm here on vacation with my family."

"Cool. How do you like it here so far?"

"It's really nice, but I'm always with my parents. I haven't had the chance to see everything I wanted to see."

"That's too bad," I said. Before I even had a chance to think, I instinctually blurted out, "Why don't you come out with me tonight?" My heart started pounding as soon as the words left my lips. I could feel the blood rush to my face, but I just ignored it. I pretended she couldn't see me blushing. There it was, I laid it all out on the line. "I can take you to all the places you didn't get to see," I continued to sell her on the idea.

"Sure," she said casually.

"Okay, great," I said. "I'm off at five o'clock. Can you come back here...preferably without your parents?"

She laughed. "Don't worry, I won't bring them."

"I'm Trevor, by the way," I extended my hand.

"Hi, nice to meet you, I'm Ashley."

***

For the next few hours, time seemed to slow down. I kept checking the time every few minutes, hoping it would be five o'clock. The anticipation was killing me. I paced around the store and caught glimpses of the people walking down the street. I wasn't exactly looking for her, but I figured she still might be out shopping. I had a huge knot in my stomach. I wanted to be outside, but I felt trapped in this crumby little snowboard shop, listening to the same music that played over and over. My mind was completely occupied with all the crazy scenarios that could possibly unfold that night. Going out with girls was nothing new to me, but something felt different about this one; I was actually nervous.

The funny feeling in my stomach never really went away, but I was reminded of it when she walked into the shop for the second time. My heart started to pound the moment I saw her again. She looked amazing. Her tight jeans showed off her petite frame perfectly.

"Hey, Ashley, I'm glad to see you again," I managed to say.

"You too. Do you still want to hang out with me tonight?"

"Of course. Let me just grab my things. I'll be right out."

As we were leaving, I proudly marched her out the front door for my fellow coworker to see. I tried not to gloat too much, but I couldn't help it.

"See ya, Corson," I said with a cocky swagger.

We decided to get some frozen yogurt and just walk around town. Banff is a beautiful place - the mountain peaks always have snow on them, the air is clean, and massive herds of elk roam down the main street.

I took her to a few places I knew, places the average tourist might not see. There was a nice spot I had discovered when I first moved there. It was a beautiful area just on the outskirts of town. It was a bit of hike to get there, but once we reached the top, there was a large flat rock where we could sit on and stare out across the valley. It was perfectly serene, devoid of any outside distractions - no bosses, no parents, and no drunk roommates. It was just us.

Our conversation flowed naturally as we got to know each other a little bit. Even when we were not talking, I still felt comfortable being with her. We gazed out at the landscape and just enjoyed the view. At a certain point, we both seemed to look at each other at exactly the same moment. A soft breeze blew a few strands of hair across her face. I took my hand and gently brushed it away. With my hand still caressing her face, I slowly moved in for a kiss. It was brief, but substantial.

I couldn't remember the last time I had butterflies over a girl before. I was utterly infatuated with her. I didn't want the ride to end, but I knew it would. The next day she would go back to where she came from and I would have to immediately deal with life without her. It was a shame, plain and simple - there was no other way to describe it. However, I took a great lesson from this experience - circumstances can change in a heartbeat.

After a while longer, we decided to leave before it became too dark. We walked slowly back to the hotel where she was staying and we said our goodbyes.

"It was nice of you to show me around tonight, thank you."

"No problem, it was my pleasure."

We shared a long hug and another brief kiss before we parted ways.

***

I showed up to work the next morning just before eight. My manager unlocked the doors for me and let me in. I went to the back to put my stuff down then began to do the usual morning duties: vacuum, dust, and Windex. Corson was there with me, although he was busy with his morning duties: taking out the garbage from the previous night and counting the day's float. He didn't ask me how my night went. All I wanted to do was talk about this girl to whoever would listen.

After I finished my duties, I unlocked the doors for the start of another day at the shop. Mornings were usually pretty quiet at the store, customers didn't start showing up until around eleven.

My manager had me in the back processing a new shipment of merchandise with him while Corson minded the store. The task was to put security tags on all the new clothing that had just come in. I did this for about an hour. Throughout the whole mindless task, all I thought about was Ashley. I replayed every vivid detail in my mind.

"You're awfully quiet this morning," my manger remarked.

"I have a broken heart," I said remorsefully.

"You do? Over who?"

"Her name is Ashley."

"I didn't know you were seeing anyone, when did you meet her?"

"Yesterday."

My manager couldn't help but laugh. "Aw, puppy love," he teased.

"I think she was the one."

"Oh okay, in that case, I apologize," he said sarcastically. "Just to remind you, you're seventeen and you don't know anything about love…and you met her yesterday!"

"Eighteen."

We continued to go back and forth. He kept teasing me and I kept talking about Ashley, it was a win-win for both of us. It was a shame to think I would probably never see her again, but that's what it was like in Banff; everyone was from elsewhere and only there temporarily. Eventually, and inevitably, they all leave.

"Yo, Trevor!" Corson yelled out. "You have a visitor!"

As soon as I heard that, I immediately jumped out of my chair and ran out of the stock room.

My heart skipped a beat when I saw her, but I played it cool.

"Hey, Ashley, how are you?"

"I'm good. I just wanted to come by and give you this card before I left," she said, as she handed me a card. "But don't read it now, okay?"

"Okay, I won't. So when are you leaving?"

"In about an hour, my family is just checking out of the hotel now. So... yeah, um, I just wanted to come by and see you again before I left."

"I'm glad you did."

"And thanks for the nice evening last night, I had a good time."

"I hope it wasn't too boring for you."

"No, it was perfect."

We stood there for a moment making heavy eye contact. I didn't say anything and neither did she, but somehow it wasn't awkward. I eventually gave her a hug, which I didn't want to let go. I pulled back slowly, as did she. Our eyes met and we gave each other a final kiss goodbye.

I stood there and watched her walk out of the store, and out of my life.

Chapter Seven

By now, the winter had arrived and the town was covered in a thick blanket of white snow. I received a discount on a bunch of equipment from the shop, so on my days off I would head to the hills and go snowboarding. Sometimes I went with my roommates, sometimes with a co-worker, but mostly I just went by myself.

At night, I was no longer going out to the bars. I actually had more fun hanging out with McKay and listening to his stories. McKay had a lot of life experience; he had graduated from university and had lived in many parts of the world including Africa, China, and now Banff. It seemed like an odd place for a guy with so much promise to end up, but I didn't really question it at the time. He could speak in depth about a wide variety of topics, including religion, politics, science, and philosophy. I hung onto every word.

From listening to him, it was obvious I hadn't really lived yet. I was eighteen, but I didn't know as much about the world as I thought I did. Nothing was more evident of this than when it was my turn to tell a story and I had nothing to say. I don't think he minded, he seemed content with imparting his wisdom onto an empty canvas.

These nights were some of my fondest memories of living in Banff. But when McKay moved away, I was once again by myself. I started going back to the bar with Rob and Dave, but it was no longer as fun. McKay had given me a glimpse of what else was out there in the world, and I was eager to discover it.

McKay once told me that when we meet people, we take the characteristics we like in them and leave behind the ones we don't like. Even though I was still going to the bar, I quit drinking. I really admired that quality in him and this was one of the many characteristics I took from him. I also wanted to have my own crazy stories to tell someday. So far my craziest story was being chased by some drunk guy one night.

***

By the time spring was in full bloom, the snowboard shop had fully converted all of its snowboard stock into mountain bike equipment, which was something I had no interest in selling. I felt like I had overstayed my welcome in Banff and there was little point for me continuing to live there. Banff seemed like a great place at first, but I felt isolated from the rest of the world. I had been there for a total of ten months and had managed to save nearly eight thousand dollars. For the first time in my life, I was on my own, and excelling. I had established my independence and was confident I could make it in the real world without any help from my parents. But Banff was a small pond; I wondered how I would do living in a large metropolis.

***

On one of my days off I decided to make some phone calls to some old friends. I contacted Will, but he was not home. I then called my friend, Darrell.

"Yo, Darrell, how's it going, man?" I asked.

"I'm still workin' on the oil rigs."

"Oh yeah, how's that going?"

"It's a rough life; I think I need a change."

"Yeah, I hear ya, man. I think I'm at the end of my rope with the whole Banff thing."

"Why don't we move to Vancouver? We can get a place together," he suggested.

"What's in Vancouver?" I asked.

"My dad lives there, we can stay with him for a while until we get on our feet."

I had briefly met his dad once before, but I doubted if he remembered me. I contemplated Darrell's proposal, I was reminded of how I ended up in Banff in the first place. A chance phone call presented an opportunity and I took advantage of it. Now a new opportunity had presented itself. If I said 'no' to this opportunity, I would also be saying 'no' to the infinite string of possibilities that would follow from it.

"Okay, let's do it," I said.

He gave me his dad's phone number and told me to call him when I arrived in Vancouver.

I immediately informed my work that I was leaving town. I packed up all my things and said my goodbyes. My plan was to take the Greyhound down to

Vancouver, but as luck would have it, my roommate Dave was coincidentally going to Vancouver at the same time and offered me a ride.

When the day finally came to leave, I put the few possessions I had into Dave's two-thousand dollar car and we made our exit.

Chapter Eight

By the time we arrived in Vancouver, it was a little after 11:00 p.m. The rain was coming down pretty hard and Dave's windshield wipers were doing the very least to disperse the water. Neither one of us had ever been to Vancouver before, so we pulled into a gas station in East Vancouver before we became too lost. Dave parked, but kept the engine running. I exited the vehicle and tiptoed through a large puddle that surrounded the car. The rain was relentless, but did nothing to wash away the sleaze that inhabited the phone booth. It actually enhanced the smell of urine and dirty concrete. Regardless of my discomfort, I had no choice but to press on.

Once in the phone booth, I wiped my soaked forehead, inserted a quarter, and dialed the number Darrell had given me. The phone rang a few times and I waited patiently. After the fifth ring, a pit welled up in my stomach as I started to worry. By the tenth ring, I hung up the phone and tried not to panic. I looked back at Dave, who was still sitting in the car. Dave was staying with one of his friends and still needed to figure out how to get there.

I took the quarter out of the coin release tray and inserted it back into the phone. I carefully dialed the number again and took a deep breath. It started to ring again. This time, on the second ring, a low-pitched gravelly voice answered.

"Hello?" the voice said.

"Hello, is this Mr. Channing?" I asked meekly.

"Yes, who is this?"

"Hi, Mr. Channing, my name is Trevor Morrison, I'm friends with your son, Darrell. He told me to call you when I was in town," I paused as if I had just cast out a lure and was waiting for a bite.

"Darrell is not here."

"Oh, okay, um, did he mention anything to you about me coming to stay with you?"

"I received a call from Darrell the other day, and he mentioned something about you and him staying with us for a while. But Darrell has not arrived yet."

"Okay, well, I'm in Vancouver right now using a payphone at a gas station and was kind of counting on him being there," I cast out another line.

"I'm so sorry about that, Trevor, why don't you come on over, you can stay here until Darrell arrives. I'll call him in the morning."

I quickly jotted down the address and jumped back into the car.

"Did you get an address?" Dave asked.

"Yeah, he lives at 1755 West 41st Street. Do you know where that is?" I asked.

"No I don't," Dave said.

"Okay, well, I can take a cab from here Dave," I said, trying to be as considerate as possible.

"That's okay, I took you this far, I may as well take you the rest of the way."

"Are you sure?"

"Yeah, no problem."

"Okay, thanks. Let's see, we're on East 16th Avenue. I think if we just keep driving down this street, it will eventually turn into West 16th Avenue. Then we can continue to drive in the direction that the blocks increase in number."

We finally arrived at Mr. Channing's modest house in an upper scale neighbourhood. When we pulled up, he was waiting for me at the edge of the garage in his housecoat. The garage door was open to reveal two Mercedes Benzes along with some other typical garage clutter.

I gave Mr. Channing a wave and unloaded my stuff from Dave's car.

"Alright, man, this is it," I said to Dave as we shook hands. "Thanks so much, brother, I really appreciate it."

Dave pulled away from the driveway and drove off. I knew I would probably never see him again.

"Hi, Mr. Channing, thank you so much for allowing me to stay with you. I'm sorry for calling you so late."

"Don't worry about it," he said, as he welcomed me into his home. I followed him downstairs to the basement.

"This is where you will be sleeping. There are blankets and towels there, and you can use that bathroom down the hall."

"Okay, thanks."

"Are you hungry, do you want something to eat or drink?"

"No, thank you, I'm fine."

"Alright then, I'm going back to bed. The alarm will be on so don't open any doors or windows. If you get hot, the control for the air conditioner is over there."

Mr. Channing was being very nice, going out of his way to make me feel comfortable. When he left, I hit the lights and laid down on the couch. I could hear his footsteps creak throughout the quiet house. I followed the sound all the way up to his bedroom, which was located on the second level. As he got further away, the sound was replaced by the pitter-patter of rain hitting the porch in the backyard.

I laid there for a moment in the dark room, my eyes still open. I looked around to get acquainted with my new environment. There was a small television, a bathroom, and some exercise equipment. It seemed a bit odd to me that I was in a city I had never been before and was laying on someone's couch that could easily be a complete stranger. I could not wait for what my life was going to bring me next.

It was the end of a long day and I was exhausted, so I closed my eyes and fell asleep.

***

"Good morning," an unfamiliar female voice said. My eyes slowly peeled open.

"Trevor?" she said again.

"Yes. Good morning," I mumbled, still half asleep.

"Hello, I'm Judy, Jack's wife."

"Hello, it is very nice to meet you. I'm so sorry about the intrusion last night. I appreciate you allowing me to crash on your couch."

"How long were you planning on staying here?" she asked. Now I was beginning to feel a little uncomfortable, but I completely understood. It was one thing to help out your son's friend, but Darrell was not her son. So to her, I was just some dude who came into her life in the middle of the night and was now on her couch.

"Um, I, well, we..." The words did not come to my mouth. I didn't want to impose and I had no idea what Darrell had told his dad. I was under the impression we would be able to stay there for a while, perhaps a month, to get on our feet. Darrell had assured me of this, he had said his dad had a lot of connections in the city and he had a lot of extra furniture we could have. Now I was not sure if any of that was true.

Judy interjected with another question that made me feel even more uncomfortable. "Where is Darrell?" That was actually a legitimate question, one that I wanted to know the answer to.

"I'm not sure," I responded.

"Well, Jack and I have to leave for work soon, so I can drop you off somewhere." It was clear she was not offering me a ride to be nice, she wanted me out of her house.

"I suppose I could do some exploring around town," I suggested.

"Can you be ready in a half an hour?"

"Sure. No problem."

Judy dropped me off at a bus stop and I took a bus downtown. As I came over the bridge, I was in awe of the magnificent skyline. The modern buildings ascended from the waterfront like jagged crystals, which complemented the monstrous snow-peaked mountain range in the background. The buildings were so enormous, like nothing I had seen before. I had always lived in small towns where the tallest building was only six stories high.

I exited at what appeared to be the busiest intersection in the downtown core. I felt the hustle instantly. There were thousands of people walking around, street performers playing music, people honking their car horns, buses releasing their air breaks, sirens going off, and even the faint chant of protesters coming from somewhere. I was definitely not in Banff anymore.

I looked up and felt so small next to all the towering skyscrapers. As I walked around, taking in the new sites, I came across one building that stood out like a shiny glass beacon among the rest. When I approached closer, I read the massive brass sign in front:

LINDBERG

I looked way up toward the sky and could barely see the top of the enormous structure. For a moment, I wondered what Lindberg did, but I kept moving.

For the next eight hours, I did some exploring. I walked up and down the blocks, checked out the mall, walked around Stanley Park, and went down to the harbor. At 5:00 p.m., I decided I had seen enough for one day so I took a cab back to Mr. Channing's house.

When I arrived, I walked up the steps and rang the doorbell. I was hoping Darrell would be there because I felt like I was imposing. After all, I didn't even know these people.

Judy answered the door and let me in. She was much friendlier than she was in the morning. Now that she was home, she could keep an eye on me. She obviously didn't trust me too much, however, I was a friend of Darrell's so I didn't blame her.

I could smell the wonderful aroma as soon as I walked in the house. I took off my shoes and followed Judy into the kitchen. Mr. Channing was making his specialty, spaghetti and meatballs.

"Wow, smells great!" I said.

"Hey, Trevor, how's it going?"

"It's going well. I had a fun day today, did some exploring downtown. How was your day?"

"It was good."

"Any word from Darrell yet?" I asked.

"Yeah, I called him today and he will be arriving tomorrow morning. We'll have to pick him up at the airport."

"At the airport? He's flying in?" I asked in disbelief. It never occurred to me how Darrell would get to Vancouver; I just assumed he would take the bus or hitch a ride with someone.

"Yeah, I bought him a plane ticket."

"Did he say why he wasn't here sooner?"

"No, I'm not sure what's going on with him, I called him today around noon and he was still sleeping."

Still sleeping? I thought. Typical Darrell, he told me to meet him on Wednesday, and it was already Thursday evening, and he still had not shown up. And he was sleeping until noon! I was quite disappointed, but not the least bit surprised. After all, he was really lazy and very irresponsible. He only thought about himself and still could not seem to manage his own life properly. I knew moving in with him was a bad idea; he did drugs, drank heavily, had no manners, and no people skills. By all accounts, he was a complete disaster. Even with these reservations, I still decided to go through with it. After my experience in Banff, I just wanted a friend, someone who could copilot the big city with me.

***

The next day, Darrell arrived at the Vancouver International Airport. I was excited to see him. It had been a while since I hung out with one of my actual friends and not just one of my roommates. I was expecting the same excitement in return, but he just hopped in the back seat and barely acknowledged me. No hug, no secret handshake, just a lazy 'wussup?' and a quick nod. I didn't take it too personally; it was just Darrell being Darrell.

Chapter Nine

Darrell had grown up a bit in Vancouver, so he was familiar with the city. Whether it was taking the bus, finding the best pizza places, or going to the best neighbourhoods to look for an apartment, he seemed to know it all. So I just followed his lead.

For the first few weeks, I conformed to Darrell's lifestyle. We didn't really do much. We would wake up and watch TV until noon, have lunch, shower, and then hit the town. We were supposed to be looking for work, an apartment, and getting our lives together, but Darrell had other plans. He was more interested in going around town writing graffiti and hanging out at the mall. I was being drawn into the 'Darrell trap' - the unmotivated carefree life.

During dinner, Jack and Judy asked us how the job hunt and the apartment search were going. Darrell always told them about all the places where we applied for work and all the apartments we had looked at. It was a complete lie; we hadn't done any of that.

I think Darrell believed his dad would allow him to live in his house forever, but I was a little more sensible than that. At night, we could hear Judy screaming at her husband. She had reached her boiling point with us staying in the house. It was time to start making some serious moves, and we knew it.

One day, Mr. Channing came downstairs to talk to me. Darrell was staying upstairs in the spare bedroom and was still asleep. I had been up for hours reading a Bill Gates biography I borrowed from Mr. Channing's personal library.

"Good morning," Mr. Channing said.

"Good morning," I replied.

"How's the book?" he asked.

"It's good so far."

"So how's the job hunt coming along?"

"To be honest, sir, we don't spend enough time looking for work. I don't really know the city that well so I end up following Darrell around and doing what he wants to do."

"So is that your plan for life, just follow Darrell around?"

"No, of course not."

"Look, I know my son has some issues, but you seem to have a good head on your shoulders. You need to take control of your life."

"Yeah, I know."

"Trevor, let me tell you a little story."

I settled in, waiting for Mr. Channing to tell his 'when I was your age' story.

"Trevor, when I was your age, I was the father of two kids, my wife had just left me, and I was broke. It was one of the lowest points in my life. Instead of dealing with the problem, I found comfort hanging out with my friends and drinking until the early hours of the morning. I had no direction in life and therefore spent most of my time in dingy pool halls, drinking, gambling, and getting into trouble. Some of the guys who I was hanging out with at the time were…well, let's just say they were not outstanding citizens. Many of them sold drugs and did all kinds of nefarious activities that were against the law. Even though I hung out with them, I knew I wasn't really like them.

"Well, one day I saw this really cute girl walking toward me. She was so beautiful, I just had to talk to her, but I couldn't."

"Why not?"

"I didn't have the courage."

"So what did you do?"

"One of my buddies dared me to go talk to her; he was making fun of me, calling me a chicken. So I got up, walked right up to her and introduced myself. I was really nervous, but I think she liked that in me. I guess she could tell I was a good person. After that, we exchanged numbers and eventually started seeing each other.

"As it turned out, she happened to be a loans officer at one of the major banks in town. So one day, I mentioned an idea to her about starting my own pizzeria. She loved the idea and set me up with a small business loan to start my own business.

"Fast forward a few years, my business was booming and I was doing well. I wasn't rich or anything, but I was making a decent living. At that time, almost all of my friends were either dead, in jail, or strung out on drugs."

"Wow, that's an interesting story."

"Do you know what the moral of the story is, Trevor?"

"Tell me."

"The people you choose to surround yourself with can determine how your life turns out. Their influence can creep into your life in subtle ways that you may not fully realize in the moment. It's important to be mindful of which direction you're being pushed and pulled in. Do you understand?"

I nodded my head in agreement as I understood what he was trying to say. It was the same message Ms. Bennett was trying to tell me. I wasn't sure if this was just general good advice older generations liked to impart on youth, or if the universe somehow placed these people in my life to warn me. The funny thing was, in both instances, Darrell seemed to be the person they were warning me about.

"So what ever happened with you and the girl?" I asked.

"I married her."

Mr. Channing left me to heed his words of wisdom. I contemplated the message at the same time staring at the picture of Bill Gates on the cover of his book. I then glanced around Mr. Channing's beautiful house. The first thought that occurred to me was, I need to start making money. From all the shopping I was doing, my bank account was quickly dwindling. Something needed to change.

At around 7:00 in the evening, I went upstairs to Darrell's room and knocked on his door. There was no answer. I opened the door and saw him completely passed out. "Hey, Darrell," I said.

"Whaaattt?" he let out a miserable groan.

"I'm going to start my own business."

He still didn't move or say anything.

"Darrell, wake up, man, this is important," he was obviously not the best choice for a business partner, but I needed him. I knew if I talked about all the money we would make, I could get him on board with the idea.

After he woke up a bit, I began my pitch. "Okay, here's what we do. We go to The Home Warehouse and get one of those high-powered pressure washers. Then we go around charging people to pressure wash their driveways. We can even approach businesses and clean their awnings, sidewalks, elephants, you name it!"

"Okay, so how do we 'go around', we would need a truck or something."

"Then we get a truck," I retorted back immediately.

I had given this a lot of thought and consideration before I decided whether the plan was feasible. However, Darrell was on board almost instantly - probably not a good sign, but I ignored it.

"Alright, so I checked online and priced out pressure washers. The cheapest ones I found cost about $1,500.00. Once we pick that up, we can get a cheap truck for around $2,000.00. We also need some miscellaneous gear, like gloves, goggles, boots, and maybe a couple signs for the truck. We could probably pick up all that stuff for around $200.00. We still need money for insurance and gas for the truck, oh, and advertising too. I haven't priced that stuff out yet, but I think our total startup cost will be under five grand."

I gave him a moment to let the information sink into his brain.

"The work won't be too bad, and the money will be good. We can charge fifty dollars an hour for the pressure washing, and we can also use the truck in other ways as well. I was thinking we could also do trash removals and small moves."

"Okay, bro, let's do it," Darrell said.

"So, Darrell, I can come up with $2,500.00, but I need you to come up with the other $2,500.00 so we can get started. What do you think?"

I knew Darrell didn't have $2,500.00 - he probably didn't even have $250.00 - but his dad did. I could have easily financed this project on my own, but by bringing Darrell on, I didn't have to risk all of my money up front, plus I would have a partner who could do half of the work.

Just as I had expected, Darrell asked his dad for the money. It took a little convincing, but after we showed Mr. Channing our business plan, he knew we were serious. After all, he knew firsthand what it was like to be passionate about an idea, but not have the capital to get it off the ground.

Over the next couple of days, we followed Mr. Channing's lead. Since he had chipped in Darrell's share of the investment, he appointed himself as a silent partner. At first, I was enthusiastic about his involvement in the company because of his life experience and business savvy. But almost immediately, this enthusiasm waned and was replaced by great reluctance. Mr. Channing soon revealed another side of himself than the benevolent mentor I first thought he was. He was arrogant about his abilities and on several occasions referred to himself as a business and marketing genius - a strange statement for anyone to utter about themselves regardless if it was true. As such, all of his ideas were implemented and ours were dismissed.

That would be okay if he truly was what he claimed to be, but I saw no proof of it. In fact, there was a lot of evidence to support the contrary. The more I thought about it, Mr. Channing was only successful because of his wife. Underneath the fancy exterior of the Shaughnessy home, Mercedes Benz, and designer clothes, he was still a street hustler, but in all the wrong ways. Landing a woman like Judy was his ultimate achievement in life. In addition to that, he was incredibly condescending. It was beginning to be Jack's company and we were just his employees.

The sole reason I entered into this venture was to avoid being an employee, so I was a little annoyed from the start. Any respect I still had for Mr. Channing was eventually lost when we were in a hardware store and I saw him casually sneak several expensive tools under his jacket and walk out without paying. I couldn't believe my eyes at first. I called him out on it, but he denied it completely. Now I had a few more pieces of the puzzle about Jack Channing; he was a thief, a liar, and delusional. His egotism and highly questionable ethics convinced me early on that we needed to remove him from the picture as soon as possible.

I swallowed my pride and worked with my new team as best I could. With our pooled money, we put together everything we needed. We found a decent truck, we picked up the pressure washer, had some signs and some t-shirts made, and we even secured our first client, Mr. Channing's next-door neighbour. I had prepared a set of flyers that we could hand deliver throughout neighbourhoods to get business. I also created a survey/thank you letter to give to clients. The survey was designed to give us insight on how we could improve our business, and the thank you letter would leave a good impression on the client so we could get more referrals.

We were officially in business.

***

Judy was so sick of us living in the house that she found us a one-bedroom apartment in the West End overlooking the Pacific Ocean. I was looking for a two bedroom, but that was not in Darrell's budget.

We decided to flip a coin to see who would get the bedroom and who had to sleep in the living room. I won the coin toss fair and square.

"Not so fast, bro," Darrell said, suddenly inventing new rules, "you haven't won anything; it's best two out of three."

The coin was flipped again and it came up heads for the second time in a row. I had officially won the bedroom. In Darrell's mind he was probably searching for another dirty tactic to change the outcome. He begrudgingly lost and was noticeably unhappy about it.

The next day, Darrell told me he had to go somewhere with his dad. Everything was always so vague with him, for all I knew, he was leaving town.

***

"Trevor, you have a phone call!" Judy yelled out from upstairs.

"Hello?" I said.

"Hi, Trevor, my name is Marc Andrews. I'm the manager of the Athletic Surplus, how are you?"

"I'm very well, Mr. Andrews, how are you?"

"I'm alive, so I can't complain. Listen, Trevor, I have your résumé here and I'm calling to see if you're still interested in the sales position you applied for?"

Things weren't exactly going well with the pressure washing business, but I wanted to stick with it. I was down to my last thousand dollars and I could really use some consistent paychecks.

"I really appreciate the call, Mr. Andrews, but I have found employment elsewhere. But if things don't work out, I would love the opportunity to work for you."

***

Darrell and his dad returned later that night. Jack had bought Darrell a bunch of new furniture and they had moved it into the new apartment, into the bedroom. There was no excuse, no apology, no nothing. It was blatant thievery, plain and simple. Lying, stealing, and manipulating were things this family was accustomed to doing in order to get what they wanted. My disdain for both of them continued to grow week after week. This was the beginning of the end.

Chapter Ten

Business was starting to pick up. In a few short weeks we made a couple thousand dollars doing odd jobs. All the cheques were deposited into a bank account Darrell and his dad had opened, which for some reason I did not have access to. My initial reaction was how most people would react. I felt it was a little sneaky to go behind my back and open up an account where one partner doesn't have access.

Mr. Channing told me I was just being paranoid and they would eventually add me to the account. He said it was just easier for a father and son to open up a business account. The fact that it was coming from Mr. Channing did nothing to reassure me. The man was a manipulator; I had watched him manipulate others countless times and then brag to us afterwards about his abilities. I decided to let it go and allow him to think he had pulled the wool over my eyes. That way, he would be unaware that I was still watching him and his son closely.

Aside from the bank account issue and the apartment issue, there were many other personality conflicts that were difficult to ignore. For starters,

Darrell was the most selfish and inconsiderate person I had ever met. A prime example of this was when we were at a nightclub once and Darrell received a call on his cell phone. Rather than going somewhere quiet to take the call, Darrell demanded the DJ turn the music down so he could hear. I guess it was just how he was raised; he did not care about anyone but himself - an impossible trait to deal with in a business partnership.

Over a short amount of time, the rift between us began to grow. There was also a lot of tension on the jobs; we hardly spoke to each other at all. When we did, it was a lot of arguing and ego clashing. Darrell had it in his mind that he was this big shot boss and I was his employee. Nothing could be further from the truth. If anything, I was more like the boss, and Darrell was my employee, but I never thought of it in terms of that. It was a partnership, albeit an inherently flawed partnership. We were like two generals, and neither one of us wanted to submit to the other.

At the end of each long day, we would come home and not say a word to each other.

One night, while Darrell was in the shower, I went into his room and looked for the bank statement for the company account. His room was filthy; there were clothes and papers all over the floor, and he had dirty dishes lying around that looked like they had been there for weeks. I found a stack of mail underneath his futon bed and found what I was looking for. Immediately, I noticed large cash withdrawals and several other charges coming from the company account.

I waited until he came out of the shower before I confronted him. The whole time, my contempt grew. When he came out, I exploded on him.

"Darrell, what is this?" I demanded as I held up the bank statement.

"What are you talking about, dude?" he asked, obviously playing dumb.

"Explain to me why I'm paying for you to eat out at fast food restaurants, get haircuts, and pay for your cell phone bill? I have yet to see a dime of the money that we earned and you're out spending it like it's your own personal expense account."

"Those are all business expenses. I needed a haircut to look professional, I need to eat to do the physical work, and I need a cell phone to stay in touch."

I wasn't sure if these were excuses he had just came up with or if they were justifications which he believed to be true.

"The phone is for company use only and you're using it for your own personal use. You can't expect me to pay for that."

"It's a company expense, we can just write it off."

"What are you talking about? Do you even know what that means?" I asked, confused.

"Fine, just take it out of my half of the money then."

"Okay, when am I going to see my half?" I said, as I threw the stack of papers on the floor.

"Dude, just relax."

I looked down at the mess of papers and saw one other letter that piqued my interest. It had a large red stamp on the front that read: 'EVICTION NOTICE'. I bent down and picked it up. I quickly read the first few lines.

"What's this?" I said confused. I continued to read. "It says here we need to be out by the 14th. That's in two days, Darrell. When were you going to tell me about this!" I yelled, completely losing my temper.

"I don't know, I guess I forgot."

I took a deep breath and restrained myself from ripping his head off.

I continued to read:

'Dear Mr. Morrison and Mr. Channing,

This notice is to advise you that you are to vacate the property as of June 14th due to ongoing noise complaints from tenants. We have made several attempts to warn you about playing excessively loud music and each warning appears to have been ignored.'

I looked up at the date in the top corner. It was dated from over a month ago. Did he really just forget or was he trying to screw me over?

My mind was racing. I needed to think clearly for a moment. All I could think about was how this loser dragged me into his world. What made matters worse, I didn't even own a stereo. Darrell was the one always blasting his music, not me. I told him this would happen.

I went to my 'room' and sat on the edge of my bed. I needed a plan. Everything was happening so quickly. The business was falling apart and I could not imagine things ever working out between us. Now I was being evicted and I needed to find a new place in less than two days. Darrell would probably just move back in with his dad and leave me out to dry. The worst-case scenario for me, I could move my stuff into a 24-hour storage facility and sleep in a youth hostel until I found a more permanent residence. If I could help it, I never wanted to see Darrell again.

***

It was Friday the thirteenth, the night before we needed to move out and I still did not have a place to go. I didn't really know too many people in the city, but I made a few phone calls to the people I did know with hopes they could help me out. I was genuinely screwed, but I was trying to remain optimistic. It's not my destiny to be homeless; something has to happen, I kept telling myself.

At around 8:00 p.m., Mr. Channing came over to help Darrell move his stuff back into his house. I imagined Judy wouldn't be too pleased with this arrangement, but that was the furthest thing from my mind.

I didn't want to be in there watching them move so I decided to take a walk and figure things out. I left the apartment and waited for the elevator. When it arrived, Mr. Channing stepped out and gave me a stiff shoulder, knocking me off balance. There was no apology. I didn't say a word either, I just entered the elevator. Mr. Channing walked about halfway down the hallway then stopped and turned around to face the elevator. Just as the elevator doors were closing, he said, "Have a nice life." The doors shut and I descended slowly down to the ground floor. Have a nice life? What's that supposed to mean?

When I went outside, I saw Darrell loading his stuff into our truck. To avoid conversation, I took out my cell phone and made a call.

Mr. Channing came out of the building a few minutes later with another load. This time he had had a little more time to think and apparently had reached his boiling point. He gave me an angry-faced glare and belted out, "You little prick!"

It was the first time I had seen him lose his temper like that. I was completely caught off guard.

"Me?" I asked startled. "What did I do?"

"You know what you did! Playing your goddamn rap music loudly!"

"Jack, I don't even own a stereo," I responded back in disbelief.

"Yeah, just like you were skimming off the top of the company account for your own personal use," he said, as he began to approach me.

"What are you talking about? I don't even have access to the funds," I said walking backwards.

He began to pursue me, still screaming. "And then you're out here talking on your goddamn cell phone and you can't even help your friend...after everything we've done for you!"

He was building up to the point of being in a complete rage and he had decided everything that was wrong with the situation between Darrell and I was somehow my fault. Aside from the black belt certification that was framed in his office, he was more than twice my size and I would rather not mess with him.

With his eyes locked onto mine, he completely snapped thrusting his big leg towards my head. I jumped back as his foot missed my head by less than an inch. We never broke eye contact.

"Mr. Channing, I don't know what is going on here, but you know me, okay?" I said, trying to mollify the tension, but I was failing miserably.

I decided the best course of action was to remove myself from the situation. I crossed the street and disappeared into the night. I could still hear him yelling at me. "You know what, Trevor. You're out of the company!"

He didn't really have the authority to make that decision, but I was not going to argue. I wanted out.

Chapter Eleven

Judging by the amount of stuff Darrell had in the apartment, I figured they would be gone soon. I needed to disappear for a while. My heart was still pounding and my legs were a bit shaky. I tried to comprehend what had just happened. I had just avoided a potentially lethal blow from Mr. Channing. I should have felt lucky, but I felt like crap.

I needed to forget about what had just happened and focus on more important matters, like where I was going to live. I checked the time on my phone; it was 8:30 p.m.

I decided to walk up the street to a local supermarket. When I arrived, the place was empty. There was only one cashier open with no customers waiting. I went over to the cash machine and inserted my bankcard. I glanced up to make sure Mr. Channing had not followed me to finish off what he had started. I entered my PIN and hit 'View Balance'. The display read, $438.43. I selected the 'Transfer Funds' option from the menu and transferred $500 from my credit card to my account, now I had a little over $900.

Right beside the cash machine, I noticed a message board. The amount of ads was overwhelming. An ad posted the day before was considered old because within a day, there would typically be three new listings stapled on top of it. I sifted through the layers, most of them junk - lost dog posters, concert listings, odd jobs, it was all there. There were some ads for apartments, mostly looking to share accommodations with a Japanese student or a female, neither of which applied to me. I was not even sure I wanted another roommate after my last experience, but with only $900 to my name, it was the only reasonable option. I found one ad that said '2 BEDROOM APARTMENT FOR RENT. $600 PER MONTH. RIGHT DOWNTOWN. MALE PREFERRED'. This seems good, I thought, and it is on top of the pile, so it must be relatively new. I tore off one of the phone number tabs and gave the number a call.

"Hi, may I please speak with Chris?"

"Sorry, Chris is not here," a woman's voice answered. "He just stepped out for a moment, can I take a message?"

"Yes, I'm calling about his apartment for rent."

"Oh wow, that was fast! He just left about twenty minutes ago to put ads around town. You're the first one to call."

"Oh really, okay well do you know when he will be back?"

"He should be back soon, I'll tell him to give you a call when he gets in. By the way, what type of music do you listen to?"

"What type of music do I listen to?" I repeated just to make sure I heard her correctly. "I listen to rap music mostly."

"That's good, I listen to rap as well. I'll tell you what; Chris should be back any minute, why don't you come over now?"

Was this a date or an apartment viewing? Either way, I at least needed to check out the place that my secret password had just unlocked.

I took my time walking to the apartment in hopes Chris would be there before me. I arrived at the apartment building and punched in the buzzer number the woman had given me.

"Hello?" a man's voice came on the speaker.

"Uh, hi, is this Chris?" I asked.

"Yes, is this Trevor?"

"Yes."

"Hi, come on up. I'll buzz you in."

I wrapped my fingers around the large door handle and waited for the faint buzzer sound. When I entered the lobby, my immediate impression was good. From what I could tell so far, the building was a lot nicer than my old apartment. The walls were white and clean, and the floor's polished tiles were spotless. I checked out every detail of my new surroundings and imagined this as my new apartment. I stood in front of two stainless steel elevator doors and waited for one to open.

When I exited the elevator, I walked down a long hallway and found unit 318. I knocked a few times. I had no idea what to expect, but anything was better than being homeless.

"Hey, Trevor, come on in," a clean-cut man said.

I entered and saw a woman with big hair sitting on a black leather sofa.

"This is my sister Anne-Marie, she currently lives here," Chris said as he introduced me to the woman who was also into rap music.

"Hi, nice to meet you," I said, as I gave her a subtle wave. "This is a really nice place you guys have."

"Thanks. Yeah, we just painted it last month."

"The colours really look good together," I said. One of the walls was a dark yellow, one was a shiny black, and the other was a dark red. There were a few Justin Bua prints hanging on the walls and some plants in the corner.

"So, what do you do, Trevor?"

"I'm the owner and operator of my own business. We do pressure washing, trash removal, small moves, yard work...pretty much anything really." That was not exactly true, but I wasn't about to worry him by saying I was unemployed and had no place to live; that might raise too many concerns about my character.

"How about you? Where do you work?"

"Have you heard of Andre's Seafood Restaurant?"

"No, I haven't."

"Well, I'm a server there."

"Okay, cool."

"So when do you need a place?" he asked.

I wanted to say 'tonight!' but I exercised better judgment. I didn't want to seem desperate. "I gave my landlord one month notice so I need to be out by June 30th, but I would like to move out sooner just to get settled in."

"Okay, well Anne-Marie is moving out on the 15th of July".

"The 15th of July?" I repeated. That was in exactly one month. "That's too bad, that won't work for me unfortunately."

The meeting wrapped up quickly, and no sooner than I arrived, I was taking another elevator ride. I stepped outside and exhaled a deep breath. I didn't want to go back to the apartment so I needed a place to sit to clear my head.

I walked aimlessly down the streets of downtown Vancouver. The bright neon lights lit up the sky and made me feel like I wasn't alone through all of this. I walked by a movie theatre and decided to check out something that was playing, preferably a comedy.

Going to the movies might not be considered the most practical thing to do at that moment, but I was out of options. I needed to be around people and do something normal, something that would cheer me up.

As the movie was playing, I tried to relax, but it was no use. There was no way to shut my brain off. I was in a serious predicament. I desperately needed both money and an apartment. In short, I needed a miracle. I kept thinking about all the long hours that I slaved away in the hot sun and the freezing rain, all the money and time I had invested in the company, all for nothing.

At around 11:00 p.m., my phone vibrated. My initial thought was that Mr. Channing was looking to apologize, or perhaps looking to kick me in the head. Either way, I didn't want to speak to him, and he was certainly not going to find me. I took out my phone and looked at the number. I didn't recognize it.

"Hello?" I said as quietly as possible.

"Trevor? It's Miguel, what's up brother?"

"Hey, Miguel, how's it going?"

"Things are good with me as always, you know."

"I'm glad to hear that, Miguel."

"Hey, Trevor, I'm sorry to bother you, man, you sound busy, but I was just calling to see if you were still looking for an apartment?"

"Yes, I'm," I said with a hushed excitement, still conscious of the fact I was in a movie theatre.

"Okay, great, there is an apartment available in my building. I know the manager so it's yours if you want it."

"Sure, when can I see it?"

"You can come over right now if you like."

I immediately walked out of the movie and called a moving company. Due to the late hour, the movers agreed to help me, but they would charge me a small fortune. I didn't have a small fortune, but I also didn't have a lot of options. I was in no position to negotiate.

I cautiously made my way back to the apartment. Mr. Channing and Darrell were nowhere in sight.

The movers arrived shortly after and we moved the little furniture I had into their one-tonne truck. I had a bed, a small couch, a TV, some dishes, two duffel bags filled with clothes and shoes, and a couple of boxes.

It was a bit unusual to get an apartment at twelve o'clock at night, especially since I had not seen it and the landlord had not even met me yet, but I didn't think too much of it.

I showed up to the address that Miguel had given me. When I arrived, I saw Miguel standing on the corner waving his hands in the air with a huge smile on his face. I hopped out of the moving truck and looked at my new home. It became immediately apparent why the landlord did not need to meet with me beforehand. It was definitely not the Trump, but as the saying goes, beggars can't be choosers.

The building was an old three story building in desperate need of a paint job. There was a pub on the ground level with stragglers hanging around outside, drinking and smoking.

"Hey, you made it. Welcome," Miguel greeted me with a big hug. "See, I told you Miguel would come through for you."

Miguel was far more excited than I was, but he would get excited by pretty much anything. "Come on, I'll introduce you to the landlord."

"Can't wait," I said meagerly, as I forced a smile.

Miguel led the way, talking a mile a minute. It was obvious he had been drinking a little bit and this had heightened his already positive energy. "Hey, you know what the best part of this place is?"

"Tell me."

"Guess again," he said with a huge smile on his face.

"Okay, let me guess. Is it the pub?"

"You got it! Plus, I live here."

I like to go out and have a good time, but I didn't want the party near my house. I could already imagine all the drunk people screaming and getting into fights at all hours of the night. But again, what choice did I have?

"Okay, so here's the deal," Miguel's tone came down a notch as if he was about to reveal the truth behind this shady midnight deal. "The owner is out of town, okay. He owns the whole building - some rich Chinese guy. No one has heard from him in months. Last I heard, he was in China and completely forgot about this building. Some people pay rent, but most don't. We have a building manager, that's who you're about to meet, but he is a bit of a joke. So, just pay the manager the first month's rent just to get the place, and then you can decide what you're going to do after that."

"So, the manager doesn't care if people pay rent?"

"No, he is a tenant like us, but he agreed to manage the property in exchange for free rent."

"Some job he's doing," I remarked.

"Yeah, he's not really altogether this one, he claims to be a servant of god. Come on, let's meet him."

Raashid was a 55-year-old immigrant - never married, no kids, no job, just lived in a tiny bachelor apartment in a rundown building that he did the very least to manage.

"Raashid, this is Trevor, the guy I was telling you about." Raashid looked very pleased to be of some assistance. I got the impression he did not have many friends and liked to help people out whenever he could.

"Hello, Mr. Raashid, it's nice to meet you, sir."

"It's nice to meet you too, Trevor," he said with a thick Middle Eastern accent and a warm smile on his face.

"So I understand you have an apartment for rent?"

"Yes, I have two actually, you can take your pick. One is not quite vacant. The other one is a large one-bedroom."

"The one bedroom sounds fine, I'll take that one."

"Wonderful. The rent is $900 plus an additional $450 for damage deposit," he said with a big smile. I had mixed feelings about Raashid. I could tell he had a kind heart, but this was still a pretty shady deal conducted in the late hours of the night with no forms to fill out and Miguel as the broker. Nevertheless, I had no choice but to trust him.

"How about I give you $450 now for the remainder of the month, and I will pay you the rest on the first of next month?" I proposed. It made sense, but it was a bit of a gamble. He could have demanded full payment and I would have been screwed, but I didn't think he would turn me away in the middle of the night.

I still needed to pay the mover $200.00, which would leave me with a little over $700.00. From what Miguel had said, Raashid was not too concerned about people paying their rent, so it made no sense for me to give him all my money.

"Okay okay, that is fine, you pay me the $450 now, and the rest later. No problem."

I counted out $450.00 cash and handed it to him. In exchange he wrote me a receipt on the back of an unused postcard and handed it to me.

"Come. I will show you the apartment," he said.

I instructed the movers to follow me with my stuff.

"Is there an elevator in this place?" one of the movers asked.

"Hey, Miguel, is there an elevator in this building?"

"Yes, but it doesn't work. Your apartment is on the second floor so it's no big deal."

On our way up the stairs we passed a coin-operated laundry room. "How about these," I asked, "do these work?"

"One of the washers works, but none of the dryers work. Someone smashed the coin slot on the washer so you just have to jimmy with it and it will work for free.

There is a laundromat just up the street; you can take your things there to dry. Oh, and be careful because someone broke the lock on the laundry room door so make sure you watch your clothes so they don't get stolen."

Moments later, we arrived at the apartment. Raashid had a hard time finding the right key among his large key ring, but we eventually got into the unit. "Okay, here you are, and here is your key," Raashid said as he handed me my key.

"Thank you, Raashid. I will see you later. Have a good night."

I flipped on the light switch, but nothing happened. Fortunately there was enough light coming in from a streetlight that was near my window so the movers could see where they were going.

After the movers finished with the rest of my stuff, I paid them and they left.

I couldn't really see much, but the apartment didn't seem too bad. It was a decent size at least.

"Hey, this is a nice place, man," Miguel said as he looked around.

I was not sure what a one-bedroom apartment looked like in Mexico, but clearly we had different standards. It was definitely not 'nice', but it would have to do. I was just happy to have a roof over my head.

"Thanks again, Miguel. You don't know how much you have saved me, really."

"Hey, no problem man. Anytime."

"I'll call you tomorrow, okay?" I said.

"Okay, man, have a good night. If you need anything, just let me know."

Just like that, everyone was gone and the place was quiet. I somehow secured an apartment at the last possible moment. As much as I would have liked to celebrate, I still needed a job. I had two weeks to come up with another $900 for next month's rent, plus the $450 I owed for the damage deposit, plus living expenses. It pained me to think about it, but I was not in a good position.

It was late and I had had a long and miserable day. I just wanted some rest. I was too tired to unpack any of my things so I just curled up on my bare mattress and went to sleep.

Chapter Twelve

When I woke up, I went around and inspected my new apartment for the first time. In the light of day, I could really notice how old and dingy the place was. The carpets were thick orangey-brown shag, probably concealing horrible stains. The kitchen cabinets had a fake wood laminate on them, which was peeling off in most places. All the fixtures and knobs had not been updated since the place was built in the 60s. There were dirty finger marks on the walls and the entire place smelled like an old shoe. I didn't even want to look at the bathroom. I didn't see any signs of rodents or critters, but I was sure they were not too far away. I was not very impressed to say the least.

I walked over to the curtain-less window in my room to check out the view. The windows, like everything else, were completely filthy. The view from my second-floor apartment overlooked the alley behind the building. As I looked out, I saw a homeless man digging through one of the dumpsters. I stared at this man for a moment and was captivated. Circumstances in this man's life forced him to do something that he would probably not want to do otherwise. Could I be this man? I thought. Is this how my life will turn out? Sure, I was not digging through a dumpster, but I was not much better off than he was.

Ever since I arrived in Vancouver, my life had trended downwards. Given another month, it was certainly plausible I would be doing the same thing he was doing. I was barely treading water, fighting for survival, and I felt like I could drown at any moment.

I took a long look around my dark bedroom. There were boxes and bags scattered everywhere with no order and no purpose, it kind of reflected my life at the moment. Standing there, taking it all in, I started to think about all the stuff I had been through over the past year since I had moved out. It wasn't obvious what my next move was going to be. Where do I go from here? How did I even end up like this?

A year ago, I was thriving. I had lots of money, ambition, and optimism, but now my life was going in the exact opposite direction that I wanted it to go. The more I thought about it, the more upset it made me. I slowly began to break down emotionally. Soon after, my emotions completely consumed me and I could no longer stand the pain. I had reached my breaking point.

I dropped to my knees, and began to cry. I was completely broken. What started out as a slow pathetic weep soon escalated into something that was beyond my control. I felt like I was paralyzed and all I could do was scream. It felt like the tears were going to ooze out of every pore of my body and just drain me until I had nothing left. There was no more fight left in me, I was done, I had been defeated.

It was time to face the cold harsh reality that my venture into the real world had ended in disaster. As the pain grew stronger, I could no longer function. Like a ton of bricks weighing me down, I was hit with the worst possible depression; it was unlike anything I had ever felt before in my life. It was almost as if any ounce of hope that was remaining had suddenly been stripped away. My future looked bleak, as if I had been left for dead and nobody was coming to save me. As hard as I tried, I could not just snap out of it. My emotions, now in overdrive, rendered me helpless as I collapsed onto the dirty floor. This was it. I was all alone in this scary world and was completely helpless. I had hit rock bottom. My life sucks.

Somehow, I managed to lift myself up and crawl over to my mattress. I guess I still had enough sense in me not to be on that dirty floor for too long. I flopped onto the bare mattress and just laid there, face down, and continued to cry for hours.

As I laid on the mattress, I thought about a lot of things. Like a mathematician who had made a few mistakes along the way, I methodically analyzed my life to see where I had gone wrong. I went over every detail, every choice I had made in the past year, every conversation, every reaction, and every relationship.

I was a big failure. I allowed a loser into my life and now my life was in ruin because of it. What made matters worse was the realization that I had no one to blame but myself. If only I could do it all over again, if only I had another chance, I would be smarter, I would do things differently, I would learn from my mistakes.

That's when it hit me. I realized I could have a second chance; I could turn these negatives into positives. I could become whoever I wanted. If this was rock bottom, then the only way to go from here was up. I could have sat there and cried all day feeling sorry for myself, or I could develop a game plan and figure out how to get out of the mess I was in. I needed to take action. I needed to force change. I was down, but not out. Like a champion who had been knocked down in a late round of a fight, I had somehow summoned enough strength to continue to endure the pain. With a stubborn refusal I decided this wasn't my life. This wasn't my destiny. There had been a mistake. This was not supposed to happen to me. No, I refused to accept this is how my life is going to turn out.

The tears stopped and I began to pick myself up again. I was a fighter, not a quitter. I was a winner, not a loser. Using these thoughts as a mantra, I began to get my head back on straight and tell myself everything would be okay. I felt like I was making progress.

Thinking back on the events that led me to where I was, there were some pretty obvious things I did wrong. I went against my own intuition. Never again would I let someone be a negative influence on me. I needed to trust my instincts and be more cautious as to who I surrounded myself with. I needed to surround myself with positive people who would help me grow, inspire me, have my best interest at heart, and not bring me down. And if I ever went into business again, I needed to choose my business partners wisely.

I kept thinking about all the lessons I could learn from my experiences so I would never be in this situation again. I needed to relearn the importance of financial responsibility. I used to be really good with my money and not spend it on stuff I didn't need. I had nearly eight grand saved up from my time in Banff, but within a few short months I had nothing left.

I had experienced a minor setback, but this wasn't the end for me. I would continue on, much wiser, as I had now gained valuable knowledge from this experience. Maybe this is what life is all about; people need to go through stuff in order to develop.

I heard a saying once that God would never put you in a situation you do not have the power to overcome. I felt like this was true for me in this particular instance. I wasn't a religious person per se, but I found comfort in the sentiment. I knew I could overcome this hardship. It was the first major obstacle in my life since I had moved out, but that's all it was, an obstacle, not the end of the road.

I thought long and hard about my life and the situation I was in and I decided what I had to do. The first order of business was to get out of the depressing apartment.

Chapter Thirteen

I made my way down the stairs and noticed the handrail had been ripped off the wall and was now lying on the stairs. It must have had an unfortunate encounter with a drunk person stumbling home last night.

I knocked on Raashid's door.

"Oh, hello," Raashid answered.

"Hi, Raashid. I'm sorry to bother you, but you mentioned there was another apartment available and I was wondering if I could take a look at it please?" I said, like a man who was on a mission.

"Oh sure, no problem. The tenants moved out this morning. Don't go anywhere; I will be right back with the key." Raashid scurried off into his lair. A few moments later he came back. "Okay, here you go. The unit number is 2E."

"Thanks, Raashid," I said as I ran back upstairs to check out the other apartment.

I inserted the key into 2E. It was on the opposite side of the hall so I knew it would not be facing the alley. When I opened the door, I felt the warmth of the sun immediately. The place was bright and the view was much better too. I stood at the window and was now overlooking a beautiful park. I guess I didn't really learn to appreciate trees and greenery until I no longer had it.

Things were starting to look better already. The place was similar to the first one, it had the same thick orange shag carpet, same fixtures, but this suite had two bedrooms. I didn't really consider how much extra the rent would be, but with the extra bedroom I could always get a roommate to make the rent cheaper for me.

I went back to the first apartment and slowly dragged all my stuff down the hall and into my new place. I arranged the few pieces of furniture I had and organized my kitchen and bedroom. I spent a few hours tidying and cleaning, disinfecting all the counters, light switches, and doorknobs. After all that was done, I tackled the bathroom.

As I emptied the last of my things out of one of the boxes, a card fell out and onto the floor. I picked it up and opened it.

Dear Trevor

Thanks again for spending time with me and showing me around. If you are ever in Vancouver, give me a call and I can return the favor. Love Ashley.

"Oh my god," I said aloud. I hadn't seen this card since I lived in Banff. I didn't even know that I still had it. I had completely forgotten that Ashley lived in Vancouver.

I quickly grabbed my cell phone and dialed the number she had left. After a few rings, a voice came on. "This is Ashley, leave a message."

***

My apartment was entirely clean. Now what? There was no sense in being cooped up in the apartment all day and I still needed to figure out how to make money. I needed to rebuild my life, and getting the new apartment was just the first step.

I put my shoes on and locked up my apartment. When I got outside, the sun was shining brightly; I had to squint until my eyes adjusted. I felt the warm breeze against my face and I took a deep breath of the summer air. Like Superman, I felt like the yellow sun gave me strength. I set off down the street with no particular destination in mind. I just needed to clear my head and gather my thoughts.

I had a million thoughts racing through my mind as I walked around exploring my new neighbourhood. The neighbourhood was like any other, there were restaurants, convenience stores, grocery stores, and of course a laundromat. I came across an internet café and sat down at a computer.

My next order of business was to get a job. Over the next couple of hours I typed out a résumé and emailed it to a dozen or so companies. I wasn't really sure what I was looking for, but given my situation, I was willing to do pretty much anything. I applied mainly to clothing stores, hotels, and restaurants. I then emailed my résumé to myself so I wouldn't have to retype it. I printed off another dozen résumés to take with me, and I left.

It was around 4:30 p.m. and I wanted to swing by the grocery store and buy some essentials. I picked up a package of hot dogs, some soap, toilet paper, some instant noodle soup, and a small pot.

I paid for the groceries and walked outside. I could feel my phone vibrate, but my hands were full. I put the bags down and quickly flipped open my phone.

Chapter Fourteen

I didn't know too many people in the city, so I was not used to my phone ringing. "Hey, what's up?" the soft voice said with no introduction. A little presumptuous, but I knew exactly who it was.

"Hey, Ashley, how's it going? I was just thinking about you."

"You were?" she replied with a flirtatious giggle.

"That's good because I was thinking about you too. I got your message. When did you get into town?"

"To be honest with you, I've been here for a few months. I would have called sooner, but I had to get my life in order."

"So did you get your life in order?"

"I'm starting to get it on track. What are your plans tonight?"

Even though I would have loved to see her, I did not have any game at the moment. There was nothing attractive about my situation, but I could have really used a friend, someone to talk to and hang out with so I wouldn't feel so alone. Besides, she didn't really seem like the type to judge, and even if she was, it would be better to find that out sooner than later. It was time to find out if my lack of funds would be a problem for her.

"I'm not really sure what I'm doing tonight," she replied.

"Do you want to hang out?" I asked.

"Sure."

"Okay, great, what part of the city do you live in?"

"I live downtown."

"Okay, I can come downtown and meet you if you want?" I asked. It was too soon to be showing her where I lived. My clothes were still relatively new so I wouldn't give off the impression I was in serious financial trouble. I needed a few more dates in before I would feel confident enough to bring her back to my place.

***

I could hardly wait for the night to come. I had a second date with Ashley, but I wasn't sure what I was going to do with her. I needed to keep the date cheap so I scheduled it after dinner to eliminate the possibility of her getting hungry.

As soon as I arrived back at my apartment, I went to the kitchen to make some food. I filled my pot with water, put it on the stove, and turned the knob on the corresponding element. Nothing happened. I tried the others, but they were all dead.

I thought for a moment then came up with plan B.

I took out my electric grill and plugged it into a nearby socket, but it didn't work either. I tried a few other sockets around the apartment, but after a while, it was confirmed. I did not have electricity.

I opened the door of my apartment and found an outlet in the hallway. I plugged in my grill and inconspicuously tucked the cord under my door. I waited a few moments to see if the grill was getting hot – it was. In that moment, sitting in the front entrance of my apartment, I reflected on how truly ghetto this was. It was one step above roasting wieners over a barrel fire in the back alley.

While the grill was heating up, I went to the kitchen again to grab the wieners and fill up a mug with tap water. By the time I got back, the grill was hot so I sliced a wiener in half, the long way, and began grilling. I sat there on the floor, hovered over my grill, monitoring the progress. A few moments later, dinner was served.

***

Ashley lived on the other side of the bridge from where I was currently living. It was a ten-minute cab ride or an hour-long walk. I needed to conserve as much money as possible so I decided just to walk to her place. I took a handful of résumés with me so I could apply for some jobs along the way.

I arrived at Ashley's place at 7:20 p.m. The sun was setting and there would only be another hour and a half until it became completely dark. I buzzed her apartment and the crackly speaker started to ring.

"Hello?"

"Hey, Ashley, it's me."

"Okay, come on up."

I entered her lobby and was impressed right away. The luxurious décor let me know I was in a classy building. It was certainly an upgrade from my apartment building – the elevator actually worked here. I got in and it accelerated rapidly up to the eighteenth floor.

I walked up to her apartment door, but didn't knock right away. I needed a moment. I couldn't believe I was actually going to see Ashley again and I wanted to make sure I was presentable. I pulled out a pack of gum, pushed a piece through the foil wrapping, and shoved it into my mouth. I chewed on it aggressively for a moment until the juices filled my mouth. I swallowed the juices and took a deep breath, inhaling the peppermint air. I straightened out my outfit and dusted off some rogue pieces of lint. I took a brief moment to gather my thoughts, then when I was ready, I knocked on her door.

"Hey, what took you so long?" she asked. "I was watching you through the peephole,"

I was greeted by a woman every bit as beautiful as I remembered.

"I'm sorry, I just had to do a systems check before I came in," I replied.

She laughed, showing off her cute dimples and perfect white teeth. She invited me in and I gave her a big hug. She smelled great. Her hair was still a bit wet; she must have just gotten out of the shower.

"It's been a while, how have you been?" she asked.

"A lot has happened since the last time we saw each other, but I'm doing well. I just can't believe I'm standing here right now. I never thought I would see you again."

"Yeah I know, who would have thought?"

I looked around her high-rise apartment and immediately noticed the vast disparity between our living conditions. Everything was new and seemed to be high-end. There was a beautiful black granite countertop in the kitchen, complemented by sparkling white tiles and a large stainless steel double-door refrigerator. The carpets were new and stain free, a nice off-white color. Plus she had electricity!

"This is a really nice place," I said.

"Thanks, sorry about the mess," she said. I looked around and the place was spotless.

"Do you want something to drink?" she asked.

"No, thank you."

"Okay, I'll be right back, I just need to finish blow drying my hair," she said as she rushed off to finish getting ready.

"You look very nice by the way," I said sincerely.

She didn't even break stride, she just continued walking into her room turning her head slightly over her shoulder long enough to give me a sexy smile before she disappeared into her room.

I sat down on her big sectional sofa and looked out at the magnificent view. I could see for miles – the entire downtown area, the water, the mountains, and even the top of the Lindberg building.

"So, where are you taking me tonight?" she asked.

The truth was I didn't want to take her anywhere, I would be happy to stay at her place. "I was thinking we could take a long romantic walk on the beach."

"Are you being serious? I would love that!"

"Good." After that, I had nothing else planned, perhaps a long romantic walk back in the other direction. I needed to keep this date as cheap as possible. I was down to my last $200. I knew there was a possibility she wanted to go out for dinner, drinks, or something that would involve me spending money. I was prepared to spend fifty dollars on this evening. I would make up the cost in other ways - maybe not eat for a week. I'm otherwise a rational man, but I can justify doing pretty much anything for a beautiful woman. She could probably get me to spend the entire $200 on her if I thought it would get me another date.

A few moments later, she emerged from her room.

"Shall we go?" she asked.

***

The sun setting off the ocean was beautiful. We took our shoes off and walked barefoot in the sand. After a while, we found a nice little spot to sit and watch the rest of the sunset. It was a clear night, but it was a getting a little cool. The breeze off the water was just enough to give her the shivers. I put my arm around her and we sat in silence for a moment.

It's funny, I hardly knew this girl and yet here we were, watching a sunset like some old couple. It was fine with me, taking her out somewhere was a luxury I could not afford at the moment. Besides, sometimes less is more. I just hoped she wasn't looking for any grandiose gestures of affection. I certainly didn't need anything fancy, I was happy just to spend time with her.

***

We arrived at the front door of her building. She took out a key card and swiped it against an electronic sensor. The sensor beeped and she opened the door.

"Do you want to come up for a bit?" she asked.

"Sure," I said casually.

We entered the apartment and she flicked on the lights and tossed her keys on the kitchen counter.

"Would you like a glass of wine?" she asked.

"That would be great, thanks."

This girl was amazing; she was really pretty, had her own place, was easy to get along with, and she drank wine - very sophisticated. I had never drank wine before, but I was not about to turn down her offer.

She poured two glasses of wine and brought them over to the couch.

"Do you drink red?" she asked as she handed me my glass.

"Yes, of course. Thank you," I said. I was trying to mask the fact I had never drank wine before. I didn't want to seem too childlike. I took a sip and tried not to grimace. It tasted like poison. I took another sip.

"How's the wine?" she asked.

"It's good, thanks," I said. Something told me the truth would not be appropriate here. The wine tasted like nail polish remover. I was not sure why people drank this stuff, have they not heard of juice? I would have preferred juice, but this would have to do. I took another sip.

"I can't get over the view you have."

"I know, it's nice right?"

"I had a few issues with my view this past week."

"What do you mean?"

"I changed apartments recently so now I overlook a nice park."

"What was your view before?"

"A dark and scary alley."

I proceeded to tell her about my situation over the last few months with Darrell, his dad, and the apartment. After all, I could hardly be blamed for that.

"That sucks," she said. "I can't believe your friend did that to you."

"Yeah, it turns out he wasn't much of a friend."

"Why was his dad so mad at you?"

"Because Darrell had been lying to him. He told his dad I was stealing and being lazy, which was not true at all. It was everything he was doing. So once his dad heard these things, his natural instinct as a father was to protect his son."

"Look at it as a blessing in disguise. You don't need to be around people like that; they'll only bring you down."

"You're right. I need to be around people like you."

"Exactly," she said, as we looked into each other's eyes. By now, we were both feeling the effects of the wine. I glanced down at her soft and full lips. I had kept our first kiss short and sweet, but this time I was not going to hold back.

Chapter Fifteen

The next morning I woke up to the sound of traffic. It was much noisier downtown than my neighbourhood.

"Good morning," she said.

"Good morning."

"Did you sleep okay?"

"Yes I did, thanks for letting me crash here last night. Your couch is actually more comfortable than my bed."

"I hope I wasn't being too loud this morning. Did I wake you?"

"No, not at all."

"I made coffee if you want some."

"No, thanks, I'm not a coffee drinker."

"Are you hungry at all? There are bagels in the fridge, I also have muffins, cereal, toast, you can help yourself, okay? I still need to get ready for work."

I crawled out of bed and reminisced about the wonderful night we shared. Finally, something was going right for me. After folding the blanket she had given me last night, I went over to the smorgasbord of food. I felt like a king.

"So, what are you going to do today?" she called out from the bathroom.

"I need to look for a job. I'll probably be downtown later if you want to hang out after work."

"Sure."

I finished my bagel and grabbed a muffin for the road. I walked her to the mall where she worked as a server at a pancake house.

"Have a good day at work, I'll see you later," I said.

After I dropped her off, I walked the five kilometers back to my apartment. I arrived back at my home a little before noon. I jumped in the shower and got dressed in my applying-for-jobs outfit.

I went up the street to the internet café, printed out another two dozen résumés, and placed them neatly in a folder. I ate my muffin to power up on carbs before I made my way back downtown once again. I handed out my résumé to a few places along the way, but my main destination was the two-block stretch in the downtown shopping district and the mall.

***

Over the course of the next week, I had a hard time coming up with ways to fill my day. I went to the public library and would read for hours. I didn't like spending a lot of time in my apartment; it felt like a prison. There was no radio, no TV, and relatively no furniture. I would also go on long walks for hours. I did some of my best thinking on those walks. Along the way, I would go into all the grocery stores and eat their free samples. I had to ration my food because my money was almost all gone. I still had not heard back from any companies that I had applied to and it was getting down to the wire.

On my way back from one of my long walks, I stopped by the laundromat and checked the ads that were posted there. One other guy was there checking the postings as well. It appeared he was looking for an apartment.

"Hey, are you looking for an apartment to rent?" I asked.

"Yeah," the guy responded, as he looked me up and down suspiciously.

"I actually have an apartment to rent and was just about to post an ad," I said, as I held up my folder of résumés.

"Really? What's the rent?"

"The rent is…" *Am I really going through with this?* I questioned myself.

I still had the keys to both units in my building. It had been over a week and Raashid had not asked for the other set back. In all likelihood, he had completely forgotten about it.

"The rent is $800 plus $400 damage deposit." I gave a lowball figure just to secure him. If this didn't work, I would not want to take my chances and post an ad, too many complications.

"Wow, okay. Yeah, that sounds good. Whereabouts is it?"

"It's only a few blocks from here; would you like to see it now?"

I'm not sure why this guy didn't think it was weird that a nineteen year old was out scouting tenants at the laundromat. I guess he was either naive or he was desperate for a place to live like I once was. Either way, it didn't matter to me. Sometimes opportunities present themselves and it's a matter of being perceptive and taking advantage of them. In this case, it was a matter of timing; I was in the right place at the right time.

When we entered the apartment, I immediately opened some windows to let the fresh air in. "The place belongs to my dad, he owns a few units in this building," I said as I began to launch into my sales pitch. I live across the hall and help him manage these units."

The guy nodded, displaying his acceptance of my story, and continued to inspect the place.

"You're getting a real bargain here too. I don't want a lot of hassle; I just want someone who will pay their rent on time," I paused a moment to let the information sink in before I proceeded.

"That won't be a problem," he responded.

"You don't need to sign a contract or anything, you can just pay month to month. All I ask is that you give me at least thirty days notice when you decide to vacate."

"Okay, that sounds good. And the rent is $800, right?"

"Yes. Plus I need a $400 damage deposit."

"Okay, I'll take it," he said.

"I can give you the key now, but I would need the first month's rent and damage deposit up front."

An hour later, the guy came back with the money.

"Okay, looks good, it's all here." I went over some other formalities to avoid further suspicion. I needed this guy to think this was as legitimate as possible. "Rent is due on the first of each month. I live down the hall in 2E. You can deliver the rent to me there. Let me give you my cell phone number in case there are any problems, just give me a call and I will take care of it immediately."

"Okay. Thanks."

"No problem, thank you. Enjoy the suite."

And just like that, my hustle-preneurship once again helped me out of a jam. Although what I did was both illegal and unethical, I was helping this kid out. He needed a place, and I needed money. Besides, the real owner wouldn't be collecting rent from that suite anyway.

I was now up $1,200.00 and feeling good. This money would be enough to tie me over for a while, but it was still no time to celebrate yet. My rent was due in a few days and I was not sure if Raashid would expect payment. If he did, then I would have to pay him $900.00 for May's rent and hope he didn't ask for the damage deposit, or the other apartment key back. I had around $200.00 in my bank account and was holding $1,200 cash, so if I decided to pay the rent, it would leave me with $500.00 for living expenses.

Another thought also occurred to me, I could use some of this money to take Ashley out to a nice dinner. I couldn't stop thinking about her.

Chapter Sixteen

The job hunt was frustrating to say the least. My résumé was still essentially a blank piece of paper. I realized if I wanted to get something out of life, I needed to apply myself. Applying did not simply mean dropping off my résumé and hoping for a callback, I needed to force the action. What I was doing was clearly not working. The next day, I went back to the internet café and revised my résumé. This time I changed the format, the wording, the font, and made my name and phone number stand out in large bold letters.

Now that my résumé looked a lot better, I wanted to update my look. I was beginning to realize the clothing I thought was appropriate was not exactly what the business world considered appropriate. I needed to adapt to my surroundings if I wanted to fit in.

It was around 12:00 p.m. and I had just left the internet café. I decided to walk downtown again and get a new outfit at the mall.

I was not sure what I was looking for, preferably something dressy that made me look more mature. I browsed around all the sales racks and discount stores to find something that looked nice without costing a lot. After about an hour of searching, I found a few things I liked so I went into the fitting room to try them on. I decided on a casual-preppy look, a white golf shirt with khaki pants.

I put on my new outfit and went back to all the same places in which I had previously applied. This time, instead of walking in and dropping off my résumé, I asked to speak with the manager. If I could speak with the manager, perhaps I could impress them like I had done in Banff.

These small changes made a big difference. Not long after I implemented my new approach, my answering machine had several messages from managers wanting to schedule an interview with me. Before, I had no callbacks and I was desperate, and now I had many companies interested in me. There had been a power shift in my favor. I changed my perception from me needing something from them, to them needing something from me. This allowed me to have a little more control over the process. Since multiple companies desired me, I could simply choose the job I wanted. This added level of confidence allowed me to excel in the interviews. I went to all of the interviews, even for the jobs I did not really want. I did this to get better at being interviewed. By the tenth interview, I was really comfortable and my answers flowed better.

The interviews were going well, but I still did not have any offers coming in. There was one place I still hadn't applied to yet because the manager was never in when I went there.

I put on my outfit and went back down to the mall. When I approached the store, I did not go in right away. Instead, I hung around outside remaining hidden behind a large plant. I wanted to stack the odds as much in my favor as possible, so stayed back to gather intel. I watched how the manager acted, what kind of mood he seemed to be in, and I observed the traffic flow to make sure it was not too busy. When all signs were green, I took a deep breath and walked confidently into the store.

"Hi, I would like to speak with Marc Andrews please," I said with the confidence of an FBI agent about to make an arrest.

"I'm Marc Andrews, how can I help?"

"Mr. Andrews, my name is Trevor Morrison. I spoke with you on the phone a couple of months ago regarding a sales position." Before Marc had time to say anything I was already into my pitch. "If you recall, I was not available at the time, but I would like the opportunity to work for you now. I guarantee you I will outsell all of your top sellers."

"Wow, that's a pretty bold statement, I like it," he said with a big smile. "I'm glad you came back, we only want the best sales people here, and you certainly seem like you're hungry for a shot at the best," he said jokingly.

"Yes, sir."

"Okay, I'm sold. When can you start?"

"Whenever you need me."

"Okay, how about you come in tomorrow at 8:00 a.m.?"

"Okay, I'll be here. Thank you so much, Mr. Andrews. I will see you tomorrow morning at 8:00 a.m."

"Just call me Marc."

"Okay, Marc, thanks again."

I walked out of the store appearing calm and collected, but inside I was about to burst at the seams with joy. Thanks again to my hustle; I had an apartment, a little bit of pocket money from the other apartment, and now a job. I was beginning to see a pattern here.

Now that I had a job, I could breathe a little easier. I had now put myself back on the path I once walked. I had to endure a few months of hell, but thankfully I made it to the other side.

I reached into my pocket and took out my cell phone. I pressed speed-dial 1 and raised the phone to my ear.

"Hello?"

"Hey, Ashley, it's Trevor, what are you doing?"

"Oh, hey. I'm just at work, waiting for my last table to settle their bill. What are you doing?"

"Nothing, just walking around in the mall."

"You're in the mall now?"

"Yeah."

"Why don't you come by?"

"Alright, I'll see you soon."

I walked around the mall for a bit and checked out a few stores. I arrived at Ashley's work a little after 2:00 p.m.

"Hey. You look nice."

"Thanks," I said. "This is my job-hunting outfit."

"So how's that going?"

"I actually just talked my way into a sales position at the Athletic Surplus upstairs."

"Really! That's great, congratulations!"

"Thanks. I'm really glad to go back to work. My first day is tomorrow."

"So we'll be working in the same mall?"

"I'm afraid so," I said sarcastically.

"That's awesome, I'm so excited. We have to celebrate tonight."

"Okay."

"Let me just cash out really quickly and we can hang out."

***

Ashley lived about five minutes away from the mall. When we arrived at her place, she headed straight for the bathroom. "I'm going to take a shower, I smell like pancakes. You can watch TV if you like. There's juice in the fridge and snacks in the cabinet beside the fridge if you get hungry."

"Alright, thanks."

TV with cable, a comfortable couch, juice, snacks - this was a life I could get used to. What may seem ordinary to some people was a privilege to me. For the past month, my diet consisted almost entirely of wieners and tap water. I would skip breakfast and lunch and have wieners for dinner. I couldn't even afford buns or mustard. I felt bad for taking so much from Ashley, but I vowed to make it up to her one day. For now, I sat back and enjoyed the ride.

Chapter Seventeen

My first day of work was exciting. It seemed like a cool environment - young staff, good music, and nice clothing. After I was given the grand tour and was introduced to everyone, I was instructed to read the company's policies and sales manuals. I sat at a small desk in the back room, which also served as the employee's lounge.

The following day was my first day on the sales floor. This was where I would be tested against the other top sellers. Each week, the employee's sales were posted in the back office. I made it a point to study that well, to see who my competition was. A guy named Josh was consistently the top seller each week. The week before I arrived, his total weekly sales were $4,168.89. I didn't care who he was or how he did it, but he now had a target on his back and I made it a goal of mine to destroy him. It was nothing personal, just business.

Since I was in the back the entire day on Monday, I only had four more days until the end of the week. The sales results were posted every Monday. I was already down a day, so I had a lot of catching up to do.

"I just sold another pair of shoes!" Josh announced to anyone willing to listen. "I'm on fire today; I'm already at eleven hundred!" he bragged.

It was rough going for me at first. I was unfamiliar with both the product and the store layout yet, but I had hustle. I would not be outworked.

After an hour or so, I started to find my rhythm. I made a couple of small sales, but more importantly I learned how it all worked. The sales floor was like a shark tank, with five sharks working at all times and the customers were their prey. To the untrained eye we all just looked like a bunch of sales people walking around aimlessly. In actuality, we were very much stalking our prey, getting into position, and would become incredibly hostile towards each other if another associate got too close to our customer. We would mark our territory with sayings like, 'I got these people', 'I talked to these people first', 'I'm already helping that guy'. I wasn't saying these things at first, but I was also not getting very many sales either. It was a sink or swim environment and I had to adapt quickly. "I got these guys," I said over the headset as I followed my prey up to the shoe wall.

The first challenge was to convince an ordinary person who walked into the store to open their wallet and buy something. There were two main strategies with this: one was to catch as many fish as possible – the ol' strength in numbers play. The other tactic was to focus on catching only the biggest fish. The latter required an incredibly keen eye to read people for buying signals, a technique I had not yet perfected in this environment. Once a big fish was identified, the goal was to get them to buy as much as possible.

I focused on numbers. I went for the customers nobody else wanted. I sometimes had five customers at a single time. It was a juggling act that required a lot of running, but my strategy paid off. Many little sales eventually added up to a lot. Occasionally, I would get lucky and catch a big fish.

Each night, I would take the product manuals home and study them. Then each day, I would spout all the knowledge I had just learned the night before. Over time, I became more comfortable with the store's products and their locations. I made some large sales, but took many smaller ones as well. I knew I was selling a lot, but I didn't know where I stood in terms of beating out my co-workers, especially Josh.

I came in on Monday morning and Marc greeted me with a warm welcome. "Good morning, champ," Marc said with a very suspicious smile on his face, as if he knew something I did not.

"Good morning," I replied.

When I returned to the back room, I put my bag down and looked over at the sales board. Josh was standing by the latest posting, analyzing the results.

"Hey, Josh," I said in a friendly tone. He didn't say anything back. As soon as he walked away, I went over to view the results. Josh sold an impressive $5,347.00 last week, crushing his last week's total by more than a thousand dollars. I then searched for my name. I was expecting it to be somewhere near the bottom. I eventually found it in the top spot - Trevor Morrison - weekly sales total: $11,582.00.

"Holy crap!" I said under my breath, surprised at the result. Am I reading this correctly? I figured it had to be some sort of typo. I could hardly contain my happiness; it felt like I had just won the lottery or something. I had to be careful not to gloat in front of anyone. It was important to remain on good terms with my co-workers. I knew keeping them happy would be a huge component in my future success there.

"Hey, Trevor. Congratulations!" Karen said to me.

"Thanks."

"Oh my god, did you see your sales last week?" another co-worker asked.

"Yes, I saw, I'm quite surprised," I said.

"Yeah, how did you sell so much?"

"Got lucky I guess," I said humbly, trying to downplay the defeating blow I had just served to the veterans. Josh was not as pleased as the others were. He was really competitive about his sales and I had just humiliated him. I had sent a message loud and clear, there was a new top dog in town.

Chapter Eighteen

I decided to pay Raashid the rent, $900 cash for the 2-bedroom suite. He didn't say anything about it costing more and he seemed to have forgotten completely about the damage deposit and the key to the other apartment that I still had. Once again, he wrote me a receipt on the back of a postcard. I quickly took the receipt and left before his memory returned. I had just bought myself another month, but I definitely needed a new place. I didn't even bother hooking up the electricity because I didn't think I would be there too much longer.

I woke up at 7:00 a.m. on Tuesday morning. It was the beginning to my weekend. My manager deliberately scheduled my days off on the two slowest days of the week so that I could be there to maximize the sales for the rest of the week. Ashley was working so I needed to find something to occupy my time. I decided to take a long walk along the sea wall.

I walked for hours – just thinking. What do I want to do with my life? I asked myself. I drew a blank and tried another way. What's missing in my life? The answer to this question came a little easier. I needed one thing - happiness. Everything else was just a byproduct. I then asked myself, how can I acquire happiness? I continued to walk, pondering these grand questions.

At around 3:00 p.m., I texted Ashley. She texted me back right away. 'HEY, I'M OFF AT 3:30. COME MEET ME :) '.

I arrived at her work just as she was leaving. "Hey, gorgeous," I said, as I gave her a big hug and a kiss on top of her head. "Mmm, you smell like pancakes and syrup."

"Eww that's disgusting. I need to go home and shower."

When we arrived at Ashley's place, I fell into my usual routine: grab some snacks and juice and make myself comfortable in front of the TV. I flipped through five hundred and thirty channels and there was nothing on. I finally settled on Oprah.

I wasn't paying too much attention to what she was talking about, I was much more interested in studying her body language. I was curious as to why some people are successful and others are not. There had to be something in Oprah that I could point to, a particular talent she possessed that others did not. It wasn't obvious to me. Was it luck? I wondered. Luck probably had something to do with it. I bet when she was my age she never imagined how her life would turn out.

Oprah's story fascinated me. Here was a woman who miraculously came through the mix from the ground up, and somehow made it to the top when so many others had failed, and she was an ethnic minority. If she could do it with two noticeable disadvantages, then surely I could do it too. I had heard ambition beats talent ninety percent of the time, so maybe that was it.

On the commercial break, I went over to the fridge to refill my juice. On the kitchen counter was a pile of opened mail. On top was Ashley's most recent bank statement. I contemplated on whether or not I should have a look at it. I wasn't interested in how much money she had, but I was curious how a minimum wage server at a pancake house was able to afford such a nice downtown apartment on her own without having a roommate. I figured the rent was at least $1,600.00 a month.

The bank statement was practically opened already; all I needed to do was casually poke it open some more and have a quick peek. What's the harm? I thought. I listened for a moment and heard Ashley still splashing around in the shower so I set my glass down and picked up her bank statement. On the top of the page I saw her name 'Ashley Taylor'. My eyes scrolled down to her account balance '$8,162.15'. I went over the statement in more detail. 'June 1st - deposit... $5,000.00'. What the heck is going on here?

I heard the water shut off so I folded up the statement and went back to the couch.

"You still okay?" Ashley came out with a towel wrapped around her.

"Who, me? Yeah, I'm fine, thanks. Just watching Oprah," I said with a smile.

"I just have to dry my hair, then we can hang out."

"Take your time."

Fifteen minutes later she came out looking amazing as usual. Her bronze skin glimmered and smelled of fresh exotic fruits.

We went downstairs and hailed a cab. The cab took us over the bridge into my neighbourhood and dropped us off right in front of Luigi's Italian Restaurant.

After we ate, we took a stroll down the main shopping street in my neighbourhood. It was not like the main strip downtown, but it had character.

"So whereabouts do you live?" she asked.

"I live just a few blocks west of here."

"Oh really, I want to see!" she said excitedly.

This was the decisive moment for me. I was hesitant to show her my apartment because it was a big contrast to her lifestyle. She was aware of my situation, but maybe she thought I was exaggerating a bit.

I reluctantly led her to my apartment building. We both didn't say much. I held the front door open for her and we walked upstairs then down the hall. I unlocked the door to my apartment and prepared for the worst.

"So here it is," I said. "It's nothing fancy… and it's just temporary," I tried to conceal my insecurities.

"This isn't so bad, it has character," she said with a smile. I didn't say anything, I was just waiting for the bad news like she just remembered she needed to pick up her Aunt from the airport or she left her hairdryer on. Some reason she had to get the hell out of my apartment.

After a brief tour she turned to me with a sincere smile and said, "I like it."

"Keep in mind this is only temporary, okay? Remember, I needed to scramble last minute to find a place and this is what was available."

"Hey, nice view. You can see the park perfectly. Oh wow, look at all the trees… my view is so boring; I'm surrounded by cold buildings."

I guess it is true what they say, the grass is always greener on the other side.

"Well before you get too excited, I have to mention something," I took a long pause before I delivered the bad news, "there's no electricity."

"That's okay, we can tell ghost stories," she said trying to lighten the mood.

"Really, you don't mind?"

"No, not at all, do you have any candles at least?"

"Of course."

"Good," she said with a sexy smile.

As the sun went down, we lit all the candles I had and put them in my bedroom.

I laid down on my bed in the dimly lit room and gazed up at Ashley who was standing at the foot of my bed in the flickering candle light. She slowly unbuttoned her shirt and it fell to the floor. She did the same with her pants. We both didn't say a word. Talking would most likely ruin this moment. I was happy just staring at her beautiful toned body in silence. She crawled toward me and got a little more comfortable.

***

At around 3:00 a.m., I heard a commotion in the hallway outside my apartment. This was not the typical drunk guy coming home from the bar commotion – it was different. I slowly got up to check it out. Still feeling a little groggy, I stumbled down the hall toward my front door. As I approached closer to the door, I could hear arguing. I looked out the peephole in the door and saw a short well-dressed Asian man saying something about rent. Oh no, that must be the building owner, I thought. I was now completely awake with my eye fixated on the peephole, trying to get a better view of the action. I checked to make sure the door was locked. I was not really sure what to expect when he knocked on my door. After all, I paid my rent and I still had my receipt to prove it. But I didn't need this hassle in my life, especially when Ashley was here. I hoped he would just go away.

I couldn't see much through the peephole, but I continued to look. I could hear perfectly through the flimsy door.

"Where's my rent money?" the man shouted with a Chinese accent.

"Ray, we tried to contact you about the rent, but you were out of town". One of my neighbours said.

"Rent is due on the first of every month; you haven't paid in over three months."

"Yes, but there are a lot of issues with the building, Ray. The elevator doesn't work, the laundry doesn't work, and there are lots of other repairs in our unit that need to be done."

"Hey, rent is rent, where do you think the money to fix all those things comes from?"

"Ray, it's late, can we discuss this in the morning? We will pay you the rent tomorrow."

"Fine," he said, as he moved onto the next unit.

'KNOCK KNOCK KNOCK' - Ray banged on my door.

"What's going on?" Ashley said as she came out to see what all the commotion was.

"Shhh," I said quietly putting my finger up to my lips.

'KNOCK KNOCK KNOCK' "Landlord, open up!"

This can't be good, I thought. I really didn't want to have to deal with that at the moment.

"Ashley, come on, let's go back to bed," I took her back to the room. "Let's just ignore him, maybe he will go away." For all he knew, nobody was even renting this unit. Maybe he would just move on to the next one.

"What's going on?" she asked in a frightened tone.

"Ashley, when you live in a crumby apartment above a pub that has no electricity, this is the kind of stuff you can expect at 3:00 a.m."

As we laid in bed quietly, we heard a key go into the lock and then the lock snapped open.

Someone was now in my apartment and he was not alone. "There's stuff here, somebody lives here," I heard one of them say. "Check the bedroom."

Someone flicked the hallway light switch, but nothing happened.

"Just pretend you're sleeping," I whispered in Ashley's ear.

"Hey! Landlord, wake up!"

We opened our eyes and saw three men standing at the foot of our bed. I tried to act surprised. "Hey, get out of my house before I call the cops!" I demanded.

"I'm the landlord and I'm with the police. You are trespassing!"

"What are you talking about? I live here," I said trying to sound confused.

"Where are the lights in this place?" Ray said.

"They don't work. Just give me a minute, I'll be right out," I said in a calm voice.

Ray and the two police officers waited for me in the hall outside my apartment where they could see me better.

"Stay here, baby, I'll take care of this, it's all a misunderstanding."

I quickly put some clothes on and went out to the hallway. "You mind telling me what's going on here?" I asked.

"My name is Ray, I'm the owner of this building, who are you?"

"My name is Trevor. I live here. I paid rent a few weeks ago to Raashid, I was told he was the property manager. I have a receipt right here," I took out my makeshift receipt and gave it to Ray. He held it under the light, skimmed it briefly, and then handed it back to me.

"Come with me. Let's go talk to Raashid," Ray said as we all went downstairs.

KNOCK KNOCK KNOCK "Raashid, it's Ray, open up!"

Raashid came to the door and opened it as if he was expecting Ray at that very moment.

"Ray, what are you doing here? Is everything okay?"

"Where is the rent for 2E?" It was apparent Ray was not in the mood for small talk.

"Stay here, I will go get it." Raashid scurried off. A moment later he returned holding a pile of cash. "Here," Raashid said, as he handed me a stack of bills. I quickly counted it and it was all there.

"See, I paid rent, here take it," I said, as I extended my arm to give the money to Ray.

"No, I don't want it like this. Give it to me tomorrow in a money order."

"Okay."

"Just drop it in the slot there by the mail boxes."

"Okay. I'll take care of that first thing tomorrow morning, Ray," I said.

I went back upstairs.

"What's going on?" Ashley said worriedly.

"Nothing, I took care of it. I paid the rent to the property manager and he never gave it to the owner. I just need to give the owner a money order tomorrow and everything will be fine."

Chapter Nineteen

The next morning we woke up and took a cab back to Ashley's place. "I'll call you later; I just need to take care of this."

As I was walking home from Ashley's place, I came across a restaurant. I looked up and it said, 'Andre's Seafood Restaurant'. I took my phone out of my pocket ; it was 10:01 a.m. Wednesday morning, July 15th.

"The fifteenth!" I exclaimed.

I went into Andre's and the hostess greeted me.

"Good morning, for how many?"

"Oh, uh, no, I'm not here to eat. Do you know if Chris is working?" I asked. "I don't know his last name, but he's a server here."

"Yeah I know him, he will be in later," she said as she checked the schedule. "Yep, he'll be in at 5:00 p.m."

"Okay, good, do you think I can leave a note for him?"

The hostess handed me a scrap piece of paper and a pen. I wrote the following:

'Hey Chris,

My name is Trevor, I met with you about a month ago regarding your room for rent. I hope it is still available because I'm still interested. Please call me A.S.A.P.

Thanks.'

I wrote my name and number at the bottom, folded up the paper, and handed it back to the hostess.

Later that evening my phone rang.

"Hello?"

"Hey, buddy, what's happening?" Chris said.

"Nothing much, I see you got my note."

"Yeah, I just got into work."

"Are you still looking for a roommate?" I asked.

"Yeah, it's tough to find a suitable match in the city. You seemed like a nice guy and my sister felt positive vibes from you. So yeah, if you want to move in, you can."

"That would be great, thanks. Do you mind if I come by with my stuff tonight? I will have all of your money."

"Sure, I get off at 10:00. Just give me a call."

I didn't want to spend one more night in my place for fear that Ray would come back in the middle of the night with the cops, so I went home, packed up my clothes and abandoned everything else.

I couldn't remember if Chris had told me to call him at 10:00 or to be there at 10:00 so I called a cab, loaded up the few things I had, and waited on the front steps until he came home. From where I was sitting, I could see Ashley's building. This was definitely an upgrade and I was happy to be downtown.

The rent was only $600 plus $300 for damage deposit. When Chris came home, I gave him $300 for the remaining 15 days of the month and $300 for the damage deposit. I was now settled into my new apartment and I still had more than half of next month's rent. I had caught the break I desperately needed.

Chapter Twenty

I arrived at work early in the morning. I had a renewed energy about me. I had settled into a nice new apartment, I had a job I liked, and I had a great girl who worked in the same mall with me. I felt like I was on top of the world.

"You see the sales results for this week yet?" Marc asked.

"No, not yet. How are we looking?" I responded.

"'We'? I like that."

"What?"

"No, that's good. You really seem concerned about the overall store performance, and not just your own," he said. "Too many people are only out for themselves and forget we're a team. In the last few weeks, you really demonstrated your passion towards the team. Last week you dominated the sales once again, but everyone else's sales have also improved since you've been here. We are up twelve percent from this time last year and I can't help but think you're an integral part of that."

"Wow, thank you, I'm flattered."

"Let me ask you something, Trevor. What do you want to do with your life?"

"I'm not too sure yet, I'm still trying to figure that out. I enjoy sales so maybe I will open up my own store someday when I get enough experience."

"How would you like the opportunity to get that experience?" he said with a big smile.

"I would like that very much, what do you have in mind?"

"We have a manager trainee program here and I would like to offer you the position to be our manager trainee."

"Are you being serious?" I asked.

"Yes, I'm confident you have what it takes to be a successful manager. When I first met you, your leadership skills hit me like a brick wall. You had such an undeniable confidence in yourself and it is quite inspiring. Not to mention you can back it up too. You're not cocky about it either, you're very humble."

"Thank you."

"So what do you say, would you like to be our new manager trainee?"

"Yes, of course," I said enthusiastically.

"Great, that's what I wanted to hear. So as you may know, with any promotion, there are some benefits. You will get a raise from $8.50 an hour to $12.00 per hour. The commission scale also increases so you can earn a lot more on top of that. You will be in charge of the daily operations of the store. So if any employees have any problems, they will go to you first. You will be in charge of the scheduling, hiring, training and of course you still have to sell."

"Okay, that sounds great."

"Here's your STAMP manual." Marc handed me a thick white binder.

"Study this. There are progress reports in there that you have to complete and get me to sign. Once you complete the course, you can be a real manager."

"Thanks again, I really appreciate it."

"Congratulations, you deserve it," Marc said with a proud smile as he shook my hand.

"There's one other thing," he said.

"Okay, what's that?"

"I want you to give a talk at our next staff meeting this Thursday. It will be a good way to introduce your new position to the rest of the team and give them a chance to learn about some of the things that make you so successful here."

"Sure no problem, what would you like me to talk about?"

"Sales," he said plain and simple.

"Okay, sure, no problem."

***

After my shift, I went over to Ashley's house.

"Hey," I said, as I greeted her with a kiss.

"What's up?" she asked.

"Oh nothing much," I said coyly. It was obvious I was hiding something because I was trying to conceal the huge grin on my face.

"What's under your arm?" she asked.

"What this? Oh this is nothing. It's just my STAMP manual."

She grabbed the binder and read the title. "Store Trainee Advanced Management Program. Oh my god, are you training to become a manager?" she said with more enthusiasm than I expected.

"Yeah, I was promoted today."

"Congratulations, Trevor. I'm really proud of you."

"Thanks."

"We should celebrate."

"Okay, what do you have in mind?"

***

The entire place was outfitted in ancient Greek décor. In the front of the restaurant was a large statue of what resembled the face of Parmenides on Zeus's body. I couldn't figure out if this was an insult to Zeus's face or Parmenides' body. I figured it was probably both.

The atmosphere was buzzing, as usual. The place was always busy. It was not so much that the food was good, but the portions were huge, and it was also really cheap. After an hour of waiting, we were just happy to get a table.

"I feel like I'm on my way, you know? I'm happy Darrell is out of my life and things are finally looking up again."

"Darrell sounds like a real loser, I'm glad I didn't have to meet him."

"I'm glad you didn't have to meet him as well. He might have sucked you into his vortex and ruined your life too."

"It's interesting how you told me how you were thriving without him, then you meet up with him and almost instantly you lose everything, and as soon as you get rid of him, you thrive again - you have a new job, a promotion, more money… and me!"

"Yeah, some people are just like that, you know? Everything they touch just turns to rubble. Unfortunately for me, I had to find out the hard way."

"Yes, but it also says a lot about your character and what kind of person you are when you are unhindered."

"Yeah, he was like a cancer to me, like kryptonite to Clark Kent."

"But now you're cured."

***

We paid for our bill and discussed what to do next. The night was still young - the sun was about to set and the skies were clear.

"Let's go down to the beach and watch the sunset," she suggested.

We walked slowly west down Davie Street, holding hands and taking in the warm summer air.

"Hey!" a recognizable voice shouted out from across the street. I turned around and sure enough, it was Darrell. He was with his good-for-nothing sister, Carla, and they were eager to approach us. "Where's my money?"

"What are you talking about?" I said. We were now standing face to face. I let go of Ashley's hand in case Darrell tried to fight me. He was a bit of a loose cannon - a dimwitted thug with a quick temper - always a dangerous combination.

"What do you mean 'what am I talking about?'" he responded, showing no attempt to conceal his ignorance.

"Look, Darrell, I don't owe you any money, okay."

"No, you 'look'. The way I see it…" he paused, as he took a moment to look around trying to act like some Mafia Don. The whole spectacle would be somewhat amusing if it wasn't for the fact that he looked like he was about to punch my lights out. I was not afraid of him, but I definitely wanted to avoid a conflict, especially tonight.

"I had to pay my dad four grand and now you owe me half of that."

"First of all, I don't owe you or your dad a thing. If anything, you guys owe me. I invested over three thousand dollars of my own money into the business and then earned another couple thousand dollars, and I didn't see a dime in return. Not to mention all the time and energy I spent as well. Plus you still have the truck and all the equipment. So if you think I owe you anything, take it out of that and we'll call it even."

I grabbed Ashley's hand again and we walked across the street. I said what I needed to say and I was not really interested in hearing whatever he had to say.

"Get 'im, Darrell," Carla chimed in for the first time, demonstrating she could be just as ignorant as her brother. "He's basically telling you to go to hell. You just gonna let him do that to you, Darrell?" she said, fueling her brother. He eventually took the bait. I turned around and saw Darrell and Carla slog across the street like the trolls they were. He didn't look like he wanted to chat anymore.

Darrell positioned himself in front of us to cut us off. Ashley and I stopped in our tracks. I let go of her hand once again and expected the worst. The night was officially ruined. He turned his hat backwards and looked up and down the street to make sure there were not any witnesses for what he was about to do. I read his body language clearly.

"I don't want to fight you, Darrell," I said passively.

Darrell did not say a thing. He was done using words. His Neanderthal instincts took over and he decided to make his move. Without provocation, he suddenly lunged forward with a powerful right fist. I telegraphed the punch before he even decided to throw it and easily ducked under it. I took a step back and Darrell charged toward me with another attack. I tried to duck again, but the second punch grazed my back. I sprang up and delivered a devastating blow of my own. My fist landed squarely on his nose, breaking it instantly. My adrenaline was now pumping at full throttle.

Darrell had a slight size advantage over me, but I was much faster. He threw another sluggish punch with bad intentions. In one fluid motion, I crouched down to avoid his punch, swiveled my torso, and launched a swift, but fierce, body blow underneath his right rib cage with enough force to deflate his lungs. I immediately followed it up with a crushing punch that landed flushly on his chin with the intent to knock him out. The combo staggered him a bit, just enough for him to reevaluate the situation.

I heard the faint yapping of his sister in the background, but I couldn't really make out what she was saying. In that moment, nothing else existed except me and Darrell. This was our moment, a chance to settle our differences and frustrations with each other - a final showdown.

He was getting the worst of the exchange so far, but he wasn't ready to give up just yet. With his face bloodied and bruised, he continued to pursue me, this time with more caution. I didn't have a mark on me, so my confidence was at an all-time high. My hands were up to protect my face, fists clenched.

Darrell was breathing heavily as he staggered toward me. I blasted him with a straight right jab to the face. His head snapped back. I faked the same punch again and his hands instinctively went up to protect his face. I quickly rotated my hips and whipped my leg against the side of his knee. He hobbled in pain a bit, but did his best not to show it.

In a moment of desperation, Darrell lurched forward and grabbed a hold of me. He pushed me backwards, forcing me up against a cement retaining wall. I pushed back, but I was outmuscled. He held onto my shirt and distributed a few dirty punches to my midsection. I raised my elbow up in the air and came down in a twelve to six motion, connecting directly on his collarbone. He winced in pain, probably a good indication his collarbone was now fractured. This allowed me to break free from his clench.

One of his hands was still fastened securely around a fistful of my shirt. As I spun around to get loose, he tore a large hole across the back of my shirt. I looked down to remind myself which shirt I was wearing. Much to my dismay, it was one of my favourites. This further enraged me. I started to swing wildly on him to defend my beloved shirt's honour. I connected with a few of them, but then I backed away. We both took a small breather to regain our composures.

I gave him a slight head fake and he put his hands in front of his face to block. I slammed my leg against his left knee for the second time. He had no answer for the barrage of devastating leg kicks I was bestowing upon him. I looked down and swiveled my hips again. This time it was a fake. With my eyes securely locked onto his left knee, I delivered a crushing head kick that nobody saw coming. My shin caught him cleanly on the temple, bringing an end to the lethargic mass of human waste. He collapsed instantly onto the pavement.

"You had enough, Darrell?" I yelled at him. "Come on, get up!"

"Screw off, Trevor!" Carla demanded, as she shoved me away from her brother. I thought about just walking away, but somehow that wouldn't be satisfying enough. I wanted to add a little insult to injury. I had just given Darrell a beating of a lifetime and it felt really good.

"It's over, man," he said mercifully with one hand in the air, the other holding his bloody nose.

"I don't owe you or your dad a thing, you understand me? If you ever come near me again, I swear I will kill you. You can curse me out, hate my guts, blame me, and fight me, but it won't solve your problems. You're a mess, bro. You need help. You're a terrible friend and a terrible person. I hope you know that. I'm so glad you're out of my life. You will never amount to anything if you continue to treat people the way you do. I hope for your sake that one day you will get your act together. Until then, leave me alone."

After my victory speech I grabbed Ashley's hand, crossed the street again, and proceeded down toward the beach. Hopefully, we could salvage what was left of the night.

Chapter Twenty-One

At 7:00 a.m., my alarm rang. I got up and made myself some breakfast - raspberry jam on white toast with a glass of orange juice. After I ate, I had a quick shower, put on my work uniform, threw on a hoody, and jogged to work.

When I arrived, all the lights were off except for the lights in the back office. I banged on the cage door a few times until Marc emerged from the back with his usual grande Starbucks coffee.

"Good morning."

"Hey, Marc, how's it going?"

"I'm alive, so I can't complain."

"Good to hear."

Marc unlocked the gate and let me in. "So today is the big day, are you ready to host your first sales seminar?" he asked, as we walked into the back room.

"You bet," I replied.

"So how are you adjusting to the new role so far?"

I didn't really have an answer for him. It had only been a few weeks since my promotion and so far I was doing what I had always done. Each day I went into work and sold shoes and clothing. There was no adjustment. "Uh, well, you know, so far so good," I said tentatively.

"So what aspects of this new role do you find most challenging?"

"To be honest with you, Marc, I don't really feel like I have fully embraced the new role yet. I guess the hardest part for me is to make that transition from being just a regular sales associate to a manager."

"Do you know why I promoted you?"

"I'm guessing it had something to do with my performance."

"Yes, in some respects that's true, but a lot of guys on our team have good performance. I promoted you because you're not just a regular sales associate."

"What do you mean?"

"You're a natural born leader. You just have to know and own the fact this is what you were born to do. You just have to own it, you know?"

I nodded in agreement, but I had no idea what 'owning it' entailed.

"So if you see someone not doing what they're supposed to be doing, get on them, say 'hey, go fix your section', or 'go talk to those people'. You're in charge and you have to let them know that. This is very important. If an employee doesn't believe you should be in the position you're in, then they will lose respect for you and it will become incredibly difficult to manage them."

"Okay, so what you're saying is that if I don't act managerial, then the employees won't take me seriously as a manager, and then they will not work hard for me?"

"Exactly. But you also don't want to be a jerk about it because then nobody will want to work for you either. There's a fine balance, like everything in life."

I sat there a moment and pondered this wisdom.

"So I recommend you take charge and be a little more assertive, but take baby steps, you don't want to come in here one day and whip everyone into shape."

"Okay."

"Don't worry, you'll get there."

Throughout the day I was getting into the routine of 'owning it'. I told the cashiers if they needed anything, to come get me first. I also observed the staff when they dealt with clients and gave them a few pointers or words of encouragement. Other than that, it was a pretty slow day, so I instructed everyone to restock shelves and tidy the store.

After closing, we all stayed behind for our team meeting. Marc went over a few administrative details and Jamie, the assistant manager, talked about some of the new products that were coming out. When it was my turn, I stood up and faced my audience.

"Hello everyone," I said trying to conceal my nervousness. "I was asked to give you guys a few examples of some effective selling techniques in hopes they will improve our store's sales. Over the next few minutes, I will go over some of the techniques I have found to be successful for me.

"Okay, so as you probably already know, there are no magic words that will get people to spend money. But, there are certainly techniques that can turn a 'no' into a 'yes'. The most important thing when you're selling is your frame of mind. For example, I never make a judgment about how much money a customer may have. I have had some average looking clients spend a lot of money. So, treat everyone with the same level of respect. Your frame of mind should always be positive. Try not to act desperate or get angry if your customer doesn't buy anything today because maybe they will come back and buy something tomorrow or the next day. But if you're rude to them, they will definitely not be buying from you and may not even come back to this store."

I paused for a brief moment and looked around to see if everyone was still with me.

"Okay, the next thing you can do is always look busy," I continued. "This is really important. Customers are attracted to hustle. So when they walk in and see you working hard, they will be inclined to think you will work hard for them as well. This may even happen on a subconscious level, but as the saying goes, 'when it rains, it pours'! I can't tell you guys how many times I've been juggling three or four customers at once and another customer will come up to me and ask for a size or something. In those cases, I usually just pass it off to one of you guys. But when I'm super busy, it's not a coincidence customers are attracted toward me. There's a pattern here and you guys can use it to your advantage. So, if a customer walks in and asks you for a size in the back, run to the back to get it for them. This pushes positive psychological buttons in their brain that makes them feel important. Happy customers spend money. If we don't have the right size for them, bring out a couple of other options of things that are in their size, or call another store and have the item they want shipped here. You worked hard for that sale, there's no sense in letting someone at another location reap the benefits of your hard work, right?

"While I'm on the subject, try to discourage putting things on hold for customers. I know our store policy is three days, but this is no good. I give people one hour," I paused for effect and let it really sink in.

"Research shows ninety percent of all 'holds' never return, so why put our inventory in a space where we can't sell it? Regardless of what they want to put on hold, tell them it's a really hot item and is a very popular size, and it will be gone by the end of the day. I tell people that we don't hold things, but that I can hide it somewhere for an hour. This does two things: first, it further solidifies the bond I have with my client, as I'm doing them a favour, and secondly, it creates a sense of urgency. If they really want it, this element of time will force the decision while their buying mood is still hot. If too much time has passed, they will have completely cooled off, reevaluate their purchase decision, and will not likely come back."

I took a deep breath and gathered my next thoughts.

"I also want to stress the importance of knowing your product knowledge. When I first started here, I would come in a few hours before my shift and just read about all the products, where they come from, how they are made, what materials are used, and when the new products are coming out. The majority of your customers will never ask about this stuff, but it's still important you know it. Knowing it will allow you to speak with much more confidence. When you speak with confidence, you establish trust. Once you've established trust, then your words become that of an expert, and the customer will believe almost anything you tell them. So if they are trying on a hundred dollar shoe, tell them all about the two hundred dollar shoe and all the wonders it will do for them. Chances are they will buy the two hundred dollar shoe instead because you've praised it so highly. Once they are on board with the two hundred dollar shoe, show them some outfits that go with it, and so on. You can build big sales by knowing your product.

"Finally, I want you all to start thinking outside of the box. There are many unconventional things you can do to get more sales. For example, I went to the Business Depot downstairs by the food court and had some business cards made up with my name and our store's phone number on it," I took one out of my pocket and showed it to them. "I hand out hundreds of these things each week and if the customers come back, they will come back to me. This is just one example of something you guys can do, and it is such an inexpensive way to boost your sales.

"So that's all I wanted to share with you guys, thanks so much for listening. Are there any questions?"

Before I knew it, my speech was over. It wasn't so bad, after a while I found my rhythm. I considered my speech a success, but I still wanted to prove to the senior managers they didn't make a wrong choice in promoting me. It was time for me to step up my hustle to the next level.

Chapter Twenty-Two

Throughout the next couple of weeks, I took notes of some of the problems I saw around the store. I typed all the notes I had taken along with a proposed solution for each.

I arrived at work at the next morning at 8:00 a.m. Marc was there early so he opened the door for me.

"So how's it going?" he asked.

"It's going pretty good I suppose, how are you?"

"I'm alive, so I can't complain," he said again, as if he was being witty.

"Good to hear," I said, almost as automatic as his response.

"Listen, Marc, I made a few observations about how the store operates and I think there are some things we can change, which will increase business."

"Great, I would love to hear them, what do you have in mind?"

"Actually, I wanted to wait for the other managers to arrive and discuss it as a team."

"Okay, good. I'll let the others know, and we can find a time at some point during the day to discuss your ideas."

"Sounds good. Thanks, Marc."

***

A few hours went by and the store was pretty quiet. I separated Andy and David so they didn't talk to each other so much. I asked Carlos to make sure all the shoes on the shoe wall had price tags on them and asked Amanda to stay up at the front to greet people as they came in. I grabbed the schedule and made sure none of the managers were taking their lunch any time soon. I went into the back and asked Marc if it would be an appropriate time to go over some of my ideas.

"Yes of course, I've been looking forward to it all day. Whenever you're ready."

I went over to my locker, grabbed four copies of my neatly typed proposal, and handed them out.

"Wow, what's this?" Jamie asked.

"Inside you will find the solutions to our problems," I began. If that didn't get their attention, I didn't know what would.

"I wasn't aware we had any problems," Jamie said.

"There are just a couple of main issues. The first thing, and probably the most important thing, is most of our staff are not selling. I have individually coached each of them and there has been little to no improvement with many of them. This draws me to the conclusion they are either lazy, unmotivated, or they just lack the ability. In any case, I strongly recommend letting certain people go and hiring some new people who are motivated to sell. Hiring a few new people may also motivate the existing staff members to be more productive as well. I elect myself to be in charge of this whole process."

"If you flip open the pamphlet I gave you, you will see I re-wrote the sales training manual. I know our current manual is handed down from corporate, but it's no good. We are the flagship store and we should be number one, but we're not. I don't think we can be number one with that manual. It's outdated and ineffective. Let me re-staff our team and train them the right way and I promise we will be number one again.

"Next, we need to reevaluate the organization of our sales floor. I don't know who came up with this arrangement, but it is illogical and needs to be changed. Right now, we have the women's department mixed in with men's athletic and men's urban. Then we have men's urban on one side, but with a part of it spilling over to the men's athletic section. This doesn't make any sense. Why don't we just put the entire men's athletic section on one side, and the entire women's section in one corner, and the entire men's urban in the other corner. That way, sections are not split up. Doesn't that make more sense than how we have it now?

"If you flip the page over, you will see an illustration I made that will give our store a face-lift. You will notice I have replaced all the shoe pyramids in the front window with several mannequins. Mannequins sell clothing, shoe pyramids do not. You will also see a large banner above the shoe wall. Currently, that space is empty and looks bare. As a focal point of our store, we should be utilizing that space for sale advertisements.

"So these are the major issues I think are wrong with the store. I'll now open up the floor for questions, comments, or concerns."

I waited, but there were none. Instead, there was a hostile tension that loomed in the air, making each agonizing second ever more uncomfortable for me. Immediately, I began to question my approach. Upon consideration, I may have been a little arrogant, but I didn't think they would hold it against me. After all, I figured that they would admire my eagerness, but I was wrong. Evidently, I still had a lot to learn about being tactful, especially among senior associates.

"Trevor, I appreciate your input, but where do you get off trying to tell us, and corporate, how to run a business?" Jamie asked.

"I wasn't implying you guys don't know how to run this store, I just wanted to present some fresh ideas."

"You're twenty years old and have been here less than six months, and already you want to entirely rearrange the way this store operates. What makes you think you can do a better job?"

"I wasn't saying that, Jamie. I was just trying to help."

"We got it, thanks, man," Jamie said, as he threw my booklet in the garbage. The others weren't as upfront about their feelings, but they seemed every bit as reluctant to implement my suggestions.

Chapter Twenty-Three

I had been working at Athletic Surplus for less than a year, but I felt like an old pro. I had learned many of the ins and outs of how the business worked and was confident in my skills at running the place. This was my show. I was at the helm of the number one Athletic Surplus in the country, and I was also the number one sales associate. I had cruised through my STAMP training and was now just waiting for the call to be promoted.

"Hey, Trevor, can I speak with you for a minute?"

"Sure, Marc, what's up?"

"So, I'm not sure if you have heard yet, but I'm moving to Toronto. I accepted an offer to be the district manager out there."

"Wow, congratulations! I'm really happy for you although I'll be sad to see you go. So who is going to take over your position here?" I asked. I was hoping he would say my name, but in all likelihood, Jamie would probably become the new store manager and everyone else would get shuffled upward.

"They actually got this new guy, Isaac. He's transferring from one of our stores out east. I've never met him, but I hear great things."

I was a little disappointed, but I didn't say anything. I figured I would just bide my time and eventually they would promote me. Right now, I was deniable. I needed to work harder so I would become undeniable. I needed to make it impossible to ignore my hustle.

***

The day Isaac showed up, I was a little apprehensive. After all, he could completely change the dynamics of the store. I figured he would have something to prove and would want to establish his dominance early on. I knew I would probably lose a lot of my freedom.

Just after lunchtime, a short Asian man walked into our store and introduced himself. "Hi, I'm Isaac, you must be Trevor? I've heard a lot about you."

"Welcome aboard, Isaac. Let me know if you need anything from me, I'd be happy to help you."

I was not sure what it was about Isaac, but something about him rubbed me the wrong way. Maybe it was the slight air of arrogance he carried around with him, probably an overcompensation to make up for his physical shortcomings.

***

It had been over a week into the job and Isaac still had not shown his face much on the sales floor. It was fine with me. He could stay in the back all he wanted and let me continue to command my squadron.

I poked my head into the backroom on some down time and asked how everything was going. He was noticeably busy on the computer and had paper work everywhere.

"Are you making some adjustments to the schedule?" I asked.

"You'll find out soon enough," he said in a condescending tone.

Screw you too, I thought. "Okay, just let me know if you need any help. I've been doing the schedule for the past few months and have memorized everyone's shift preferences and availability."

Isaac said nothing.

The following morning, I came in at 10:00 a.m.

"Hey, man, what's up?" I said to Carlos.

"Hey, why did you cut my hours!" he demanded, ignoring the civil pleasantries.

"I wasn't aware your hours had been cut, Carlos."

"Yeah, well they are. Everyone's hours were cut."

"Okay, let me see what's going on."

When I went to the back, I saw Isaac at the computer again. He didn't say anything to me or even look at me. I walked up to where the schedule was posted and looked for my name under the 'manager trainee' slot. It wasn't there. What the heck. I scanned down the list and saw my name listed alphabetically with the others. Okay, no big deal. I glanced across to my hours for the upcoming week, it read '20'.

"Hey, Isaac, did you make this schedule?"

"What's that?" he said, trying his best to ignore me.

"The schedule? Did you make this schedule?" I asked, trying to conceal my anger.

"Yes."

Okay, now this guy was really starting to piss me off. First he ignored me, now he was trying to play coy with me as if he didn't know he just demoted me without cause and cut my hours in half.

"Is there any reason why my name is no longer under the 'manager trainee' column and why my hours have been reduced?"

"Just doing a little bit of house cleaning. Don't worry, you'll be manager trainee again."

"House cleaning?"

"We just need to take one step back in order to take two steps forward."

"In case you don't know, I'm the number one sales associate in the country; you can't just cut my hours."

"I'm sure you are."

"It's not an opinion, it's a fact. Look it up."

"I don't have to. Things are going to be run a little differently around here from now on."

"Whatever," I said under my breath. I walked onto the sales floor noticeably pissed off. I had worked really hard to get to where I was at, and then some pompous jerk came in and undid it all almost overnight.

***

Every night at closing, the big cage gate was protracted from the wall and locked into place, securing the store from any entry and exit. Typically, we would leave all the TVs and music playing during closing, but ever since Isaac took charge, he put an end to that. For the next half an hour, I cleaned up the store and restocked the shelves just like everyone else, in silence. I was robbed of any power I had. It was no longer enjoyable being there, but I still needed the money. My plan was to just ride it out and get my old position back.

One night at closing, Isaac came out in his grand bravado to make a big announcement. "Listen up, boys and girls, nobody leaves tonight until all this new merchandise is security tagged and put onto the floor." There was no discussion, it was an order.

I looked at all the boxes we received and estimated it would take us about an hour and a half to tag and stock all of these items. We were all scheduled to be off at 9:30, less than twenty minutes away.

I stayed and tagged with the rest of them for the next twenty minutes. When it was 9:30, I yelled out to Isaac.

"Hey, Isaac!"

"What?"

"I need you to come check my bag and let me out," I said, in a somewhat cocky tone. The rest of the staff continued to do what they were told. The Athletic Surplus had a habit of not paying overtime and I was not interested in working for some tyrant for free. I had to keep a promise to myself, to never be taken advantage of again.

"Where do you think you're going?" he asked. "I told you nobody leaves until all this merchandise is tagged."

"My schedule says my shift ends at 9:30, so I'm off now."

Isaac stood there for a moment. I had blatantly defied his authority in front of everybody. He walked over to the cashier desk, grabbed a plastic hanger, and whipped it against one of the clothing racks. It shattered in several small pieces.

"Is everything alright?" I asked smugly, holding open my bag so he could perform the security check. My eyes were staring directly through his. I was not backing down, and he knew it. He opened the metal gate and allowed me to leave. Without even the slightest attempt at making eye contact, he slammed the cage door shut and aggressively fastened the lock.

"See you guys later," I said, as I looked back, waving.

The next day, I expected some sort of retaliation – bathroom duty, stockroom duty, heavy lifting... When I arrived to work, I went to the back and put my things in my locker. I grabbed the schedule to see whom I was working with that day. I noticed my hours were once again reduced down to fourteen. The number one sales associate and former manager trainee now works twice a week. It sure didn't take long for things to change around there. This was a lesson I was already familiar with, so I was prepared for it.

"Hey, Isaac, can I talk to you for a minute?"

"What?" he said coldly.

"Is there any reason why you cut my hours again?"

"I made the decision to reduce your hours, along with everybody else's last week."

"Yes, but I had twenty hours, now I have fourteen."

"Oh, the twenty was an oversight."

"You know what, Isaac... you're a little weasel. I was cool with you until you started to mess with me.

Your big ego couldn't handle the fact that I outshine you. Or maybe you were picked on in school and this is your way for getting back at the popular kid. It's no wonder nobody likes you. You disgust me you little worm. You should be fired," I said looking down on him.

"Are you done?" he asked.

"No, go to hell, I quit!"

Chapter Twenty-Four

It's a wonderful feeling to stand up for yourself, but it's a scary feeling to lack the security of a steady paycheck. I woke up early, had a quick shower, and got dressed in my white golf shirt and khaki pants. I found the nearest internet café and updated my résumé that I had saved in my email account.

Once I was satisfied with the finished product, I printed out several copies and immediately hit the streets. The first place I applied to was Mike's Athletic Store.

"Good morning," I said to the woman behind the counter. May I please speak with the manager?"

"One moment please."

I glanced around and tried to imagine myself working there. It was a lot smaller than what I was used to, but it was right on the main strip downtown. I thought it would be nice to get out of the mall and breathe some fresh air. Plus I lived right across the street - I could go home for lunch.

"Hi, my name is Jay, I'm the manager here."

"Good morning, Jay. My name is Trevor and I would like to speak with you regarding an employment opportunity. Are you hiring at the moment?"

"We are, but only for a supervisor position."

"Well, you're in luck, Jay; I'm exactly what this store needs. I managed the Athletic Surplus for the past year and was consistently the number one seller in the country."

"Do you have a résumé?"

"Yes," I carefully took out a freshly printed résumé and handed it to him.

As Jay was looking over my résumé, I continued to sell myself.

"I'm familiar with all the products you sell, I'm trained on the same computer system you guys use, and I'm an expert on store merchandizing, scheduling, and training."

Jay looked up briefly, but didn't say anything.

"So why did you leave Athletic Surplus?" Jay asked a very good question.

"A new manager was brought in recently and we had a personality conflict. I was no longer happy being there, so I decided to move on. I'm still very passionate about selling athletic gear, so I immediately came here to apply."

"Okay, let me get back to you, I'll let you know by the end of the week."

"Sounds good, thank you so much for your time, Jay."

I left Mike's and handed out the remaining résumés to every cell phone shop, restaurant, and clothing store in the neighbourhood. I had nothing left to do except wait for someone to call me.

A few days went by and I bumped into Jamie, one of my old managers at Athletic Surplus.

"So, I hear you applied at Mike's," he commented.

"How did you hear that?"

"Jay is a friend of mine. He called me and was asking about you."

"Okay, so what did you tell him?"

"I told him the truth."

"Which is…?"

"I told him you're a hard worker, good with people, and a great seller."

"Did you tell him why I left?"

"Of course, I told him the whole story. He asked me if he should hire you."

"What did you tell him?"

"Don't worry, I told him to hire you."

Later that day, I received a phone call from Jay; he offered me the supervisor position and I accepted it. I had once again landed on my feet.

***

"Trevor, I was looking over the sales for last week. My top guy sold around $3,300 and you sold close to $12,000. That's incredible, you just about sold more than the rest of the staff combined."

"I think I know the reason," I said.

"Yeah, what's that?"

"Over the past week, I really paid attention to how this store functions. I got a feel of the traffic flow, how the staff operates, the merchandising, and the sales manual. I made several notes on these observations as well as several other ideas I had for improving our store's productivity."

I handed him a similar package to the one I made for the managers at Athletic Surplus. I wanted to learn from my mistake last time so I treaded softly. I did not want to outshine my new boss or be overly critical of anything he did in particular.

"Jay, I don't mean to overstep my boundaries here, but seeing as I'm the newest member of the team, I figured I would offer you a fresh perspective. I hope my sales over the past week have demonstrated to you what is achievable in such a little store. My goal is to get everyone to be a sales superstar.

"I had a look at the sales manual and quite frankly it's no good. I created a new manual that's ready to go. I think we should bring on some new people and train them using the effective selling techniques I have developed. I can retrain everyone, or host a sales seminar if you like."

"Who did you want to let go?"

"Jon and Marcy are the two most obvious choices. I think we can work with the others."

"Okay, let me have a look at this stuff and I'll get back to you."

Chapter Twenty-Five

My bags were packed and I was ready to go. I took one final look around my apartment to make sure I wasn't forgetting anything.

"Are you ready?" Ashley asked.

"I think so."

"Come on then, the cab is waiting for us."

We both had three days off together so we decided to take a trip to Whistler. We took the Greyhound up and booked the cheapest hotel we could find. The room seemed nice on the website. It was right in the village and it had a hot tub in the room.

It was a two-hour long bus ride, so we had a lot of time to talk.

"We should have rented a vehicle," I mentioned, while I adjusted my position in the uncomfortable Greyhound seat.

"Yeah, but that would cost a lot more money. Besides, taking the bus isn't that bad."

"Yeah, I suppose you're right," I paused for a moment and chose my next words very carefully. "If you're so cautious about money, how are you able to afford to live in such a nice apartment by yourself?"

"It isn't that expensive."

"Do you mind me asking how much you pay for rent?"

"I don't pay that much, maybe $500 a month."

"What do you mean 'maybe $500 a month'? You don't know how much you pay?"

"Fine, I pay $500," she said, noticeably annoyed. She clearly did not want to talk about it, but why? My curiosity got the better of me as I sat there trying to decide whether I should continue to push or just let it go. A moment went by and then I said, "$500 a month. That's cheap."

"Yeah," she replied.

Another moment went by, and I decided to press even further.

"So how did you find a place for $500 a month?"

"Look, you obviously don't take hints very well," she snapped back at me.

"Why are you getting so angry? What is the big mystery about your rent?"

"My parents own the place, okay."

"Okay, so what's the big deal?"

"I didn't want you to get the wrong impression of me, like I'm some spoiled rich kid. Especially since you're working really hard to make it on your own and here I'm getting handouts from my parents."

"We're taking the Greyhound to Whistler, I would hardly call you rich."

She didn't respond for a while, but I could tell something was on her mind. "I didn't want to take my car," she said, under her breath.

"Excuse me, your car? Since when do you have a car?"

"It was a graduation present."

"Wow, that must have been nice, my parents didn't even show up to my graduation."

"I'm sorry to hear that."

"Don't be, I didn't invite them. So what kind of car did you get?"

"Why does that matter?"

"I'm just curious."

She left me hanging for a bit, but then finally told me. "It's an X5."

"X5? What is that?"

"It's a BMW."

"You own a BMW, a BMW X5 mind you, meanwhile we're sitting on the Greyhound like a couple of chumps. What year is your BMW X5?"

"Why do you always ask so many questions?"

"I like to know things. I pay attention to the subtlest of details."

"I can see that."

"So you were saying..."

"It's new okay."

"How new?"

"Brand new alright, can we just drop it?"

For the next ten minutes, neither one of us said a word to the other. Her eyes were fixated on the scenery, as she stared out from her window seat.

I was a little surprised that she lied to me, or rather concealed the truth from me. I could understand her reluctance to tell me about her living situation for fear I would form the wrong judgment about her. After all, I had a similar fear, but at least I had told her.

"You know what would be good right now?" I finally broke the silence and tried to lighten the mood.

She looked over at me, but didn't say a word.

"Heated leather seats!" I said with a big smile on my face. "I bet your BMW X5 has heated leather seats, doesn't it?" she rolled her eyes and looked back out the window. "Yeah, I bet it does."

"You're a jerk," she said as she laughed at my persistence.

"I'm just saying. Next time, do you think we could take the X5? My back is killing me in these seats," I said, as I made another adjustment.

"Fine."

"See, it's not so bad. I still love you. I didn't get any wrong impression of you."

"Yeah, but now you just like me because I have money," she joked.

"I liked you when I thought you didn't have money, remember? I've seen where you work, there's nothing glamorous about serving pancakes and coffee in the mall."

"Shut up."

"I'm just saying."

I didn't mention the money or her parents for the rest of the trip, but I wanted to.

***

We had a great time in Whistler. We went snowboarding, did a little shopping, and ate out at some nice restaurants. It was nice to get away, but it was obvious I needed to make more money. There was only so much I could do on ten dollars an hour.

We arrived back to Vancouver on Sunday night. There was a line of cabs already waiting at the bus station, so we quickly ran to the first one to avoid getting drenched in the rain. The cab dropped Ashley off first. She took a few bills out of her wallet and paid the cab driver.

"That should be enough for you to get home, including the tip," she said, as she kissed me goodbye.

A few minutes later, the cab pulled up in front of my building. I unloaded my bag and snowboard equipment from the trunk and hauled it up the front steps and into the lobby. I struggled to maintain my grip the whole way down the hall. Finally reaching the front door of my apartment, I set down all my wet gear. I unlocked the door, opened it slightly, and put my foot in it to prevent it from shutting. Once I picked up all my stuff off the floor, I kicked the door wide open, and dragged everything inside. It felt good to be home. I was cold, wet, and exhausted. The place was quiet and empty. I flicked on the lights and called out to my roommate. There was no answer. He was probably at his brother's place watching the football game.

I left all my stuff at the front entrance and then ran a hot shower. After that, I went to the kitchen to pour a large glass of chocolate milk, then went into the living room and flicked on the TV. I sank deep into the couch and began to drift away.

My slumber was interrupted by a loud knock at my door. I got up, sauntered over to the door, and looked through the peephole. A sloppy, heavy-set man was standing on the other side of the door. Judging by his untidy grayish goatee, I estimated he was in his late forties.

I opened the door and the man asked, "You, Trevor Morrison?"

"Yes," I said suspiciously.

"You've been served," the man said in a monotonous tone. He handed me a package and did not say another word. He turned around and walked back down the hallway. I've been served, what does that even mean, I thought. I opened the package and began reading.

'Dear Mr. Morrison, on behalf of Power Crew Services,

The purpose of this letter is to inform you that my client, West Coast Press, is seeking damages totaling $3,653.16 (plus interest) for services rendered unpaid. A settlement conference has been scheduled for January 7th. Failure to show up will result in West Coast Press being automatically awarded the entire damages plus other costs that may follow. Failure to pay will result in West Coast Press being legally permitted to garnish your wages until the debt has been settled.'

"What the heck is this!" I said aloud. My heart sank into the bottom of my stomach. I immediately grabbed my phone and hit speed dial 1.

"Hello?"

"Ashley, guess what?"

"What?"

"Remember that business I had with Darrell?"

"Yeah."

"Well apparently he racked up a bunch of debt with some advertising company and never paid them. Now they are suing both of us for over thirty six hundred dollars!"

"Are you being serious?"

"Yeah."

"Geez, even when this guy is not in your life, he finds a way to bring you down."

"Tell me about it."

"I don't get it though, why are they suing you?"

"I guess it's because my name was still on file as a co-owner and co-operator of the business."

"Can't you just tell them you left the business?"

"I'm going to try, but they probably won't believe me because I'm not credible."

"I can testify for you then."

"I appreciate that, but I don't want to get you involved."

"You should speak with a lawyer."

"I can't afford a lawyer."

"Do you have a pen?"

"You know a lawyer?"

"Yeah, my dad. Do you have a pen?"

"Yes."

"Okay, write down this number," she said. I quickly jotted down the number she had given me. "I'll call my dad right now so he will be expecting your call. Call him tomorrow morning before noon."

"Thank you so much, Ashley. I don't know what I would do without you."

"Don't worry about it. Just call him tomorrow and he'll tell you what to do."

"Okay, I'll call him then I'll call you afterwards. Thanks again, Ashley, have a good night."

I hung up the phone and returned to the couch. What a weasel; I knew he would try to screw me over somehow.

My plan was to just attend the settlement conference and explain my side of the story, that I had nothing to do with the business. I figured Darrell would be there and it would be so obvious he was lying.

Chapter Twenty-Six

I sat down on the edge of my bed. I was holding my cell phone in one hand and a small piece of paper with a number scribbled on it in the other. Beside me was the Notice of Claim document that was served to me the previous night. I had everything ready to make the call. I stared down at my phone and prepared for what I was going to say. This would be the first conversation I had with the father of the girl I was dating. I hoped he would understand my situation. After all, it was not as if I was calling him to bail me out of prison or something. Here I was, a young guy trying to make an honest living, and someone screwed me over. I took a deep breath and dialed the number.

"Thank you for calling Bernstein, Taylor, and Associates, how may I direct your call?"

I cleared my throat and said, "Yes, hello, I would like to speak with Mr. Taylor please."

"May I ask who is calling?"

"Yes, my name is Trevor Morrison."

"One moment please."

I took another deep breath.

A moment later, a deep voice came on the line with authority. "Howard Taylor speaking."

The direct and concise greeting was from a man who was obviously aware of the importance of time. This made me even more nervous because I knew I was wasting his.

"Hi, Mr. Taylor, my name is Trevor Morrison, I'm friends with your daughter Ashley," I said, as I waited for my cue to proceed.

"Mr. Morrison, hello, what can I do for you?"

"Well, sir, I'm being sued and was wondering if you could please give me some advice."

"Who is suing you?"

"West Coast Press," I said trying to match his conciseness.

"How much in damages?"

I grabbed the paper and read it to him. "$3,653.16."

"Do you have the Notice of Claim handy?"

"Yes."

"Okay, read it to me."

"Dear Mr. Morrison, on behalf of Power Crew Services. The purpose of this letter is to inform you that my client, West Coast Press, seeks damages totaling $3,653.16 plus interest for services rendered unpaid. A settlement conference had been scheduled for January 7th. Failure to show up will result..."

"Okay okay, that's enough," Mr. Taylor interrupted. "Did you sign a contract?"

"I don't know, I can't remember."

"You'll need to find that out."

"Okay, and if I did?"

"Then you're liable for the damages unless you publicly terminated the business relationship with Power Crew Services. Did you do that?"

"No, but I do have a Record of Employment from my employer. Could I use that to prove I ended the business relationship?"

"Look, I'll be frank with you. You don't really have a case here."

"Okay, that's what I was afraid of. Thank you very much for your time, and I look forward to meeting you... perhaps under different circumstances."

"Alright, good luck."

I hung up the phone and got ready for work.

***

"So, Jay, did you consider my recommendations for the store?"

"Uhh, well, yeah, I think we're just going to leave it for now."

"Really? What about Jon and Marcy? Those two don't sell anything."

"I'll talk to them. We also have a new assistant manager transferring over from one of our other locations."

"Why do we need an assistant manager? Me and you are running this store just fine."

"It wasn't my choice. The owner wants each store to have a manager and an assistant manager."

"Why couldn't I be the assistant manager?"

"You don't have the experience."

"Experience? I practically ran the Athletic Surplus."

“You were there for only a few months, you gotta pay your dues first.”

I was starting to see a pattern with my life. It didn’t matter how hard I worked, my fate was always in someone else’s hands. I worked really hard, was kind to everyone, and put forward a lot of really great ideas, but it still wasn’t enough. I was not able to realize my full potential until someone else gave me the opportunity to do so. It definitely wasn’t fair.

Chapter Twenty-Seven

The date for the settlement conference fast approached. I was prepared for the worst, but I was still optimistic about my chances to absolve myself from Darrell's debt. I didn't have any experience being in court, but the whole idea was exciting to me. I loved to argue and I had done nothing wrong. This should be an open and shut case.

The elevator door opened and I walked into my lobby looking and feeling like a million bucks. I was wearing a traditional three-piece, three-button suit that I had bought on Boxing Day from a suit store in the mall located next to the Athletic Surplus. I checked my mailbox one last time for my Record of Employment I had requested from Athletic Surplus several weeks ago. A large portion of my case was resting on this document and I still did not have it.

I opened my mailbox and was relieved to see the law gods smiling down at me. It must be my lucky day, I thought. After three weeks of waiting, there it was, my Record of Employment. I was not sure how much it would help, but I would rather have it than not. I placed the envelope in my inside jacket pocket and I marched toward the court, ready for war.

I entered the stone courthouse for the first time and was awestruck by its size. The place was spotless and very quiet. I walked through the grand entrance to get to the map of the courthouse. I pulled out the letter I received from Mekhail and Co. LLP to confirm what conference room the hearing was being held.

I descended slowly down the escalator and looked straight ahead at the huge floor to ceiling mirror. I made a few adjustments to my tie and suit jacket before I stepped off at the bottom. I walked towards the first hallway on my left. The walls were covered with framed artwork from elementary school children. There was a big opening in the centre of the room that extended all the way up to the glass ceiling, allowing the natural sunlight to shine through. Everything else was what I expected to see, lawyers, cops, and a group of other people who seemed like they would rather not be there.

The first door on my left was room 135. I kept walking down the hall until I arrived at my destination, room 107A.

Outside the room, there were a few chairs. A short man with large glasses sat beside a middle-aged woman. The man had thin blonde hair parted to one side and wore a loose fitted hunter green suit with an outdated tie. The woman wore a navy blazer and matching skirt.

"Are you here for West Coast Press vs. Power Crew?" the man asked.

"Yes, I am."

"I'm Jerry Mekhail, I represent West Coast Press." The introduction was more of a formality than friendly. I didn't smile or say anything.

I took a seat and made sure my cell phone was turned off. Darrell was nowhere in sight. He must be running late, as usual, I thought.

"West Coast Press vs. Power Crew Services," a lady announced.

Without saying anything, I rose from the chair and walked into the room. Mr. Mekhail followed behind me and the middle-aged woman followed behind him.

"Please take a seat," the Judge said.

Inside the small conference room was a large circular table with several chairs around it. The walls were white and bare. In the corner was a stenographer, ready to type everything we said.

"Please state your name for the record," the Judge commanded.

"My name is Trevor Morrison."

"Jerry Mekhail, Counsel for West Coast Press."

"My name is Wendy Strobe, advertising manager for West Coast Press."

"Mr. Morrison, where is your partner, Darrell Channing," the Judge asked.

"Mr. Channing is no longer my business partner and I haven't spoken with him in over a year."

"Very well then, let's proceed without him."

Proceed without him? This can't be good. It never occurred to me that he wouldn't be there. In retrospect, it seemed so obvious to me. Of course he wasn't going to show up. How could I be so naïve?

"Mr. Mekhail. Your client seeks damages of $3,653.16 plus interest against Power Crew Services, you may proceed."

"My client, West Coast Press, met with Mr. Trevor Morrison and Mr. Darrell Channing early last year to run a number of advertisements for their business. I have a copy of those ads your honour," Mr. Mekhail said as he flipped open an inch thick folder. He pulled out the necessary documents and set them aside. "I also have a contract Mr. Morrison and Mr. Channing signed with my client stating they would agree to pay for the services my client provided. The first couple of payments were made, but then there were a total of thirteen additional renewals over a period of two months that were left unpaid."

"May I see those?" I interrupted.

"What would you like to see, Mr. Morrison?" Mr. Mekhail said, in a condescending tone.

"I would like to see the contract you claimed I signed, and also the renewal requests that were made."

Mr. Mekhail slid over the documents. My heart skipped a beat when I looked down and saw my signature next to the title 'El Presidente'. This was clearly something a young eighteen year old who was trying to be cool would write. I even remembered signing it. I looked at the other set of documents that were stapled together, five pages of orders for advertisements, the date, time, and authorized signee… 'Darrell Channing'.

"Okay, I admit that this is my signature on the contract, but I signed as an authorized signee for Power Crew Services. I was no longer with the company at the time any of these orders were placed.

As you can see, Darrell Channing made all of these orders. Therefore, he should be solely liable for the accrued debt."

"Be that as it may Mr. Morrison, you still signed the contract and are jointly liable for the debt."

"Why did you allow Darrell to continue to renew the ads thirteen times without payment?" I asked to the Advertising manager.

"Mr. Morrison, that is completely irrelevant. My client's business practices are of no concern here. Let's just stick to the issue at hand, shall we?"

I stared down at the desk and felt the presence of everyone's eyes looking at me. This added to my anxiety as I was obviously being outmatched. I tried to block out those thoughts as I searched for my next words. I kept remembering what Mr. Taylor had said, 'Did you sign a contract? You're liable for the damages unless you publicly terminated the business relationship with Power Crew Services'.

I took a deep breath and looked up. The bright florescent lights made my eyes squint and made the tiny little room very hot. My new wool suit was causing me to sweat profusely so I undid the buttons on my jacket to air out a bit. It was at that moment when I saw my Record of Employment sitting neatly in my inside jacket pocket, shining like a ray of hope. A wave of confident came over me. I grabbed it immediately and prepared for one final effort to exonerate myself.

I raised the document high in the air and announced, "I have here a Record of Employment that states I was employed full time by Athletic Surplus. This document proves unequivocally that I was no longer in business with Power Crew Services, and therefore proves I'm not liable for any of the damages." I set the document down on the table, leaned back in my chair with a smug look on my face, and folded my arms.

"Mr. Morrison," Judge Winston interjected, "we believe you that this is not your debt. Nevertheless, you still signed the contract. You can take this to trial, but honestly you don't have a case."

"Fine, I don't want to waste any more time with this. I'll pay you half of the debt, and you can track down Darrell for the other half."

"I have a problem with that," Mr. Mekhail announced. "Either one of you is fully liable for the debt. If you want to track down Darrell, then you can do so."

"I can do that?" I asked, showing my interest in getting revenge on Darrell.

"Yes, you can seek indemnity," Mr. Mekhail replied. "If you agree to pay this debt, then I can help you track down Mr. Channing."

I looked over at the Judge to confirm this. The Judge nodded.

That would be great, I thought, I would love to sue Darrell. Besides, at that moment it seemed like my only option. "Okay then, I don't want any trouble. I'll agree to pay the entire debt. However, I can't afford to pay you all at once. I'll get a second job if I have to."

"Why don't we agree on you paying me one hundred dollars a month, due on the fifteenth of every month?"

"Why the fifteenth?" I asked, as my curious nature took over.

"Because I assume you, like most people, get paid twice a month, once in the middle of the month and once at the end of the month. The end of the month is usually when most people pay their rent and other bills, so the fifteenth is the best time to collect."

"Makes sense," I said. I liked the way he thought, very calculated and very logical.

"So, the first payment will be due next week. You can deliver it to my office. Here's my card with my address in case you don't have it already."

I took the card and briefly looked it over. I made my exit and proceeded up the escalator.

What just happened? I asked myself. I came here to defend my innocence and I ended up absorbing the entire debt. How am I going to pay this debt? There's no way I can afford to pay a hundred dollars a month.

Chapter Twenty-Eight

There have been a few situations in my life that have been less than ideal. In each case, I have had a choice: do something, or do nothing. I was now facing one of those instances. I needed to make more money, that was a fact, and what I was doing was not working.

I once again went out to the internet café and updated my résumé with my latest work experience. I printed out a dozen copies, but only applied to all the restaurants in the neighbourhood.

A few days later, I received a phone call from Kim, the manager of Ray's on Top Restaurant. Despite its uplifting sounding name, it was a double entendre – the restaurant was owned by a guy named Ray and was literally located on top of a drug store. Ray's was a local hotspot for the 'in crowd' because of the attractive staff, positive vibes, and unique menu. I was invited to go in for an interview.

"I see you applied to be a server," Kim said.

"Yes, that is correct. I believe my skill set makes me an excellent candidate for a server position."

"Unfortunately, we only hire servers who have had prior serving experience; however, I wanted to discuss another position we have available. It is an entry level position, but you could eventually be trained to be a server."

It was the same old story. I knew I could do the job, but there was always something, or someone, holding me back.

"What is the position that's available?" I asked.

I was willing to take anything at that point. After all, if I worked as hard as I had in the past, I would surely be promoted to a server. I needed the money and I knew servers made a lot more than I did. Ashley made close to two grand a month at the pancake house. I needed to start making that kind of money.

"We have a part-time busser position available. The busser's job is to ensure all the tables are ready for our guests. They are also responsible for food running, stocking cutlery, and assisting the bartender and chef with a variety of odd jobs. So if you're looking for a job that offers diversity, we would love to bring you on board. So what do you say, are you up for the challenge?"

***

I started out just working some night shifts and weekends. The pay was minimum wage, but I received a small percentage of the tips every night, usually around ten bucks a night.

As usual, I worked really hard trying to impress everyone. I went beyond what was expected of me. I did everything before the manager even thought to ask me. I swept and mopped the floors, restocked all the dishes for the kitchen staff, helped the dishwasher load and unload, cleaned the bathrooms, watered the plants, changed lights, you name it. From the moment I started, until the end of my shift, I wanted to make it very obvious no one would outwork me.

"Trevor, I just want to let you know we appreciate all your hard work," Kim said to me one day.

"Thanks. You know, Kim, my real talent is in sales. I would really like the opportunity to become a server."

"Alright, just keep doing what you're doing and we'll talk about it."

***

My shifts were from 5:30 p.m. to 10:30 p.m. I would finish around the same time as many of the other staff so I would sit on the patio with them. We would drink, flirt, and tell stories. I was not much of a drinker, but I did not want to miss out on this great networking opportunity. I would just listen mostly and see what types of things I could learn from them.

One guy designed websites, another was a photographer, two guys were in med school, there was a writer, a personal trainer, and then there was me. I was not really sure what my thing was. I guess I was just a dude. I realized I didn't really have much going for me. The passion was there, but it was being wasted on doing these odd jobs I had.

"So Trevor, how come you're not a server yet?" Kevin asked me.

"I don't know. I talked to Kim and she said to give it time."

"How much time does she expect you to wait? How long have you been here?"

"It's been about two months."

"Do you want to know why you're not a server yet?" Tyler interrupted. He paused to take a drag of his cigarette.

"Enlighten me," I said.

"It's because you're a good busser." He paused again to allow his big philosophical revelation to sink in. "If they promote you, then they will lose their all-star busser. Think about it, man."

I thought about it for a moment and he was right. How am I going to make the transition from busser to server? Do I stop working hard? Do I threaten to quit? I gave it more thought when I got home and decided what I was going to do.

The next day was a Saturday. I was scheduled for the lunch rush from 12:00 p.m. to 1:00 p.m., then again for the dinner rush from 5:30 p.m. to 10:30 p.m.

I worked the lunch rush part of my shift then went in the back to wash up. On one of the back tables was a food and beverage manual. I looked around to make sure no one was watching me and then I tossed my apron over it. I looked around again then picked it up with my apron wrapped around it.

On my way home, I passed by Mike's Athletics to check in with my other co-workers.

"Yo, what's up, Trevor?" Jay said.

"Nothing much, I'm just getting off work. How's it going with you?"

"It's going well I suppose."

"That's good."

"So I talked to the owner, Mike, and he wants to renovate the store. We will have to close down for a while."

"Really, for how long?"

"Just for a couple of weeks. He wants us to start packing things up in boxes as soon as possible. Are you available tomorrow?"

"I can be. I work lunch and dinner at the restaurant, but I can help you in between those times."

"Okay, great. How about you come in tomorrow at 8:30 a.m.? You can leave to go to your other job, but then come back here after."

"Okay."

"I'll be here all day. I've scheduled a few other people to work as well. Mike and his wife will be coming down to help, and the new assistant manager will be here all day too."

"Okay, no problem, I'll be here."

The following morning I showed up bright and early. I met the new assistant manager, Damian. He seemed really friendly.

"So here's the plan, Trevor," Jay said. "All this stuff has to go, so I just need you to take all the stuff off the racks and put it into boxes. Leave the hangers on, and make sure you label all the boxes. If you need anything or have any questions just let me know."

"What are we going to do with all the shoes in the back?"

"They're staying here. We'll cover them with large plastic sheets so they won't get dusty."

"But if they're here, the construction workers might steal them."

"One of us is going to be here at all times."

"Oh, okay."

“Yeah, we’ll all take turns. So starting Monday, I need you to be in at 8:30 a.m. to let the construction crew in.”

“No problem. What about the rest of the week?”

“I’ll call you tomorrow and let you know.”

Chapter Twenty-Nine

Sitting around in the back room didn't sound like much fun to me, but it was easy money. I brought the food and beverage manual from Ray's and studied the ingredients for hours. Jay would call from time to time on the store phone just to check in on me. He was probably more concerned about the merchandise and wanted to make sure I hadn't left.

"How is everything?" Jay asked.

"So far so good, I suppose. They turned off the heat so it's pretty cold back here, and there's limited lighting, but otherwise I can manage."

"Okay well, just stay until closing. I think the workers will be done by around 11:00 p.m."

"Okay, and what about tomorrow?"

"I need you to do the same thing tomorrow. Just show up at 8:30 and I'll relieve you around 4:00 p.m."

"Okay, no problem."

The six by six square foot back office was cold, dark, and did not have good ventilation. I sat at a small desk surrounded by boxes stacked from floor to ceiling. The large plastic sheets set up to protect the shoes from getting dusty did their job; they were covered with white dust from the gyprock. However, I would get it all over my clothes anytime I brushed up against it, which would happen pretty much anytime I moved. Twelve hours went by and I could not imagine doing another day like this. It was beyond unbearable.

The following day was more of the same. I was counting down the minutes until Jay would come in at 4:00 to relieve me. I felt like I was going crazy sitting back there all alone in the dark.

***

"Yo, Trevor, how's it going?" Jay said over the phone.

"I'm hanging in there. How's it going with you?"

"I'm just at the Metro Mall location helping them out and was wondering if you can you check if we have some shoes in stock?"

"Okay."

"You got a pen?"

"Yes."

"Good. I'm going to read you off the model and the sizes."

"Okay, shoot."

I took down the information and left the phone off the hook. I grabbed a flashlight and walked down the narrow hallway in the back of the store. I found the general area that had all the shoes Jay wanted. I wiped the dust off the plastic sheets with my hand and held up the flash light.

I returned a few minutes later. "Yeah, Jay, we have them."

"Okay good, I need you to box those up for me and express them over here today. Can you do that?"

"No problem."

I hung up the phone and went back with the flashlight. I set the flashlight down and peeled back the tape that was securing the plastic sheet to the bottom of the shelf. I lifted it up just enough for me to crawl carefully underneath it, making sure the tape from the top did not come off. I did this a few more times in different locations in the stock room and put together everything Jay had requested.

I called the shipping company we used and scheduled a pick-up. In the meantime, I found a flattened box from out back and put it together. I loaded all of the shoes in the big box and made sure the sizes and models were correct. The shipping company arrived shortly after, and in no time, the shoes were en route. Mission accomplished. That only took up about twenty minutes of my day. After that, it was back to reading the food and beverage manual until Jay arrived.

***

"Thank you for calling Mike's Athletics, this is Trevor speaking, how can I help you?"

"Yo, Trevor, it's Jay."

"Hey. Did you get the shoes I sent?"

"Yeah, I got them. They were all covered in dust."

"Sorry, but everything is covered in dust back here."

"Just make sure for next time there's no dust on the shoes before you send them."

"Jay, you have no idea what it's like back here, the place looks like a disaster zone. I have almost no room to move, in fact, if it weren't for my chair's ability to swivel, I would be trapped at my desk. It was hard enough trying to find a box to put everything in, not to mention getting the shoes off the shelves."

"Those sound like a lot of really great excuses, but I'm not interested in hearing any of them. Just so we're clear, there better not be any dust on them next time."

"Sure, no problem," I said with a dull tone.

"I'm pretty busy here, so just stay there until the workers are done."

"You're not coming at 4:00?"

"No, I can't, we're swamped over here."

***

I learned after the first day not to wear my good clothing. I threw on the same hoody and jeans I had worn the previous couple of days and went to work, already filthy. After a few hours in the back, I decided to get some fresh air. I locked the back entrance and stood out at the front of the store in the sunshine. If the workers were going to steal shoes, they would have to walk right past me holding them.

"Hey, Anne," I called out to one of my friends who happened to be walking by. She was talking on her cell phone and didn't hear me.

"Anne!" I called out again, but she still didn't hear. She stopped at the corner and was waiting for the light to change. I walked up to her and tapped her on the shoulder. "Hey," I said again.

She quickly looked at my clothes, said, "Sorry, no change", and walked across the street. For a moment, I just stood there, humiliated. I decided to go back inside.

***

Over the next week, I worked seven days straight, working fourteen hours a day, and still there was no sign of Jay. I had given up on the idea of him coming in to relieve me. It felt like I was serving a life sentence in solitary confinement. The sooner I got used to it, the easier it would be. After a while, I adapted to it. It was still bad, but not as unbearable as the first couple of shifts had been. The worst part was the isolation and the boredom, but also breathing the dust and fumes all day was seriously affecting my health. I would routinely have coughing fits and headaches.

I didn't even know my schedule for the next day until about 6:00 p.m. That's when Jay would usually call and inform me he needed me to come in the next day, bright and early. I didn't want to complain, so I did everything he asked of me without question. But it was really starting to irritate me that he was making me work every single shift. I was running out of things to do. I was so sick of looking at the food and beverage manual from Ray's. I had memorized every ingredient in every item on the menu, including the drinks. I was not sure how much more of this I could take. I was at my breaking point.

***

Later that night, the phone rang.

"Thank you for calling Mike's Athletics, this is Trevor speaking, how may I help you?"

"Yo, Trevor, it's Jay."

"Hey."

"Listen, man, I'm gonna need you to come in again tomorrow from 8:30 a.m. until noon. Then I'm gonna need you to cruise out to the Metro location and help with the receiving. They just received a huge shipment and need all the help they can get. I'll be there at noon to cover you until 4:00. Then I need you to come back to our location and relieve me the rest of the night."

I paused for a minute and said the only word that came to mind, "No."

"What do you mean 'no'?"

"No, I'm not going to do it."

"Excuse me?"

"It's not part of my job description to sit in the back of the store all week breathing in dust for fourteen hours a day, and now you want me to go out to Metro and help with receiving. Forget it."

"Well, I'm adding it to you job description. I don't want to argue with you, but you'd better be there," he said, before he slammed the phone down.

The decision had been made; I was not going out to Metro the following day. I figured as long as I was not going to Metro, I might as well take the entire day off. After all, I think I deserved it. I was done babysitting the construction workers while Jay did nothing. He was the manager, let him figure it out. I had done my fair share of the shifts. In fact, I had done all of them.

I took the next couple of days off and did not hear from Jay once. I figured he had the new assistant manager sitting in the back all day. On the third day, the phone rang. It was Jay.

"Hey, Trevor."

"Hey, what's up?"

"Can you come down to the store really quickly; I need to talk to you."

"Sure, I'll be there in five minutes."

When I arrived at the store, I was surprised to see it open and operational. The renovations had been completed.

"Hey, man," Jay said in a somber tone.

"The store looks nice," I said, looking around.

"Yeah, just come to the back with me please," Jay said nervously.

I didn't say anything; I just followed him to the back.

"Have a seat," he said. "So, you were scheduled to come in this morning at 8:30."

"Really? I had no idea. Did you call me?"

"I shouldn't have to call you; it is your responsibility to check your schedule."

"I didn't even know there was a schedule or that the store was open. For the past two weeks you called me to let me know my schedule, isn't that right?"

"The bottom line is you were scheduled, and you missed your shift. I got a call this morning from Jon. He was waiting outside for over an hour and a half before I came down here to open up the store."

"I'm sorry, I had no idea. You know, you could have just called me to come in this morning, I live five minutes away."

"Unfortunately, Trevor, we can no longer keep you on."

"Excuse me?"

"Don't make this harder than it already is."

"What are you talking about, Jay?" I asked.

"Effective immediately, you're no longer employed here."

"For not showing up this morning?"

"Yes."

"You know, Jay… I can't help but think this has something to do with our little dispute the other day."

"No, it's not about that at all."

"Really?"

"I have the policy right here," he handed me the store policy manual. It was already opened to the relevant page. It read, Each employee is required to show up on time for scheduled shifts. Failure to do so may result in disciplinary action, including termination.

I grabbed the schedule and saw my name in the 8:30 time slot. I looked down the list and saw Jon scheduled for that morning as well. I didn't feel like arguing with him anymore. "Alright, man, whatever."

"No hard feelings, Trevor. For what it's worth, you were a great employee," I didn't say anything, I just felt sick to my stomach. I got up and proceeded to walk down the hallway between the rows of shoes.

Before I left, I said goodbye to some of my former co-workers. Jay was still in the back. I didn't expect him to have the courage to come out for at least twenty minutes.

"Hey Jon, sorry to keep you waiting out in the cold this morning, I didn't know I had to work."

"What are you talking about?"

"You weren't waiting for an hour and a half this morning?"

"No, when I got here, Jay was already here."

"Really?"

"Yeah, why?"

"How did you even know to come in today?" I asked.

"Jay called everyone and told us our schedules."

"Apparently he didn't call everyone."

I stormed into the back office pushing the door open aggressively. Jay had a look on his face as if he had just been caught with his hand in the cookie jar.

"I wasn't scheduled for 8:30 this morning and you know it. You were here and you penciled my name in the schedule in last minute."

"What's done is done, Trevor. Please leave now or I'll call the police."

I didn't want any trouble, so I left. I needed to get my life back on track. I needed that job, or more specifically, I needed the money. I still had another job, but I only worked about sixteen hours per week there, hardly enough to pay my bills. I needed to figure out what my next step was going to be.

Chapter Thirty

For my next shift at Ray's, I decided it was time to prove to Kim why I deserved to be a server. I figured if I could be a server, then all my financial problems would be over. I would make enough to pay my rent, all my bills, and Darrell's debt. If I did not get promoted to be a server, my plan B was to try to get as many hours as possible until I could find another job. It seemed like everywhere I went, I was being kicked around. It was frustrating and disheartening. This was definitely not how I envisioned my life turning out.

"Good morning, Kim," I said with a big smile.

"Someone is in a good mood today."

"I'm always in a good mood when I come here. The warm smell of our in-house chicken soup at lunch, the chopped onions, carrots, and celery, mixed with chicken stock, and a pinch of basil. Or maybe it's the smoked salmon with peach-salsa and gruyere cheese with three ounce..."

"Okay okay, I get it. I'm impressed. When did you learn all that?"

"I have memorized every single ingredient for every item on the menu."

"What about the drinks?"

"Oh, I memorized those as well. You want a blue lagoon? You'll need one ounce vodka, one ounce Blue Curacao liqueur, lemonade..."

"I see you've done your homework."

"Yes, I have. Any chance I can start my server training?"

"I'll tell you what, finish your lunch shift then I'll train you on how to use the computer system."

"Are you being serious?"

"Of course, you deserve it, don't you?"

"Thank you so much, Kim."

***

After the lunch rush, the restaurant died down completely. It was strange how it could go from a metropolis to a ghost town in less than an hour. There were a few people still dining, but I had completed all of my duties and there was nothing left for me to do.

"So, Kim, how about that training?"

"Have you cleared and set all the tables... wait, I shouldn't have to ask you that, I already know the answer. Come on, let's get you trained on the Squirrel."

"The layout of the restaurant is programmed into the computer. So just click on your table and select how many in your party. Typically, you're going to order the drinks first, so click the 'Drinks' tab and all of our drinks come up. Over here is where you can customize your orders or add notes for the bartenders, like 'easy ice', 'double shot of something', and so on. You can do the same for the entrées as well."

After about thirty minutes on the basic computer system, I felt I had a good grasp of how it worked. Everything was very logical and straightforward.

"Wow, you learn fast," Kim said.

"I guess you could say I'm really motivated."

"Good, how about I start you off with a few tables tonight?"

"Okay, sounds good. I'll see you tonight."

After my training, I decided to meet Ashley at her work. I walked past Mike's and glanced inside. I saw Jay standing around with Jon and Marcy. Nobody was doing anything. He was not a leader; he had no business being in that role. He should have taken my advice and gotten rid of those people, but instead, he got rid of me. Maybe my leadership threatened him. I was a leader being led by a follower. What a sad realization.

"Hey, babe," I said.

"Hey, hon. What are you doing here?"

"Just wanted to see you."

"Really?"

"What time are you off?"

"I'm off at 3:00."

"Do you want to hang out?"

"Sure."

"Okay, I'm going to walk around the mall for a bit and I'll come back in a half hour. You should be off by then right?"

"It all depends on how fast my last table settles their bill."

I wandered aimlessly through the mall, poking my head into a few stores. I had no intentions of buying anything. In fact, I could not afford to buy anything even if I wanted to.

When I came up to the end of the strip, I was within fifty feet of Athletic Surplus. I was trying to be inconspicuous so I hid behind the same large plant that shielded me from view the first time I'd come here. From my vantage point, I could look into the entire store without the risk of being detected. They were like fish in a bowl, completely oblivious to what was going on outside their little athletic world. There was a bunch of new people working there. I wasn't too sure if the other people were let go or they just got sick of Isaac and quit. A moment later, Isaac slithered out from the back room like the snake that he was. The very sight of him made my blood boil, yet I could not look away.

"Hey, there you are," Ashley said, completely startling me. "What are you doing?"

"Who? Me? Oh, nothing, I was just… waiting"

"Did I catch you in a moment?"

"Uhh…"

"It seems like you're hiding behind this big plant. What are you looking at?" she asked as she looked across the way at the Athletic Surplus. "Come on, it's their loss."

"Sorry for not showing up, I lost track of time."

"No worries, this mall isn't that big and I sort of had an idea of where to look for you. So what's new?"

"Lots, actually. I was fired today," I said with a slight smirk on my face.

"You were fired? From where, and why?"

"From Mike's, but it wasn't my fault."

"How is it that you keep getting fired?"

"I don't keep getting fired, I quit Athletic Surplus, remember? Besides, that wasn't my fault either and you know it."

"Trevor, I'm going to ask you a question and I want an honest answer. What if it has always been your fault?"

I paused for a moment of honest reflection. "You know what, at the end of the day, I can say I worked really hard and did my best."

"Maybe that's your problem."

"What do you mean?"

"Maybe next time you should try doing what I do."

"Oh yeah, what's that?"

"Show up on time, do a reasonably good job, and don't rock the boat."

"That sounds like a recipe for a mediocre life. I don't want a mediocre life. I don't want to be an average Joe. I want to do something special in this lifetime, something that matters and makes a difference."

"Hey, that's a noble ambition, but while on your path to greatness, you will have to work for other people. My formula may not make me rich, but it will also not make me poor either. I have never been fired from a job, whereas you've been demoted, messed with, yelled at, and now you've been fired. I'm just saying..."

"You make some good points, but what I'm doing can't be all bad. I was promoted today at Ray's – I'm a server now. My first shift is tonight."

"That's great, congratulations. Welcome to the server's club!"

"So, do you want to hear my plan?" I asked.

"Okay, what's your plan?"

"I'm going to be a server… while I go back to school."

"You're going back to school, what made you decide that?"

"I'm just tired of being jerked around. I've worked retail and although I like sales, there's no future in it. I don't want to be selling shoes in the mall when I'm forty."

"Okay, so what are you going to school for?"

"I want to be a lawyer."

"Yeah, I could see that. I think you'd make a good lawyer."

"I got a taste of court from the whole Darrell situation and I liked it, as weird as that sounds. Plus, it has a lot of the elements that I would want in a career - you can be your own boss, nobody messes with you, you can make lots of money, garner respect..."

"So do you know what school you're going to apply to?"

"No, I have to look into all that. I also need to get a computer and a desk."

"How are you going to afford a computer? And school?"

"I don't know, I'll probably have to take out a student loan, maybe get a better job."

Chapter Thirty-Two

I decided to take a different approach to finding a job this time. Instead of handing out résumés to all the shops in the mall, I applied online for some office jobs. I picked a bunch of companies I wanted to work for and submitted my résumé to them.

A few weeks went by and I did not have one single call back, so I changed my approach again. This time, I changed my résumé to make it look more professional. I then put on my suit and applied to a lot of the businesses in person. On my way home, I stopped by the bank to make a withdrawal. I entered the bank and looked around. It seemed like a really professional environment, people in suits talking about their business and their finances. It never occurred to me to work at a bank, but the more I thought about it, the more it made sense. I looked in my folder and had one résumé left.

I walked up to the customer service desk and asked to speak to the manager.

"Do you have an appointment?" the receptionist asked.

"No, I don't. I just wanted to speak with the manager about any employment opportunities that are available."

"If you give me your résumé, I'll make sure he gets it."

I gave the receptionist my résumé and went home.

I waited a week before I started calling places back. I felt like I had nothing to lose, so I called the manager at the National Group Bank every day and left him a message on his answering machine.

'Hi this is Trevor Morrison calling. I dropped off my résumé last week and was just wondering if you've had a chance to review it. I'm really interested in pursuing a career with your branch. Please give me a call so I can further introduce myself.'

A week's worth of those messages filled the bank manager's voicemail, but there was still no word from him. I decided to put my suit on and go pay the manager a visit.

"May I help you?" the receptionist asked.

"Yes, my name is Trevor Morrison; I have a two o'clock appointment with Derek Jones. Can you please let him know I'm here?"

"Yes, certainly Mr. Morrison, please take a seat."

"Thank you."

I took a deep breath and sat down outside the branch manager's office - so far, so good. I had made it past the first line of defense. Now all I needed to do was to turn on some charm and convince the branch manager his business would fail without me.

I glanced down at my phone every few minutes. The anticipation was killing me. I had been waiting for over fifteen minutes. Occasionally, the receptionist would look over at me. I just looked back at her and smiled. It was obvious the manager was in no hurry to see me, but I continued to wait.

After a few more minutes, his door opened and he walked out. He noticed me sitting in one of the leather chairs outside of his office, but he continued to walk pass me. He said something to one of the financial advisors, then headed back to his office.

This was it; it was my time to shine. "Good afternoon Mr. Jones, may I have a moment of your time?"

"Certainly," he said reluctantly with a fake smile. "Please come in and have a seat."

"Thank you."

"So what brings you into my office today?"

"Well, sir, I'm interested in working for you and I wanted to meet with you in person to discuss a possible employment opportunity."

"Okay, do you have your résumé with you?"

"Yes, I do. Here you go," I handed him another copy of my résumé.

He took a moment to review it. "So what did you have in mind?" he asked.

"I want to start off as a teller, but I would eventually like to work my way up to become a financial advisor one day."

"So you're interested in pursuing a career in finance?"

"Yes, sir."

"That's excellent. I think we might have something for you. Let me hang on to your résumé and I will have Lizzie give you a call later this week to discuss what we have available."

"Thank you so much for your time today, it really means a lot to me."

"It was my pleasure."

It took a little bit longer than I had expected, but my persistence paid off. I had my foot in the door. Where others saw a dead end, I saw an obstacle and figured out a way around it.

Lizzie called a week later to discuss the position. After a few minutes of talking, I had talked my way into a job with the largest bank in Canada.

"So what will the schedule be like?" I asked.

"We work on a forty hour work week, with a half an hour paid lunch break. The shifts are Monday to Friday 8:30 to 4:30, and we're closed on the weekends."

"Oh, okay, that sounds good. Do you offer any part-time employment at all?"

"No, unfortunately not, we only have full-time shifts available."

"That's too bad. I probably should have mentioned this earlier, but I will be attending classes in the Fall. I won't be able to work during the day."

"We do have a credit card division. It's still customer service, but it's in an office environment, so you wouldn't be dealing with customers directly."

"An office environment," I repeated with a smile. "That sounds perfect."

"I know they offer part-time schedules and cater to a lot of students."

"That would be great."

"I'll forward your résumé onto that department and will have someone give you a call."

"Thank you so much, Lizzie. I really appreciate it."

I figured out life was all about creating opportunities for myself. Rarely are things handed to people. I figured if you're not where you want to be in life, it's because you don't want it bad enough, plain and simple. A little persistence, a clean shave, and a smile can do wonders for a person. I now had my office job, which paid me much more than being a server.

I was all set to go back to school in the Fall. I was excited, but a little nervous. My plan was about to be realized. I was about to take the first step in my journey to become one of the most successful lawyers in the country.

Chapter Thirty-Two

The next four years of school were incredibly challenging. Taking four classes per semester and two courses in the summer proved to be too much for me. I was burnt out. There wasn't enough time in the day to take on that kind of course load, especially when I was working thirty hours per week at the National Group Bank call centre.

I had never lasted so long at a job before this one. I had learned the hard way that the nail that sticks out gets hammered first. So, instead of trying to rearrange the entire business model of the company I worked for, I took Ashley's advice – I kept my mouth shut and did what was asked of me. It seemed strange to me that a company was not interested in hearing about ideas from their employees, especially if those ideas would be beneficial to them. After all, a good idea is a good idea regardless of where it comes from. I vowed if I ever have my own company, I would be sure to foster a culture where even the guy sweeping the floor can submit his idea.

I struggled to pay my bills, but working at the bank helped out a lot. Maybe that was why I stuck around so long. I made more money working part-time than I did working full-time at the retail shops and restaurants I worked for in the past.

I worked nights, weekends, and picked up the odd overtime shift here and there. I was able to make enough to cover all my expenses, including paying back Darrell's debt. I still had not collected a cent from him. I gave up searching for him when it was obvious he did not want to be found. I heard from a mutual friend he had left the country. I wouldn't expect anything less from a little rodent like Darrell to scurry off into some far corner of the world to avoid his responsibilities.

My schedule was packed. Every minute of every day was assigned towards doing something. I didn't know the meaning of rest, or having a day off. During the week I had a routine - wake up at 6:00 a.m., run for thirty minutes, then workout for forty-five minutes. After that, I would have a protein shake, a large breakfast, shower, and then go to school. Some mornings I had no choice but to skip my workout routine. It was the only expendable thing in my day. Ironically, it was working out that allowed my body to keep up this pace. Even then, I was always exhausted. Any remaining time I had would be spent with Ashley.

Even getting to school was exhausting. I had to walk fifteen minutes to the Skytrain station, take the Skytrain three stops, and then get on the sea bus. The sea bus ride was thirty minutes across the water to North Vancouver. Once I got off the sea bus, I would get on another bus, ride another thirty minutes to the Phibbs Exchange bus terminal, where I transferred one more time to a bus that would take me the rest of the way to school. I did this same process in reverse to go back home. The moment I would get home, I had to quickly eat lunch, then get ready for work. I would work all night, come home, and make something to eat. It would be around midnight by the time I was done. Then, I would study until two or three in the morning. Some nights, I was just too tired to study, so I would go to bed and study on the way to school.

The bus rides were miserable too. It would be raining most mornings, so I would stand in the rain until the bus came, then try to fight my way on an already packed bus. I would have to squish in there with a hundred other dripping-wet students who were often sick. Being coughed on, sneezed on, and farted on was unavoidable.

If I were lucky enough to get on the early bus, I would have to stand the whole way. This was not ideal, but it was the only bus that would get me to class on time. Most days, the early bus was too full to board, so I had to wait for a backup bus to arrive. On these days, I would end up standing in the rain for an extra fifteen minutes. Taking the second bus did not get me to school on time, but at least I could get a seat and catch up on some reading. That was one big advantage for me. That time was just too valuable to waste sitting there staring out the window for two hours each day. Besides, staring out the window was often discouraging.

Periodically, I would look out the window to see how close I was to the school. I would wipe the condensation from the window and catch a glimpse of some rich kid driving their Mercedes or Lexus. I couldn't help but think of how lucky those kids were.

They had the easy life. I bet they wouldn't even last one day in my situation. They would probably never know what it was like to have to overcome hardship, not know where they were going to sleep that night, and they probably never had to go to bed on an empty stomach.

It's ironic that the ones who lack adversity in their lives often go the farthest. This is not because they are more talented and things come effortlessly, it's because there's less resistance. The fortunate ones get the best grades not because they are brighter, but because they don't have to work thirty hours per week and don't have to waste two hours each day commuting on public transit. They have time to socialize and develop connections. They have time to volunteer and build their résumé. They have parents who know people in high places who will usher them into cushy jobs with high pay. They will eventually rise through the ranks, not because of their hard work, but through connections, impressive job titles, and glad-handing. These people eventually go on to run our banks and rule our countries, but they're not necessarily the best people for the job.

The more I thought about it, the more depressed I got. The only thing I could do was to continue to work hard and hope for the right opportunity to come my way.

After four years of university, I was fully adjusted to the school life. My grades started off average, but I eventually learned what the professors were looking for. I wrote the LSAT and applied to all the law schools in the country. I received offers from a few of them, but I accepted only one offer from the University of

Ontario School of Law. This was not my first choice, but it was the only half-decent school that accepted me. Graduating university and getting into law school was very gratifying. It was confirmation that I had bounced back after having some major setbacks along the way. Graduating from law school had been my primary goal for the past four years and in a few short months, it would be the first day toward achieving that goal. I was nervous about moving to a new city because I had no idea what to expect, but I was determined to make it, the way I had always done – through my hustle.

***

"Thank for calling the National Group Bank of Canada, my name is Trevor, how may I assist you today?

"Hello. I received my bill today and you're charging me interest on my account. You better reverse it or else I'll cancel my card!"

"Sir, you're being charged interest because you didn't pay your bill last month. It's legitimately charged and unfortunately we cannot reverse it."

"Look at my account history, I never miss my payments."

"Yes, but you've missed it this month. Are you familiar with how credit cards work, sir? If you don't pay in full and on time, you will be charged interest."

"I don't care about all that."

"Okay well, we do. The bank is lending you money interest free and all you need to do is pay it back each month. That seems like a pretty fair deal to me."

"I was on vacation."

"That is hardly a compelling argument, sir. It is still the cardholder's responsibility to make sure they pay their bill on time, right? It's not the bank's fault you went on vacation and forgot to pay your bill."

"I don't need you to lecture me on how to pay my bill! Let me speak to your manager!"

I exhaled a deep breath and transferred the call.

"You alright there, Trevor?" Tami asked.

"No, not really. This job is going to kill me."

"You better take it easy on yourself or else you may end up like Debbie."

"Why, what happened to Debbie?"

"She had a heart attack, didn't you hear?"

"Another one?"

"Yeah, must have been on your day off. The paramedics had to haul her out of here on a stretcher."

"Dang."

"Try not to take the job so personally," Eduardo said.

"These people are so dumb. It's really wearing me down having to deal with them. And it's always the same story, isn't it?"

"You've been here a long time, how long has it been?"

"It will be four years in July."

"That's a long time."

"Yeah, soon I won't have to deal with it." I decided to take another call.

"Thank you for calling National Group Bank of Canada, this is Trevor, how may I assist you today?"

"I forgot my PIN."

"Okay, I can definitely help you with this today ma'am."

"You know, there are too many goddamn PIN numbers to remember these days. I got about a dozen different PINs for work, emails, online banking, and debit cards. I've got PINs coming out the ying-yang…"

***

"Thank you for calling National Group Bank of Canada, this is Trevor, how may I assist you today?"

"Why won't my card work?"

"Are you keying in the correct PIN number?"

"What's my PIN number?"

"Unfortunately, I do not have access to that information, but I can tell you how to obtain another PIN."

"Alright what do I need to do?"

***

"What's with people not remembering their PIN number? I get like five hundred calls a day because people don't remember their PIN," I said.

"Yeah, and another five hundred calls for people demanding we reverse interest," Eduardo added.

"I try not to think about it," Tami said.

"I'm sorry, I hate to be one of those co-workers who complain all the time, but when I'm gone, I won't miss this place, believe me."

"When you become a successful lawyer, can you take me with you?"

"Yeah sure, you can be my secretary," I joked. "Eduardo, you can be my assistant."

It was time for my break. I grabbed a banana from my desk and went over to the computer room – a tiny corner with two computers set up for personal use.

After about ten minutes of browsing, the system automatically logged me out. "Hey, what the heck!"

"Excuse me, Charlie," I said to my manager, who happened to be walking by.

"Yes, what's up, Trevor?"

"I was just reading an article and after ten minutes the computer just signed me off. Do you know why that happened?"

"Yeah, it's a new feature to help people achieve more efficient break times."

"So the system has now been programmed to automatically log users out after ten minutes just to help cut down on them taking extended breaks?"

"Exactly," he said with a big smile.

"Oh okay, thanks."

Throughout all my work experience, I really learned a lot. I learned what not to do when running a company. The National Group Bank didn't treat people like adults, they treated us like little kids. It was the largest bank in the country, made billions of dollars, and yet invested almost none of that to its front-end employees. Was profit maximizing really all that great for them? What about trying to run the best company possible, even if it meant not making as much money? That seemed like more of an achievement to me.

***

"Thank you for calling National Group Bank of Canada, this is Trevor, how may I assist you today?"

"Yeah, I'm looking at my bill and I think my card had been compromised."

"Okay, I'm sorry to hear that, sir, I can definitely take a look at that for you."

"There's a charge for twenty nine dollars for 'purchase interest', I never shopped there."

Chapter Thirty-Three

I headed into boardroom A for a four o'clock meeting that I was scheduled for. Shannon, one of the temporary managers, stopped me. She had been recently promoted to fill in for my manager, Charlie, who was on parental leave. It was her first week on the job and there were plenty of things she hadn't fully grasped yet - schedules being one of those things.

"Trevor, we have a coaching session at 4:00," she said.

I could see the meeting was about to start and I already had one foot in the boardroom. I reminded her I had a meeting scheduled, and not coaching, but she insisted I was wrong. I was a little annoyed, but did my best not to display my emotion. We walked back to her desk. I remained standing because I knew she was wrong, she just needed to be convinced of that. She opened up the scheduling software on her computer and found my name.

TREVOR MORRISON: MEETING - 4:00 p.m.

"Hmm, that's odd, I thought we had coaching," she remarked.

I didn't say anything.

"Okay, go to your meeting and then come back here at 5:00."

I walked back to the meeting and listened to some frivolous company propaganda for a little shy of 60 minutes. The meeting let out a few minutes early and much to my surprise, there was Shannon, waiting for me by the door as if I was some convict she was responsible for escorting.

"Are you ready for coaching?" she asked.

"I guess so."

"Coaching will actually be in boardroom B. Unfortunately, it will be more of a verbal warning, and I don't want to do it out in the open in front of everyone. Please follow me."

I followed Shannon into boardroom B. When we arrived, another two managers were already waiting there, Alfredo and Martin.

She informed me they were just there to observe and take notes.

I took a seat and crossed my legs.

When Shannon began to speak, her voice became low and somber, in order to emote the seriousness of what she was about to discuss with me. The whole thing was rather amusing to me since I knew what she was trying to do. She was the newbie in the management pack and wanted to flex her muscles. She had chosen me to be her sacrificial lamb – a bad choice on her part.

"Trevor," she said as she exhaled. "There are a few things we need to address with you. First of all, we have a list that gets produced each month that displays calls that are less than 20 seconds and your name appears on the top of this list every month. There's not even a close second. Now, the policy states you are to remain on the line for at least 20 seconds before disconnecting. Are you aware of that?"

"Yes, of course. My manager discussed this with me already a few weeks ago."

"So, please tell me why you disconnect so soon."

"Okay, I will tell you what I told him. It's simple, really. In the past, if I received a call where I couldn't hear anyone on the other line, I would wait 20 seconds before disconnecting. I did this for years. After all those years, you know what I discovered? There was not even one instance where someone came on the line after 10 seconds. As it turns out, 20 seconds is an arbitrary number. Whoever came up with that policy got it wrong – it's inefficient. So, in an effort to improve call efficiency, I disconnect after 10 seconds in order to take more calls for the company."

"I understand that, but the company wants you to wait at least 20 seconds before disconnecting. I don't want to see your name on this list again, okay?"

"Okay."

"The second thing, Trevor, is your idle time is very high. This implies you are chatting with your co-workers and avoiding calls. In some cases, you sit in idle mode for 20 minutes. I pulled a record of all the times you are sitting in idle and it appears you keep going in and out of ready mode in order to reposition yourself at the back of the queue. This is a very serious offense, Trevor. What do you have to say for yourself?"

"If I go in and out of ready mode, then there must be a really good explanation for doing so since I obviously have no problem sitting in idle for 20 minutes, as your records indicate.

"Furthermore, having a high idle time does not necessarily imply I'm "chatting" as you put it. I happen to do a lot of my work after the call rather than during it. Some people choose to do it during the call, and that's fine too. There's no right or wrong way, just a difference in style. Regardless of which style I choose, in both cases I would be unavailable to take another call. At least my method avoids the customer getting annoyed while they pointlessly wait on the other end. So, I think my method is much better than the alternative. It's win-win for everybody."

Shannon had nothing really to say about that so she went on to her next point.

"The third thing I wanted to bring to your attention is a particular call."

Shannon already had the call cued up, so she pressed play. During the call, the customer expressed the desire to cancel their account. I suggested to the cardholder they keep the card for another six months since they had already paid up front for the card's annual fee. The card was up for renewal in six months, so by cancelling later, they could still benefit from the usage of the card. The cardholder agreed with my suggestion and requested to have the card cancelled automatically in six months, without the need for her to call back. I agreed and disconnected the call.

When the call ended, the room was silent. I continued to sit there coyly with a bored look on my face.

Once again, trying to increase the dramatics of the situation, Shannon let out a big sigh. "Trevor, please tell me why you told this woman you would cancel her account in six months."

"Because I will cancel her account in six months," I said directly. "Are you accusing me of something, Shannon?" I asked. At this point, I was getting rather tired of this game we were playing.

If a customer called in to cancel their account, it is our job to prevent it as much as possible. It was actually one of the stats they use to measure our performance and base our pay grade on. As such, there is financial incentive for an employee to manipulate their stats in order to increase the size of their paycheck. It was no secret employees did this, and she was insinuating I was guilty of doing it too. I played dumb so I could get her to accuse me directly.

"What is it you think I did wrong during that call?" I asked.

"Well, from an auditor's standpoint, it looks like you told the woman you would cancel her account in six months, but didn't."

"How could I cancel an account today, six months from now? It's illogical. If we were to go to my desk right now, I could show you a note with her account details written on it. I fully plan to cancel her account, as promised."

"Okay, but if you were ever hit by a bus, we wouldn't know you had a piece of paper in your desk. In the future, just write the referral."

"Okay, fair enough."

"Finally, I want to bring up your usage of the phones for personal calls on company time. What is your understanding of that policy?"

"Keep it to a minimum."

"Exactly. We recognize during a shift, people will need to make personal calls, but we want you to make them from the phones outside the office."

"Okay."

"In the last two weeks, you made a total of 42 minutes of outbound calls."

"Uhh... okay?" I said dumbfounded.

"Trevor, these are serious problems."

Ordinarily, I would have let it go, but I had received my acceptance letter into law school a week prior so I knew I would be quitting soon. I had nothing to lose - complete freedom to speak my mind. So I used this opportunity as a forum to do so.

"Shannon, first of all, I don't appreciate all the dramatics, okay? I know what you are trying to do and it's unnecessary. When I came in here, you made it seem like you had me on camera stealing from the company.

"As far as these things being 'serious problems', I have to say, I don't share your concern. You brought up four issues that are so petty that they are not even worth mentioning at all. Then you base your case around some skewed data that hardly presents an accurate reflection of the whole picture."

I could tell she wanted to speak, so I raised my hand to stop her. "Please, let me finish. Your record of my outbound calls is from a random two-week period where I happened to be off the phones for 42 minutes, but it's not as if I'm consistently doing it. Not to mention, 42 minutes over a two-week period is not really a big deal in the broader scope of things. That's 21 minutes per week, which works out to a couple of minutes per day. Are you suggesting that you're doing your job the entire time you are here? You wouldn't be able to come up with a span of 21 minutes in your week where you are not doing your job? Because that would be a lie. Nobody works 100% of the time. I constantly witness managers talking to other managers for 45 minutes per day about Canucks games, or what they did on the weekend.

"Let me give you some free advice. What you did just now was completely inappropriate. You can't treat people this way. If I were to quit or be fired, believe me, I would be fine. However, some of the people out there do not have this same luxury so I will speak for them. Do you know how many people here are stressed out, on some kind of anti-depressant, have major medical issues from being at this job, or have quit entirely because of the impossible standards this company expects? This slave-master mentality this company operates under has got to stop, it's not right."

"Did you know I did your job for five years, Trevor?"

"With all due respect, Shannon, that was a long time ago. Many relevant aspects of the job have changed since then. There were not as many products and procedures, there were no time limits for the calls, there were no sales, there was a different scoring matrix, and not to mention, a completely different management team. So, I disagree, you did not do my job."

Alfredo chimed in for the first time in a somewhat aggressive tone. "Look, people get promoted because they are doing a good job. People who do poorly, don't. It's illogical."

"I'm sorry, I don't see the relevance of that statement," I said.

Alfredo was completely caught off-guard by my apparent lack of respect for authority. He was trying his best to intimidate me, and I swatted him away like the annoying pest he was.

All the things that made me a bad employee were the exact qualities that made me a good entrepreneur. I relished in that fact and made no apologies about it. For most of my life, I was trying to conform to something I was not. I was trying to fit in and be a good employee, but in that moment it became clear I was not meant to be an employee. I needed to do my own thing. I needed to start my own company.

PART II

Riches

Chapter Thirty-Four

I checked to make sure I still had my boarding pass. I gave Ashley one last hug and kiss goodbye before I boarded the plane.

"It will only be for three years. And I'll visit you every few months, or you can come visit me once you're done your MBA."

"You promise?"

"Of course, Ashley. Being with you is the best thing that has happened to me. You've been with me throughout all the ups and downs over the past five years. I just have to go away for a while, but I'll come back for you. Okay?"

"Okay, I love you."

Leaving her was the hardest thing I have ever had to do. So much can change in such a little amount of time. It would be a shame to lose her, but that was the reality I was facing. I had every intention of going back for her because she was worth it. She was with me when I had nothing, a rare quality to find in a woman, especially one who had everything. I was just trying to be realistic about all this. There was a real possibility we would grow apart once the separation had gone on for a few months. Time has a funny way of doing that, making us forget.

***

I arrived in Ontario one week before classes commenced. The air was crisp and the leaves were starting to turn brown and fall off the trees. The campus looked really beautiful this time of the year. It was not as large as my previous school, but it was big enough to make me feel insignificant. I was essentially starting from scratch here. I didn't know a single person and did not have any of my usual comforts from back home. I had worked for the number one bank in the country, had a great girlfriend, and lots of friends. But I traded it all in to follow my dream. There was no doubt in my mind I would end up back in Vancouver, but I just needed to focus for the next three years and get the credentials that I desperately wanted.

I had gone there a month prior to secure an apartment. I had found a nice one-bedroom apartment on the seventh floor of a brand new apartment building on campus. It had a small gym, sauna room, entertainment room, and in-suite laundry. Rent was a lot cheaper out here than in Vancouver, so it was definitely an upgrade.

***

"Hey, man," a friendly looking guy greeted me in the hallway outside my door.

"Hey."

"Looks like you're movin' in," he said, looking at all the stuff I was carrying.

"Yeah, I just got into town today," I replied, as I fumbled with my keys.

"Where are you from?"

"Vancouver."

"Oh really, that's where I'm from too."

"Really, what a small world."

"Here, let me help you with that."

"Thanks."

I unlocked the door and propped it open with a dustpan.

"Looks like you need some furniture," the man said, looking around my empty apartment.

"Yeah, do you know of any places where I can get some cheap furniture?"

"I do actually. One of my uncles owns the largest furniture store in town. I can get you a sweet deal."

"Really? Thanks, man."

"I'm Steve by the way."

"Nice to meet you, Steve, I'm Trevor. Do you live on this floor?"

"No, I live on the fifteenth floor, but my buddies live next door to you. I'll introduce you if you want."

"Sure."

"Actually, we're about to play some poker and we could use another player. Do you want to join us?"

"Um, okay, yeah, that would be great."

***

"Hey, I found a fourth for our game."

"Hello," I said, as I gave an awkward wave.

"Trevor, this is Dan and Jeremy. Dan and Jeremy, meet your new neighbour, Trevor."

"So what are you guys playing?" I asked as I took my jacket off and grabbed a seat at the table.

"The game is No Limit Texas Hold 'em, have you played it before?"

"Remind me," I said coyly. The truth was I used to host tournaments and cash games at my house every week to make a little extra money. With my winnings, I would play in the big tournaments at the casino once in a while. I did pretty well too, but I kept that information to myself.

"The buy-in is twenty dollars, is that okay with you?"

I reached into my pocket and grabbed a fist full of whatever I could find. I had three five-dollar bills and a bunch of change. I noticed a few stares, but nobody said anything. I counted out twenty dollars and put it into the pot.

"Alright, hurry up and deal," Steve said to dealer.

For the first couple of hands, I played the rookie card like a pro. I checked out of turn, asked dumb questions, and pretended to forget which direction the cards were supposed to be dealt. I had these guys believing I really sucked, but there was money on the line, and I wanted it.

"So you're a student?" Dan asked.

"Yeah, I'm starting law school next week, how bout you guys?"

"Hey, me too. I'll probably see you in some of my classes then," Dan said. "Jeremy and Steve are in business school."

"I see. Oh, is it my turn?"

"Yeah, it's on you, what do you want to do?"

"Um, I'll check."

"Well, Dan just raised, so you either have to call, re-raise, or fold."

"Oh, sorry. Okay, I'll call."

"Flip 'em, let's see what you have?"

"I have a straight, is that any good?" I asked.

"Good enough. Take it down."

That was another one for me. I had been conning these guys all night and was the current the chip leader. Perhaps it was not the best way to make new friends.

"So what do you guys do for fun around here?" I asked.

"Around here? Nothing," Jeremy said.

"We go to New York and Las Vegas a lot though," Steve said. "New York is only a few hours drive from here."

"I haven't been to either of those cities."

"Really? You should come with us next time we go."

"Sure, that sounds like fun."

Chapter Thirty-Five

Classes were starting soon and I still needed to settle in. I picked up all my books in the morning, but I still needed some furniture. The last two nights I had slept on the floor with a rolled up towel as my pillow while using another towel as a blanket. It reminded me of earlier times when I was broke. I managed to save up a little money over the past few years, but not much, just a couple thousand dollars. I was relying heavily on my student loans to get me through the next three years.

Just outside my building was a small drugstore where I bought a bunch of cleaning supplies and some groceries. On my way out, I inserted a quarter into the payphone and dialed the number to my only friend.

"Hey, Steve, I'm sorry to bother you, but I was wondering if you could let me know where your uncle's furniture store is?"

"Where are you?" he asked.

"I'm at the drugstore payphone."

He laughed a little, and then said, "Okay, why don't you come up to my apartment and wait for me while I get ready, and then we can go together?"

"Alright thanks, I'll be there in a minute."

When I entered Steve's apartment for the first time, I was completely blown away. He lived by himself in a large two-bedroom apartment. The first thing I noticed was his elaborate entertainment system."

"Wow, this is a nice place, man. It's almost three times the size of my place."

"Thanks. Wait until you see the view."

I walked across the dark polished hardwood floor, toward the large window. The curtains were open, revealing the entire campus. A small telescope was set up, pointing down to the Student Union Building. I peered into it and saw a bunch of scurrying students.

"Is this the penthouse?" I asked, looking up at the fifteen-foot high ceiling.

"It's one of them. There are four units on the top floor."

"You want the grand tour?"

"Sure."

The living room was equipped with an array of high-end electronics including a 60" TV, surround-sound speakers built into his walls, and a massive catalogue of movies. He had a large sectional sofa with a simple glass coffee table and a stylish area rug underneath it. I followed him through the living room to a large sliding glass door. He slid the door open to reveal a beautiful patio that was larger than my entire apartment. The patio housed a large hot tub, basketball hoop, a sun tanning area, and a flower garden.

"Check this out," he said, as he showed off his prize possession. "I had this installed a few months ago."

The L shaped bar was completely stocked and fully functional. It was custom made out of stone and had a built-in barbeque, mini-fridge, sink, and dishwasher.

"Come on inside, I'll show you the rest."

Steve led me back inside, through the living room, past the kitchen, down the hall, and into his office. One of the walls in his office had a colorful abstract painting in the centre of it with two bookshelves on opposite sides. In the centre of the office was a large executive desk with three monitors mounted to a single base.

"What's with all the monitors?" I asked.

"Oh, I need them for trading."

"Trading?" I asked.

"Yeah, I trade equities."

"What does that mean?"

"Oh sorry, I trade stocks."

"Do you make any money at it?"

"I do okay, made thirty thousand last week," he said casually.

"Wow, good for you." My mind was still trying to comprehend such a large figure. I didn't even make thirty thousand the entire year.

"Come here, I'll show you what I do. The monitor to your left is where I check all my SEC filings, news, and charts throughout the day. The middle monitor is where I do all my order entries, and the monitor on the far right is set up for my alerts and level IIs."

I had no idea what he just said, but for the chance to make thirty thousand, I wanted to learn more. I stood behind him and tried my best to make sense of all the flashing lights, graphs, and letters moving rapidly across the screen. I felt like I was in the cockpit of an alien spaceship.

"If you want to learn more about this stuff, I can show you."

"Seriously? That would be great, thanks."

"No problem. You can also help yourself to my book collection. I think you will like everything on the top shelf."

***

We entered the elevator and Steve swiped his key fob against a sensor and pressed PP1.

"What did you just do?" I asked inquisitively. I lived in the same building, but I did not have to scan my key to use the elevator.

"Oh, I have a private parking garage. You need to swipe this thing to gain access."

The elevator took us down one level below the main parking garage. The doors opened and we stepped off the elevator. I was shocked at what I saw. In front of us was an assortment of beautiful exotic cars.

"Dang," I said under my breath.

"Nice, right?"

I was speechless. Who is this guy? For a young guy in university, he sure had a nice car collection. The first vehicle to grab my attention was a polished black H1 Hummer. It was by far the largest vehicle in the fleet, but certainly not the most extravagant. The cherry red Ferrari 599 GTO won that title. He also had a Mercedes E class, a Lexus RX Hybrid, and an equally impressive collection of street bikes.

Steve extended his hand, pressed a button on his key chain, and the Lexus came to life.

"Come on, we'll take this one, we can put some small stuff in it. I'll get my uncle to deliver all the larger things."

On the way to his uncle's furniture store, we talked a lot more about trading stocks.

"My strategy is simple really, I find 'diamond-in-the-rough' companies and bet large on them."

"Are you successful most of the time?"

"Usually. Sometimes I take losses, but my gains far outweigh my losses. I don't want you to get the wrong idea, if you don't know what you're doing you can go broke very quickly. In fact, a buddy of mine lost a half million dollars playing my strategy. I can teach you everything I know, but you must have the right kind of personality for trading. I trade mostly on instincts, and I can't teach you that."

"I know exactly what you mean," I said, remembering my sales seminar.

"If you want to invest a little bit of money to get your feet wet, look into XNR."

"XNR? What does that mean?"

"Oh, sorry, XNR is the ticker symbol for Xaner Pharmaceuticals."

"Okay, what do they do?"

"This company is about to introduce a drug that will revolutionize the way people treat diabetes. It's still undergoing trials, but they are in their phase 3 of testing."

"Sounds interesting."

"Yeah, this thing is going to be huge, I have a couple hundred grand invested in it."

***

Thanks to Steve, my apartment was now set up with the essentials. I picked up a cheap couch, bed, and desk. He even gave me an old coffee table he wasn't using. I planned to go into town and pick up some dishes and bed sheets later, but first I wanted to try out my new cell phone.

"Hello?"

"Hi baby," I said.

"Hey! How are you?" Ashley said excitingly.

"I'm doing well, how are you?

"I'm good. So is this your new number?"

"Yeah, I just got it today; I wanted you to be the first person I called."

"Aww, that's sweet. So how are you finding everything so far? Have you made any friends yet?"

"It's great so far. I've met a few really nice guys in my building actually. One of them is starting law school as well. And this other friend of mine, Steve, this guy is loaded. He lives in the penthouse of my building, which is huge by the way, and he has over a half a million dollars worth of cars in his own private garage."

"Wow, sounds like a cool guy."

"Yeah, he's awesome. He hooked me up with some really cheap furniture from his uncle's store and even got me into trading stocks."

"Oh baby, be careful, I don't want you to lose all your money."

"To be honest, I have no idea what I'm doing, I just listen to him and so far he has been right. He told me to put some money into this pharmaceutical company and a week later the stock went up almost four hundred percent!"

"So how much money did you make?"

"I just put a couple thousand dollars of my student loan money and I made around eight grand."

"Wow, that's fantastic!"

"Yeah, I know. Steve has been teaching me a lot. He has his own personal library and lent me a few books on trading."

"I'm happy to hear that, hon. I just worry you will lose all your money, or you will be too focused on stocks and not do well in school. Don't forget why you're there. You worked really hard to get there."

"Yeah I know, but I love making money too."

"Okay, as long as you know what you're doing, I trust you."

Chapter Thirty-Six

I logged onto my computer to check on how my stocks were doing, something I found myself doing every five minutes throughout the trading day. Trading was definitely addicting. I didn't want to admit it to Ashley, but she was right. The stock market was consuming all my time, my valuable time. I reviewed a few charts, analyzed some numbers, and made my best attempt to make sense of it. A few moments later, I picked up my phone and texted Steve. 'HEY STEVE, I AM WORRIED ABOUT HEX CORP. IT'S DOWN NEARLY SIX POINTS'.

Almost instantly, he responded. 'DON'T WORRY BUDDY, WAIT FOR THE NEWS TO COME OUT MONDAY, IT SHOULD FLY!.'

'I HOPE SO.'

'HEY, WHAT R U DOING 2NITE???' he asked.

I replied back, 'NOT MUCH, YOU?'

'U WANT 2 COME OUT W/US 2NITE?'

'SURE, WHERE TO?'

'VEGAS BABY!!!'

I didn't reply right away. I sat there for a moment, staring at my phone. I could think of a dozen reasons why I shouldn't go: I was behind in my readings in almost every course, I had a paper due, a quiz to study for, and I didn't really have the money to spend on a whimsical Vegas trip. I contemplated some more, and finally replied.

'OKAY I'M IN!'

I hopped in the shower and lathered up my face for a shave. A few moments later, I heard what sounded like a dozen people pounding on my door. It was loud enough for me to hear it over my music and the running water.

"Alright-alright, I'm coming. Geez, someone is excited."

I wrapped a towel around my waist and opened the door.

"Hey, nice towel," Steve said, as he and his friends barged in. "I can't believe you're coming to Vegas with us," Jeremy said.

"Yeah, it should be good," I replied, still dripping wet.

"This trip is going to be crazy!"

"So did someone check the flight times?" I asked.

They all looked at each other as if I had just said the most ridiculous thing.

"Not exactly," Steve replied with a smirk. "You don't have to worry about a thing. Just sit back, relax, and uncle Stevie will take care of you. Now hurry up and get dressed."

I quickly put together my Vegas outfit. I decided to go with a pink dress shirt with the sleeves rolled up over a white tank top. I left the top two and bottom two buttons undone. For pants, I wore a straight-front classic off-white khaki. After a few sprits of cologne, I was ready to go.

"Who are you, Don Johnson?" Steve joked at my outfit.

"Yeah, we're going to Las Vegas, not Miami Vice," Dan said.

"That's okay, you guys just aren't men enough to wear a pink shirt with white pants."

"Apparently not. Anyways, do you have all your things?" Steve asked.

"Yeah, I'm good," I replied.

"Alright, let's go."

We all piled into the elevator like a bunch of rowdy fans at a sporting event. It was obvious I was the only one who didn't already have a slight buzz. Aside from their amplified enthusiasm, I could smell the vodka on them. Steve pressed 'L' to take us down to the lobby. When we got outside, there was a shiny black limousine parked out front. "What's this?" I asked excitingly. "Is this what we're taking? I've never been in a limo before!"

"Just get in," Steve said.

I looked at Jeremy and Dan and they had a look on their faces like I hadn't seen anything yet. They seemed amused at how excited I was getting. This was obviously nothing new for them.

"If you like this, wait until you see the next surprise," Steve said.

"What surprise?"

"Trevor, tonight is going to be a magical night, full of surprises. It's your first time to Vegas and don't worry, we'll make sure you have a good time."

Steve grabbed a bottle of champagne from the limousine's mini-bar and sloppily poured out four glasses.

"Toast!" Steve announced, as he raised his glass in the air. We all did the same. "To Vegas and the wonderful sins it will bring us!"

***

We arrived at the airport thirty minutes later. I hadn't been to the airport that often, but I knew enough to know we were not going the regular way. I could see the departure terminal, but we were not driving towards it. "Hey, where are we going?" I asked in confusion.

"Trevor, have I ever let you down before?" Steve asked.

"No."

"Alright then. You've seen my apartment, right?"

"Yeah."

"You've seen my cars, right?"

"Yeah."

"You're in a limo tonight, right?"

"Okay?"

"My friend, you have only experienced a little taste of what my lifestyle is like, just a nibble."

I didn't say anything.

"Now let me ask you something, sir. Do I look like a man who flies commercial?" Steve said. It was as if he had timed it perfectly. The limo pulled around a row of hangars and I saw a private jet being fueled in one of the hangars.

"Oh my god!" I blurted out in amazement.

The guys all chuckled. "I thought you might like that. Welcome to the good life, sir!"

We quickly finished our drinks, raced out of the limo, and piled into the plane. Every last detail of the plane gave off the image of success. The spotless black carpet complemented the rich mahogany wood. There were about a half a dozen large white leather captain's chairs in the plane, including a couch with throw pillows, and a bedroom at the back. Some of the seats had their own desk and TV. There was also a full bar, which I was sure was about to get a lot of use. It was unlike anything I had ever seen in a plane before. I took a seat and was now facing a 50" LED TV screen. Steve grabbed the remote and turned the TV on. He flipped to a sports station and ironically, it was playing the World Series of Poker in Las Vegas. He muted the volume and put on some music.

It was hard for me to comprehend this whole experience. It didn't seem real. I was completely overwhelmed and was very quiet, a sign I was out of my comfort zone. Everything seemed so nice and new. I looked at the impeccable carpet and recalled the dirty apartment I had in Vancouver with the orange shag carpet. If someone had told me back then that in a few years, I would be flying to Las Vegas in a private jet, I would have thought they were crazy.

"This is your captain speaking," a voice announced over the PA system. "Gentlemen, we'll be reaching an altitude of thirty three thousand feet on a non-stop flight to Las Vegas. Please make sure your seat belts are secure as we are about to prepare for takeoff."

The plane maneuvered into position then accelerated down the runway at an alarming speed. A few moments later, we had liftoff. I looked out my window and saw the city lights below getting more and more distant. I imagined what my classmates were doing. Most of them were probably at home studying, oblivious to the fact I was flying over them in a private jet.

A few hours later, another message broadcasted over the PA system. "Hello, this is your captain speaking. We are approaching our destination. We will begin to reduce altitude, please fasten your seat belts."

The tires hit the runway smoothly and I felt an immediate pullback from the massive stopping power of the plane. We went from 400 miles per hour to a crawl in less than twenty seconds. Our excitement was escalating in anticipation. During the flight, we had continued to party and were completely drunk by the time we landed. We spilled out of the plane and felt the warm Las Vegas air hit our faces. I took a deep breath and stretched my arms. I could get used to this lifestyle, I thought.

Steve seemed to be thoroughly enjoying himself as the host of our little adventure to wonderland. He had probably done this a hundred times, but he seemed to find pleasure in bringing this lifestyle to others who weren't as fortunate. He exited the plane last and stood at the top of the stairs of the G550 plane.

"Gentlemen," he shouted out to us down below as if he was the king of the castle. We all turned around, eager to discover what was in store for us next. "Since we are all gentlemen here," he announced, "I think it only seems fitting we begin our evening with an elegant trip to the gentlemen's club. What do you say boys?" he yelled, like a coach trying to rally his team.

Steve came down the stairs and was congratulated for planning such a spectacular night.

"The limo awaits, sirs." Steve extended his arm toward another shiny black limousine. We stepped into the limo and sped off toward the bright lights.

Chapter Thirty-Seven

As we drove through the Vegas strip, I was starting to see why Steve came here so much. My eyes darted around trying to take in as much as possible. The bright lights created an ambience like I was in a fantasyland. So far, the mystique of Las Vegas was living up to the hype.

"We're here," Steve proudly announced, as we pulled up to the Tiger Room Gentlemen's Club.

"You're going to love it here, Trevor, just you wait. The women here are the best," Steve exclaimed. "And they will do something strange for a little change, if you know what I mean."

Inside the gentlemen's club, it was everything I imagined. Scantily clad women were hoisted in the air on giant swings, women in cages, women on stage, and of course, a room full of drunken perverted men. I wasn't sure how many of them were actually gentlemen, but I was there too, so I was not in a position to pass judgment.

Steve said something to the hostess, and an exchange took place. He turned around and winked. Instantly, we were led to our private booth. Steve whispered something else into the hostess' ear and then she left. I generally liked to be in control of the situation, but I was not complaining. I was happy to just sit back and let Steve do his thing. This was his world and he was in his element. A few minutes later, a server returned with a tray of eight overflowing shot glasses. She unloaded them onto the table so we each had two apiece. We all took one and raised it in the air.

"To the good life!" Steve yelled out over the loud music. We each put a glass to our lips and quickly tilted our heads back.

"Come on guys, we got one more, let's do this."

We all grabbed our second shots and followed Steve's instructions. By this time, we were all thoroughly wasted.

"So where are the women, Steve?" Jeremy called out.

Steve didn't say anything; he just gave me a sinister smile, like a mastermind who was watching his elaborate plan unfold. Just then, two beautiful exotic women came over. By my guess, they appeared to be of Russian descent. They brought a couple of their friends as well. Steve leaned across the table and asked me, "Will they do?"

I quickly evaluated the women who were being presented to me, as if I was a powerful emperor. I gave a quick nod and a smile to display my approval.

"Come on, dude, let's go, get up," Steve said.

I wasn't really sure what was in store for me, but I had an idea. We both rose from the table and I followed Steve and the two Russian women. Just to the right of the bar was a small inconspicuous doorway labeled 'PRIVATE'. The two women led us through the doorway, down a dimly lit corridor where they finally presented us with our own private room. One of the girls gestured for us to go in. Steve looked at me like he was the happiest man on the planet and said, "After you, sir."

I walked into the dark room and noticed a small elevated platform in the centre of the room with a pole that extended to the mirror-covered ceiling. There were a couple of large velvet sofas around the platform so I walked over and took a seat. The walls were black, but were covered in tiny lights, like the night sky. That's cool, I thought, I should get that for my place.

Steve came over and sat down on the couch to my left.

"You having a good time so far?" he asked me.

"So far, so good."

"Just wait, you haven't seen nothin' yet."

Another attractive woman entered the room wearing a really short miniskirt and some kind of mesh top. Her bra glowed under the black lighting. She came over to us carrying a tray with a couple of drinks on it, but did not say a word. She set the tray down on a small table in between the two couches and then proceeded to disrobe. The two Russian women followed suit. The waitress wasted no time getting friendly with Steve. She straddled his lap and started kissing him. One of the Russian girls tried to do the same with me, but I was very careful not to cheat on my girlfriend, who had popped into my mind more than once that evening.

"Will you excuse me?" I said quietly as I stood up to leave. I don't think Steve noticed - he was preoccupied with more important matters. I retraced my steps and found my way back to the club.

I saw Dan sitting by himself at our table. "Hey, where's Jeremy?" I asked.

"I think he went off with some chick. Where's Steve?"

"He's in the back having the time of his life."

"Why aren't you back there with him?"

"It was too much for me, man. I had to get out of there. Why don't we take a walk, see if we can find Jeremy."

"Alright."

After a few laps around the club, we finally found Jeremy off in a dark corner, making out with some woman. We walked over to where Jeremy was sitting and I tapped him on the shoulder.

"Hey, Jeremy, I'm sorry to bother you, but can we talk to you for a second, man?"

"Heeeyy! What's up?" he said, obviously intoxicated. He slowly wobbled up to his feet.

"How you doin', buddy?" I asked.

"I'm great, man," he slurred.

"Are you having a good time?"

"Yeah, why what's up?"

"We're bored, do you want to grab some food?"

"Yeah, okay, but we need to find Steve. Where is he?"

***

After a long night, I was looking forward to going home. The limo was on time, but we were all a little late. I told the others I had one more stop to make before I left. I walked up to the cashier window and laid down eight grand in chips, all five hundred dollar denominations. The floor manager came over to supervise the transaction while the young trainee cashed me out. The manger was making small talk with me - the kind of small talk cops make when they're trying to catch you in a lie. Eight thousand dollars was not a lot of money to a casino in Vegas, but still they would rather you not walk out with their money.

"You catch the lucky ladies?" the floor manager asked. I didn't say anything, I just smiled and winked at him. A few minutes later, the teller counted out eighty one hundred dollar bills and placed them in front of me.

"Do you have an envelope?" I asked. The teller said 'no', but handed me an elastic band. I immediately folded the stack of bills in half, wrapped the elastic band around it twice, and shoved it into my pocket. I did a small lap around the floor to make sure no one was following me, then made my exit.

I finally left the casino and was surprised to see the sun coming out. I looked at my phone to check the time; it was a little after 7:00 a.m. With all the oxygen being pumped through the casino, I didn't feel exhausted at all.

We piled into the limo and flopped on separate seats. The energy in the limo was a lot lower than it was on the drive in from the airport twelve hours ago, but we were all happy to relive the events of last night.

We shared stories all the way back to the airport. I was up around eight grand so my trip was a success. Unfortunately, the same could not be said for some of the others.

***

"Wake up boys," the pilot said. I slowly rose from my reclined chair and looked out the window. We had arrived home, safe and sound. We were in the hangar again. Parked beside the plane was another limo, which was there to take us home. I looked around at everyone else - they were all still sleeping.

By the fourth limousine ride, the excitement of being in a limo had worn off. It became clear to me why Steve lived so lavishly. He was on a never-ending mission to one-up the last time. When the extravagant becomes ordinary, a person must have to do wilder and crazier things to reach that next level of excitement. For Steve, he had discovered a way to capture those same feelings he once had. By inviting us along, he could catch a glimpse of the same excitement of doing it all for the first time. It never occurred to me how difficult it would be to live a life like that. That might explain why money does not buy a person happiness. I never really understood that until now.

Chapter Thirty-Eight

Back to normal life. I could hardly wait for the exam period of my first year of law school to be over. It was definitely a lot of hard work, a lot of reading, but what made it more difficult was my attention was divided between taking notes and trading stocks.

Now that the summer was just around the corner, I could focus more on making money. While most of the other first year law students would be busy working all summer at various law firms throughout the city, I planned to sit in my housecoat and trade stocks. I had done hundreds of trades over the course of the semester and had gained a lot of really valuable knowledge and experience. With the success of my first few trades that Steve picked for me, and my Vegas earnings, I had been able to continue my winning streak and build up my trading account to around twenty-five thousand dollars. I quickly realized Steve was not trading so much as he was gambling. He would scour the message boards to find out what stocks were being talked about and get in before it was pumped up. I did the same thing at first until I realized the game. If you got in too late, or the pump was ineffective, the stock fizzled, and then it was a mad dash to sell off everything before it bottomed out. Steve enjoyed the rush and could afford to take on these kinds of risks. He had a safety net to catch him if he fell. I did not have the same luxury. I couldn't afford to gamble with my tuition money, so I came up with a different strategy.

I called my strategy 'Doggy-doodoo Trading'. It was a combination of swing trading and short selling, although I focused much more heavily on the long side. I even told Steve about it, but he said it was too slow for him. Be that as it may, I was not taking on huge risk. The technique was a holistic approach that begins with sure footing, with the goal to get to another sure-footed spot without stepping in some doggy-doodoo. Regardless of any past success I had, I knew I could always step in some crap if I wasn't careful or being too fancy.

With each trade, I proceeded with extreme caution. I would examine the entire market to get a sense of the overall sentiment. This required a thorough analysis of individual human psychology and the psychology of crowds. My objective was to predict how people would react to certain news items, then try to stay ahead of the crowds at all times. After I developed a picture in my mind of the market sentiment, I would look at how specific sectors were doing, then break it down into individual companies I had a particular interest in trading.

I used technical and fundamental analyses to determine if my next step would be on solid ground, or doodoo. For instance, just because a company had an upward trending chart pattern, good customer reviews, and solid earnings, it didn't mean they were a good investment. A company like this might attract an average investor and fill them with false hope, but not me. Sometimes a company like this would rely too heavily on just one of their products. Eventually, a competitor would come out with a better version of the product and make the old product obsolete.

So far, my strategy had paid off. In my first year of trading, I was up one hundred and five percent, crushing the S&P 500 composite index.

***

'This is Ashley, leave a message'.

"Hi, sweetie, it's Trevor, remember me? Um… sorry I haven't called you in a while, I've just been really busy with exams and whatnot. So, I hope you're doing well and I'll look forward to hearing from you. Okay, talk to you later. Love you. Bye."

A few days went by and I still had not heard from Ashley. A million thoughts ran through my head as to why. Most of them were not good. I ruled out the possibility of her being in a serious accident because her parents would have called me by now and her voice mail would have been full.

***

"Alright, is it my turn? How much did you bet?" I asked.

"I bet five hundred."

"You're still chasing your straight, aren't you?" I replied.

Just then my phone vibrated in my pocket. Considering the people who usually call me were in the same room as me, there was only one other person it could be. I took out my phone and looked anyway.

"Hold on a second guys, my girl is calling me, I have to take this."

I excused myself from the table and walked across the living room, outside to Steve's exquisite patio.

"Hey, baby," I said.

"Hey," she replied very stoically. The instant I heard her voice, I knew something was wrong.

"Are you okay?"

"I don't know."

"Why are you being so quiet?"

"I don't know."

"Are you sad?"

"I don't know."

"Ashley, please can you talk to me. You don't sound happy."

"It's just… well, I've been thinking a lot."

She didn't have to say another word, I already knew what was coming. My heart sank to the bottom of my stomach.

"Okay, and what have you been thinking about?"

"Us."

"You're scaring me, babe. What's wrong with us?"

"It's just… hard, you know?"

"I know, but it's only a couple more years."

"Trevor. A couple more years is too long for me. This past year was hard enough; I can't imagine what another two or three would be like."

"Alright so what are you saying?"

"I don't know, I just think maybe we should see other people?"

"See other people? I don't want to see other people. Are you seeing someone?" I swallowed hard and tried to block out the thought, but I had to ask.

"No, but it has been over a year now and we kind of lost touch. You used to call all the time, but now I don't hear from you for weeks. Even when I call you, you're always busy."

"I know. I'm sorry."

"And I want to go out, but I also don't want to feel guilty for talking to anyone, and I don't want to have to worry about what you're doing."

"You don't have to worry about what I'm doing. I'm not doing anything."

"I just feel maybe we should be more open to the possibility of seeing other people."

"Why do you keep saying that? I don't want to see other people."

"Alright well, I'm just not sure I can go another two years like this."

"Like what?"

"Trevor, don't make this harder than it already is."

"I can't believe what I'm hearing right now."

"I'm not leaving you for anyone else. I'm leaving because I need to. I don't think I can do this long distance thing anymore."

"Alright whatever, do what you have to do."

I hung up the phone and exhaled a deep breath. I took a moment to gather my thoughts before I went back inside. I had experienced my fair share of pain and sorrow in my life, but nothing like this. It felt like a part of my soul was ripped out and taken away from me. I leaned against the railing and gazed up at the stars. I didn't have to think too hard to realize there was only one way to fix this. One of us would have to drop out of school and move across the country, and that just didn't seem realistic.

The sliding door opened slowly and Dan stuck his head out.

"You okay, bro?" he asked.

"Yeah, I'm fine," I said, as I came back inside.

"Dude, what was that all about? Is everything okay?" Steve asked.

"That was my girl; she just broke up with me."

"Sorry to hear that, man. How long have you guys been dating?"

"About five years. Six if you count last year."

"Don't worry, man; maybe it's for the best. If it is meant to be, then you guys will get back together."

"Yeah, maybe you're right."

"Hey, bro, I know you're going through a lot right now, but do you still want in on this hand?" Jeremy asked.

"Screw it, yeah. How much to call?"

"Dan bet five hundred, now it's on you."

"Okay, I'm all in."

"Dude, are you sure?"

"Yeah."

"I fold," Jeremy said.

"I'll call," Steve said. "No offense, Trevor, but I'm not sure you're thinking straight right now."

"How much is your all in?" Dan asked.

"For you, $4,850," I replied without showing any emotion.

"Wow, that's a lot of action," Dan said as he pondered the call. "Okay, screw it, I'll call."

"Let's see 'em, everybody flip their cards over."

The board read 10/K/Q. Steve revealed his cards, A/K suited - top pair with a high kicker. Dan had pocket jacks, not a great pair in this situation because he only had one out - any nine would complete his straight. If another jack came up, it would actually give Steve a straight so he did not want that, unless an ace followed it on the river. That would result in a three-way tie and everyone would get back what they had put in. As for me, I had 10/6 off-suit - a serious underdog with bottom pair.

"Alright, are you guys ready for the next card?"

"Just hurry up already," Steve demanded.

"Okay, the next card is..."

Jeremy revealed 6 of diamonds, which put me in the lead with two-pair. In order for Steve to win, he would need a jack - but Dan already had two of them - or pair up again, which would trump my two-pair.

"Okay, flipping last card..."

The final card was a 6 of clubs, giving me a full house, and the win.

"Oh my god, I don't believe this!" Steve shouted. He stood up from the table and put his hands on the back of his head.

I remained relatively emotionless. Winning a pot of that size somehow did not bring me the joy I thought it would. Five years ago, that money would have changed my life.

"That's not fair! Steve protested. "I want a rematch."

"Okay, let's play again," I said calmly, still in my seat.

"The buy in is five grand this time!" Steve announced as he sat back down, eager for a chance at redemption.

"That's too rich for my blood," Jeremy said.

"Yeah, me too, count me out," Dan said.

"Okay, Steve, looks like it's just you and me, heads up."

"Let's make this interesting," Steve said. "Since these guys are out, let's raise the stakes. Ten grand buy in. Blinds are fifty and a hundred."

"Fine. Deal them up!" I said, like a man ready to die for his cause.

The deck was shuffled and the cards were dealt. I looked down at my hand, I had Q/8 suited.

"Bet," I said simply. "I'm feeling good about this hand. In fact, it's my lucky hand. I'll bet... five grand," I pushed my chips slowly toward the centre of the table.

"Call!" Steve quickly called, showing confidence in his hand.

"Good, I'm glad you called. I'm going to bet another five grand on the next card and I want you to call again," I retorted back in an attempt to demonstrate the strength of my hand.

Dan, the dealer, laid out the first three cards, 8/6/10.

"That's the exact flop I wanted to see, I'm all in," I said.

I had middle pair and I doubted the flop helped Steve in any way. There's no way he would call with 7/9 pre-flop. Steve had become too predictable, typically only playing over-cards.

Steve took a moment to analyze the situation. "Take your time, Steve," I said with a cocky bravado.

"Shut up," he fired back as he contemplated his next move carefully.

He eventually mucked his hand.

Two new cards slid in front of me. I stacked them together and flipped up one of the corners. The first card was an ace of spades. I slid the next card over, it was an ace of diamonds.

"I'm all in," Steve announced, as he attempted a last ditch effort to make a comeback.

"Are you sure?" I asked.

"Bring it on," he replied.

"Okay," I said as I flipped over my cards.

"DAMMIT!" Steve screamed out. The rest of the cards were drawn and I took down another massive pot. In the last three hands, Steve had lost around fifteen thousand dollars. My stack was looking good, sitting at twenty-five thousand dollars.

"Don't worry Steve, I'll give you a rematch. What do you say, double or nothing?"

"No way, forget it."

"Okay, how about this, I'll put up my twenty-five grand. If you win, you get it all."

"Okay… and if I lose?"

"If you lose, you let me pick out one of your cars and let me drive it until I finish school."

"Hmm, interesting proposal," Jeremy said.

"Which car?" Steve asked, questioning the bizarre wager.

"A car of my choosing."

"And what if you crash it?"

"I'll drive carefully."

Steve didn't say anything.

"Look, Steve. You know you can beat me, I just got lucky on that last hand."

"Shut up, quit conning me!"

"I'm not, I'm just saying. It sucks to lose like that on one hand. You must be feeling very unsatisfied right now," I said, as I continued to bait him.

"Okay, let's do it. Shuffle up and deal."

Over the course of the next hour, we battled back and forth. Both of us were being overly cautious. Dan and Jeremy were happy just to be watching, almost as if they were witnessing a part of history in the making. The amount of money at stake would change my life. I tried not to think about it too much, but this was an epic battle, the type of poker game you would tell your grandkids about one day.

The first hand was dealt and I got pocket 2s. Not a great hand. I would usually fold it immediately, but I wanted to outplay Steve.

Steve looked at his hand, then up at me. "Two grand," he said nonchalantly.

"Call," I said immediately.

"Oh, man, here we go," Dan said excitingly.

The first three cards that were laid out were A/4/5. Steve looked down at the board, then at his cards, then up at me.

"It's on you, Steve," I said.

"Okay, I'll bet... another two grand." Steve splashed the pot with a fistful of chips. That was my first clue.

I knew if Steve played poker anything like he traded stocks, he would be impatient. Impatient people get agitated over time, which in turn affects their judgment. I needed to make him more anxious, so I stalled.

He represented top pair at that point, probably had the ace. I looked carefully at him, studied his behaviour, hoping he would reveal information to me through subconscious clues, which I could then exploit. We both sat there staring at each other for over a minute. The more time that passed, the bigger advantage I would have.

"Are you gonna play, or are you just going to stare at me all night?" he said. That was the second clue - he didn't have the ace, mid-pair probably.

I didn't answer. I just continued to study him, watching his breathing, reading his body language, looking for something, anything, which would reveal what cards he was holding. Eventually he would slip up and tell me what I needed to know. Just then, I noticed his jugular vein on the left side protrude and begin to pulsate rapidly - an obvious sign he was nervous. That was clue three, he didn't have a pair. I focused on the vein, which made him even more uncomfortable, that's when he revealed the fourth clue. He clasped his hands together in front of his face and tucked his thumbs inside. He was on a straight draw, representing 6/7.

I calmly announced, "Bet - four thousand."

Steve quickly studied his cards and then made a rash judgment call. "Okay, I call."

"Oh, man, this is getting crazy," Jeremy said.

"Okay, are you guys ready?" Dan asked, before laying down the next card, which was a 7 of clubs.

I was incredibly nervous at that point, but did my best to conceal it. This time I did not get lucky. I had to rely on skill alone. In order for me to outplay him, I needed to convince him my hand could beat his. My heart felt like it was going to pound out of my chest. Since I put Steve on 6/7, I figured he had just hit top pair. Now I was a serious underdog with only six cards in the whole deck that could save me. I needed any 3 to complete my straight, or one of the remaining 2s left to give me three of a kind. Suddenly I questioned why I even agreed to play this hand. Steve was the one who lost big; he should be on tilt, not me.

"Alright, here it is, the last card for all the marbles." The next card that was dealt was a 9 of hearts, which didn't help either of us.

Now it was Steve's turn to study me. I saw his eyes dart around, looking for clues.

There's a saying in poker that is used as a general rule to gauge whether your opponent has a good hand or not. The saying is, 'weak when strong, strong when weak'. It means a player who has a strong hand will try to make their opponent believe they have a weak hand, almost like setting a trap. If it works correctly, their opponent will take the bait and enter into the hand, presumably with a weaker hand. If a player conveys a strong hand, it is usually taken as a sign he is actually holding a weak hand, but wants his opponent to think it is strong in order to get his opponent to fold.

I obviously didn't want Steve to call, so I needed to trick him. If I played weak, I ran the risk of him calling. If I played strong, he might think I was trying to mask a weak hand and call. So the traditional 'weak when strong, strong when weak' would not do. I needed to use reverse psychology to trick him into thinking I was masking a mask. In order for it to work, I needed to act as if I had a strong hand, but with bad acting. If the acting was bad enough, then Steve might think I was setting a trap for him. He might think I really did have a strong hand, and then fold.

I began my shoddy portrayal of someone holding a strong hand. Steve looked at me, then down at the board, then back up at me. He had a glimmer in his eye like he was proud of himself.

"Aaahh, no you don't, Trevor. You think you're pretty sneaky, huh? You have the straight, don't you? I'm not gonna fall for your tricks."

"What are you talking about, I don't have the straight."

"Yeah, right! I'm way too clever to fall for that trick mister reverse psychology. You're trying to trick me into think you have a weak hand by portraying a strong hand."

Without saying anything, Steve threw his cards in the centre of the table. "Fold," he declared. He revealed his cards, showing his massive lay down, and a massive mistake.

"Good read, man. Your 6/7 wouldn't have beaten me," I said, trying to affirm his decision.

"Did you have the straight?" he asked.

"Yeah, I did. Good lay down."

Steve sat back down in his chair, shoulders slumped, feeling completely conquered.

"Which car are you going to pick, Trevor?" Dan asked, almost more excited than I was.

"I don't know, I haven't decided yet."

"Hey, it's not over yet. I still have a thousand dollars. I'm about to stage an epic comeback."

"Alright, hurry up and deal, let's get this over with," I said.

Steve was down, but not out. He sat there twirling his lone thousand-dollar chip. I could barely see him over the mountain of chips that was in front of me. I tossed a thousand dollar chip into the pot. Steve had no choice but to call. Since there could be no more rounds of betting, the cards were dealt to us facing up. The queen of hearts and the ace of spades landed in front of me. Steve's two cards were the 9 and 10 of clubs. We both stood up with great anticipation. The flop was laid down slowly - 7/8/Q. I was looking good so far with top pair. Steve still had outs, but he desperately needed the jack.

The turn card was drawn from the deck and snapped down on the felted tabletop. It was a 9 of hearts. The suspense was deafening. The 9 of hearts gave Steve another breath of life. Now any 9, 10, or jack could win him the hand and potentially put him back in the game. The final card was slowly drawn from the deck. My sweaty hands were clasped together behind my neck. As the river card was revealed, I breathed a sigh of relief. It was the queen of diamonds. Steve collapsed into his chair in agonizing defeat. I went over and shook his hand. Even though Dan and Jeremy were not in on the hand, and had both recently lost five grand to me, they were surprisingly happy for me.

"Let's go, Steve," Jeremy said.

Steve reluctantly peeled himself up and grabbed his keys. He had yet to say anything. I reminded him this was not a complete loss; after all, he didn't lose any more money and I was not keeping the car.

When we arrived at PP1, I casually strolled around the lot, carefully examining the exterior of each car. The first vehicle I sat in was the Hummer.

"Hey, how's the gas mileage on this thing, Steve," I called out, with a huge smile on my face. Steve didn't reply. The other guys and I were having fun toying with him.

I walked over to the Mercedes and peered into the window. The whole time, I knew which car I was picking, but I was enjoying the process. "How's the handling on the Lexus?"

Again, Steve did not say anything.

"So what do you think so far?" Jeremy asked.

"Well, I can't see myself taking the Hummer if I can get the Lexus, and I can't see myself taking the Lexus if I could get the Benz. But as hard as I try, I can't think of a single vehicle here I would rather take over the Ferrari."

Steve disarmed the Ferrari and I got in. "Yeah, this is the one for sure. I'll take this one, Steve."

"Oh, he's taking your favourite!" Jeremy said.

"Whatever, I'll just buy another Ferrari," Steve said, resorting back to his perennial self-defense mode, where money masked his insecurities.

"Thanks, buddy," I said, as I took the key from him. "I promise I'll take care of her."

Chapter Thirty-Nine

I pressed a button on the dash and the car came to life. The large engine behind me growled. I adjusted the mirrors and fastened my seat belt. I could not believe I was about to drive a Ferrari. I looked down at the little horse on the steering wheel and felt happy.

The big steel gate of the parking garage retracted into the ceiling and I crept out in first gear. I flipped a switch and the bright headlights illuminated the darkness as I prepared for my maiden voyage.

The paddle shifting took a little time to get used to, but after a few minutes, I felt like a pro. I merged onto the freeway with no intended destination. I promised Steve I would be careful, but as soon as I hit an open stretch of road, I had no choice but to break that promise. I gently pressed my foot down on the gas pedal and the engine screamed. The sound was almost deafening. Stationary objects whizzed by my periphery so fast I could hardly tell what they were. I kept my eyes straight ahead and took off down the deserted road, easily exceeding the legal limit.

From the side view mirror, I could see the headlights of another vehicle accelerating toward me. I reduced my speed in case it was a cop. The car tailed me for a couple of miles then came to a stop right beside me at the next intersection. I looked over at a gorgeous girl with long straightened hair driving a brand new BMW M3. She looked over at me and smiled. I smiled back and we shared a moment together. The light turned green and she winked at me. The rear wheels of her Beemer screeched as she peeled out. When her tires finally found traction, she took off. I sat there mesmerized. I had to remind myself I was behind the wheel of a brand new Ferrari.

"Oh it's on," I said to myself. I engaged the racing suspension and slammed my foot on the gas pedal. Almost instantly, I reached the maximum RPMs for the first gear and immediately shifted into second. The car continued to accelerate. I flipped the paddle and entered into third gear. My foot was still firmly on the gas. The BMW, already in fourth gear by this time, was way ahead of me. I weaved in and out of a few cars and had the Beemer within my sights. I shifted into fourth and watched the distance between us become shorter. You're mine now, I thought.

As I approached mind-numbing speeds, I gained considerable ground on the M3. I pulled right up beside her for a moment. She looked over at me and smiled again. This time, the smile was different. It was much more sinister. Without notice, she slammed on her brakes causing her vehicle to drop out of my sights. Through my side view mirror, I could see she had made a sharp right turn to divert her course onto the 302 exit. Within an instant, she was gone.

I continued driving north on the freeway with the city lights behind me. Other than a few warehouses, there was not much out there. I took the next exit and veered off the main drag. I found a long stretch of open road with no traffic and no cops. It was a great place for me to get away from people and allow me a chance to think. I was feeling ambivalent. I was excited to have won over twenty-five thousand dollars in cash and prizes, but it wasn't enough to take my mind off Ashley.

I gave the gas pedal a slight nudge and the car accelerated instantly past 100 kilometers per hour. My head jolted back and I was thrust deeper into the fine Italian leather.

The more I thought about the whole situation, the more upset I became. I recalled the first time I saw her in Banff, the long walks on the beach, all the ups and downs we had shared together. As soon as things were starting to go well for me in one aspect of my life, another aspect failed miserably. How could she just end it after just one year apart? I questioned.

I pressed my foot down even more and flipped the right paddle again. The smooth engine didn't skip a beat as the needle climbed past the 150 kilometer per hour mark. The gas gauge seemed to be decelerating at an equal and opposite rate. This short ride had probably cost me over thirty bucks in gas so far. The money didn't bother me, but I remained a little concerned about running out of gas. I was now deep into the forest on the outskirts of town, surrounded by trees. The thought of being stranded out there had occurred to me more than once. How long would it take me to walk back? Would I even get cell reception out here?

Those thoughts were quickly replaced by thoughts of Ashley. I thought about our trip to Whistler, meeting her parents, her cute smile. That will be someone else's smile now, someone who does not leave her to go to the other side of the country for three years. How could I have been so stupid?

A collection of fluid developed in the corner of my eye. I gave a quick squint and forced a single tear out and down the side of my cheek.

I thought about the hot woman in the BMW. What were the odds that as soon as I was single, another woman would be presented to me? I knew it was too good to be true the moment she sped off in the other direction. Maybe I just repel women.

I sunk deeper into a state of self-loathing. This time I didn't hold back. "AAAAAAHHHH!" I let out a big roar that was immediately swallowed up by the powerful twelve-cylinder engine. Letting out the scream was not as effective as I thought. I seemed to have a sickness that only excessive speed could cure. I tightened my grip on the steering wheel and slammed my foot down on the gas pedal. I accelerated up to 240 kilometers per hour and the adrenaline was enough to push out any sadness I was feeling. If I lost focus at this speed, I would be dead.

I ripped around a corner feeling the massive thirty-inch tires grip the road. As soon as my tears stopped, it began to rain. A few drops of rain splattered across my windshield as if the world felt my pain and was crying back.

The trees on either side of me whizzed by as I took the car near its limit. What was once a calm and peaceful night in the forest was now interrupted by over 600 horsepower. The car howled in the night like a lone wolf. The ground was getting a bit slick as the rain started to come down harder. I reduced speed, but I was still going well over 100.

I looked up at the moon, which was now being consumed by clouds. The rain started coming down harder. I fiddled with some knobs to activate the windshield wipers, but I was having trouble. I only took my eyes off the road for a moment, but when I came around a corner and looked back at the road, I saw a huge creature standing in the middle of the road. It appeared to be a deer, but I couldn't quite focus on it as I rapidly approached it. I was now running on pure instincts.

Without thinking, I slammed on the brakes, causing the back end of the Italian import to drift outwards. To avoid a complete tailspin, I released my foot from the brake and down shifted into third. The car made all kinds of noises as the RPMs reached over 6000. I gave it a little gas and squeezed the steering wheel. The tires screeched, but I regained traction, and not a moment too soon. I cranked on the steering wheel just enough and avoided impact with the giant beast. It was a good thing it didn't have antlers or else it would have peeled the top off the car like a jagged can opener.

I brought the car to a complete stop and was now perpendicular with the road. I looked out the passenger window and saw a massive doe looking back at me almost as if to say thanks before she gracefully galloped off into the night. I took a deep breath to try to get my heart rate back to normal. That was too close for comfort. I was once again reminded of the importance of exercising caution and staying focused.

Chapter Forty

"The Canada Act, otherwise known as the Constitution Act, includes the Canadian Charter of Rights and Freedoms. As you all know, the Charter protects an assortment of civil rights and obligations. Since the enactment of the Charter, the face of Canadian constitutional law has changed drastically," the monotonous professor continued.

The words went through my ears like dust in the wind. I had my head buried deep in my laptop. I was considering buying stock in a company and was reading some of their most recent SEC filings. It was kind of like doing law research, so I allowed myself to continue. Besides, at least I showed up to class.

"Hey," Dan whispered into my ear. "Don't look now, but there's a hot girl at three o'clock."

I immediately looked to my right and saw a slender woman with soft eyes and full lips. She was stunning, which was enough to make most men tremble. She had a naturally dark complexion and was impeccably dressed, obviously someone who was into fashion and did everything in her power to convey the image of self-assurance.

"Why don't you talk to her?" he said.

Without hesitation, I leaned over towards her and said, "Hey, how's it going?"

"Hey," she replied, without as much as a smile.

"What's your name?" I whispered again.

"Jessica."

"I'm Trevor," I offered my name even though she didn't ask for it. I sensed a lot of reluctance from her, not even a forced friendliness. She seemed genuinely unfriendly – hot, but unfriendly. She will make a great lawyer, I thought. I decided to leave her alone.

***

"Alright, after this hand, blinds go up to twenty-five/fifty," Steve said.

"So, Trevor, what are you going to do once you graduate?"

"I'm not sure yet, I was thinking about moving back to Vancouver to do my practicum."

"Really, why don't you just stay here?" Dan asked.

"I don't know, I guess I miss my home."

"Bet – fifty."

"Why don't you guys move to Vancouver? Steve, you're from Vancouver, don't you plan to go back?"

"I don't know, I haven't been back in a while," Steve replied.

"We should all take a trip out there this summer. Steve and I can show you guys around."

"Call."

"We'll all be graduating at the same time and none of us really have any commitments here," I said.

"Except for the contacts, the comfort, the internships..." Dan replied.

"Yeah, but you can get those things anywhere really. I mean, look how fast I met you guys."

"Yeah, but we're your only friends."

"That's not true, I met someone today. Her name is Jessica."

"Ha, good luck with that!" Dan said.

"Why? Who's Jessica?" Steve asked.

"She's some really hot girl in our constitutional law class. Trevor tried to talk to her, but she completely ignored him."

"That's not true, she didn't completely ignore me. Besides she was probably just really enjoying the lecture and I was distracting her."

"Yeah, the lecture on constitutional law was riveting," he said sarcastically.

"Anyways, the point is, that there's no need to stay in this city. Vancouver has a lot to offer. It's a bigger city and there are a lot more opportunities there."

"I'm not totally against the idea. I could move there if everybody else does," Jeremy said.

"What do you want to do with your life, Jeremy?" I asked.

"I don't know; probably just get a job somewhere. Maybe start my own business."

"What kind of business?" I asked.

"I have a few ideas. I was thinking about buying a glass factory."

"A glass factory?" I asked, just to make sure I heard him correctly.

"Yeah, you know, windows, windshields, maybe even cookware."

"Would you sell glass cups?" Steve asked in a mocking tone.

"Sure, I'll sell those too."

"Alright, so you have your glass company, then what?" I probed further.

"First I would buy one, then another, then another. Eventually, I'll have a monopoly on the glass supply industry in a certain region."

"Okay?" I said puzzled.

"Here's the smart bit. Whenever business is slow, I'll go around town, or hire someone to go around town, and smash a bunch of windows. Then, I sit back and watch the money roll in."

"This is your plan?" Dan asked, as if he was not quite sure whether to take him seriously or not.

"Um, Jeremy…" I paused for a moment to find my words, "… don't you think that would be a little…transparent?"

"What do you mean?"

"Let's say you own all the glass companies in the city and suddenly the police receive a flood of reports stating that everyone's windows are smashed out. You're the first person they're going to come looking for."

"No, I've already thought of that. That's why all the glass companies will be under different names."

No one was convinced this was the next big investment opportunity.

"And this isn't just limited to a glass company either. The same concept works with a tire factory, or a graffiti removal company. When business is slow…" He stopped when he realized none of us were on board with his scam/business proposal.

"Whatever, you guys are just haters."

"Look, Jeremy, those are some really creative ideas, but do you have any that aren't so... illegal? I'm a student of the law; I can't get behind an idea where you go around undermining the whole system."

"Alright, what did you have in mind?"

"I have a plan..." I said mysteriously, as I slowly looked each person at the table in the eyes.

"Are you going to tell us what it is, or are you just going to eyeball us all night?" Steve said.

"It's not quite ready, but I have been trying to work out a business plan for the past few months. This can't leave this room..."

Chapter Forty-One

It was a little past ten in the morning and I was home watching the market, still in my housecoat. Fortunately, class was cancelled so I was able to relax at home without having some tweed jacket professor blabbing in my ear.

There was a knock at my door, so I got up to answer it. It was Dan. I invited him in and offered him a smoothie, but he declined. He put his bag down on the floor and began his interrogation.

"Dude, I saw some girl sneaking out of your apartment early this morning, who was that?" he asked.

"It was just this girl from class."

"Who?"

"I don't know, I didn't catch her last name, Jessica something," I said with a slight smirk, then I took a drink of my morning smoothie.

"You mean that hot girl from our class?"

"Yeah, you know, it's no big deal."

"What? No big deal? Of course it is. How the hell did that happen? Tell me everything."

"Oh, Dan, don't bother yourself with all the details. All you need to know is that it happened, and it was amazing."

"Shut up. I want details and I want them now."

"There's nothing much to tell really. I was out at a bar on campus last night with some friends from my study group and we bumped into each other."

"And?"

"And... apparently we hit it off. She's actually a really cool girl. I think you would like her," I said, as I took a sip of my smoothie.

"Go on."

"Yeah, it's funny actually because we didn't see each other the whole night until after we were all leaving."

"Oh, so you didn't bump into each other 'at' the bar, you bumped into her 'outside' the bar?"

"I guess so, why? What are you getting at?"

"I'm just trying to get clear with the details. Please continue."

"Like I was saying, we were all leaving and then I hear some woman call out 'hey', so I turned around and there she was."

"Where was your precise location?"

"I was in the parking lot, just down the street from the bar."

"What was your proximity to your car?"

"I had one foot in, why?"

"Oh, so you had one foot in?" Dan said, as he made a face.

"Yes."

"Alright, so it was at this point where you apparently 'hit it off', is that correct?"

"Yes, that is correct."

"I'm sorry to say this, Trevor, but you're dealing with a certified gold digger."

"What makes you establish that conclusion?"

"Let's go back to the beginning and run through the chain of events leading up to last night," Dan said, trying his best to sound like a trial lawyer cross-examining a witness.

"One day, you're in class minding your own business and you see a hot girl. You say 'hello'. She is not rude, but is… shall we say, unfriendly?"

"We shall."

"Okay, so she is unfriendly. She obliges to your small talk, but gives you the very least amount of attention possible, one notch above completely ignoring you. Is that a fair assessment?"

"I believe it is."

"Then, after a chance encounter outside the bar one night, she decides she is going to call out to you, 'hey'. Isn't that right?"

"Yes, that's right."

"Was it not established," he said, as he raised his voice, "that her sudden change of heart coincided with your apparent proximity to a two hundred and fifty thousand dollar automobile, WHICH, by the way, she did not know you had when you first met her in class?"

"That seems accurate."

"Once she sees you, she does the exact opposite of ignoring you, and shows you all kinds of love and affection. Next thing you know, she is seen tiptoeing out of your apartment this morning with a slightly dissatisfied look on her face. I rest my case."

"I must admit, it's a wonderful theory, and very well executed I must say. But I think you may have been a bit too hasty with a few of your inferences."

"Is that a fact?"

"Yes, sir, I believe it is."

"Alright then, please enlighten me on the precise details you have inferred from said event."

"Like you said, I was minding my own business one day in class, when you inform me of a hot chick sitting next to me. I didn't even notice her at first; you had to point her out to me. Isn't that right?"

"Yeah yeah yeah, get on with it."

"That means she sat down after we sat down. She could have taken any seat in that room, but decided to sit down right next to me. Shortly after, I proceeded to engage in a little light conversation with her, but she remained focused on the lecture.

"In our haste, we mistakenly interpreted this as being bitchy, or as we agreed, 'unfriendly', but we would not be doing our due diligence if we were to draw such a harsh conclusion based on such a brief interaction. After all, here is an obviously bright woman who was trying to understand the complexities of constitutional law when I rudely interrupted her. We certainly can't fault her for putting her education first. Besides, it could be argued she is experienced in the delicate art of seduction and was merely enticing her suitor by playing hard to get.

"A few weeks go by and the guy of her dreams, me, has not said another word to her since our first encounter. She feels she has no choice but to take actions into her own hands. Fortunately for her, she happens to see me at the bar one night.

"At first, she was too shy to come over and talk to me, but that all changed by the end of the night when she had a few more drinks in her. She finally built up enough courage to talk to me, but it was too late, I had left. Deciding this was her moment, she searched the bar, but could not find me anywhere.

"Feeling as though her window of opportunity was closing, she went outside, desperate to find me. As fate would have it, she was in luck; there I was, walking down the street. She called out to me, but I did not hear her at first. She then dashed toward me, calling out again, 'hey', just in the nick of time, before I was about to drive off."

Dan laughed and rolled his eyes, "yeah, that sounds about right. You are going to make a good lawyer someday, or maybe a good fiction writer, but unfortunately, I'm not convinced. Do me a favor, Trevor. As a social experiment, ask her out on a second date, but this time show up at her house in an old rusted Datsun. Tell her the Ferrari was a rental and see if she will sleep with you again."

Chapter Forty-Two

It was 11:00 a.m. when we arrived in Vancouver and thankfully, the sun was shining. The flight was long, but we slept through most of it. Outside the YVR airport was a row of yellow cabs lined up waiting. At the front of the line was a shiny stretch limousine ready to take us anywhere we wanted. The driver quickly got out and rushed over to help us with our bags.

"Where to today, my friends?" the driver asked.

"1390 The Crescent, please."

"The Crescent?" Dan asked. "That sounds fancy."

The limo pulled out of the lineup and headed north toward Steve's parents' house. Steve's parents were on vacation and would be gone all summer so we had the entire house all to ourselves.

As we drove down Granville Street, I had butterflies in my stomach from being in the city again. Just looking at the skyline brought back so many memories. I couldn't quite see Ashley's building, but I looked for it. I wondered if she still lived there. It had been two years since we had last spoken and I wondered what she had been up to.

The limo entered the Shaughnessy neighbourhood. I gazed out at the beautiful houses; each house was bigger than the last. I hadn't spent a lot of time in this part of town, but I had an idea of the property value.

"It's this one on the right," Steve instructed the driver.

As we got out, we looked up in amazement. I think we all had an idea of what to expect when we pulled up to his parents' house, but this exceeded all of our expectations.

"So this is the house you grew up in, Steve?" Dan asked.

"It's one of them."

Steve hopped out and punched in the code for the security gate. The limo driver waited for him to get back in before he slowly crept down the long wrap-around driveway. The limo finally came to a stop under the large covered entryway. We each grabbed our luggage from the trunk and wheeled them up to the front door of the hotel-sized house. Steve unlocked the door and deactivated the alarm. As soon as we stepped inside, we all looked up at the magnificent entrance. At the top of the forty foot high ceiling was one of the largest crystal chandeliers I had ever seen. It dangled in between two massive dome skylights.

"Wow, this is a nice place, Steve. Are you going to give us the grand tour?"

"Yeah, sure. If you guys want to set your bags down, I'll show you around."

We set our bags down on the polished white marble floor and followed Steve through the house. Everything seemed expensive, and each piece of furniture had a story. Even the coffee table was not just an ordinary coffee table – it was imported from some far off region of the globe.

"In here is our kitchen. If you guys ever get a fridge, get this one, it has an airtight seal and controls the exact temperature for you. And it's super quiet."

"How much does that cost?" I asked.

"This one was customized to match our cabinets so I think it was about ten grand."

It took us about twenty minutes to walk in and out of every room on the first floor. "Wait until you guys see the downstairs," Steve said, as he raced down a winding staircase. When we arrived, we saw a large swimming pool surrounded by lots of plants. It looked like an oasis in the jungle. On the far left of the illuminated blue water was a mountain of stonework and greenery that had a waterslide through the centre. One entire wall was made of glass, which offered a full view of the spectacular backyard. It was a large green pasture with a beautiful assortment of trees and flowers.

We proceeded to walk down the hall from the pool area, where Steve briefly introduced us to the family's home gym. It was complete with nearly everything a major fitness club would have. "Okay, are you guys ready for my favourite room in the house?" Steve asked. We unanimously nodded our heads and mumbled something, indicating our mutual agreement.

Steve peeled open two heavy double doors to reveal the most elaborate home theatre any of us had ever seen before. It was designed to look like a scaled-down version of a real movie theatre. We stood at the back of the theatre behind three rows of large leather chairs cascading downward. At the front was a small stage with curtains, and by my guess, a 100" LED TV screen.

"Come on, I'll show you to your rooms... we can take the elevator."

***

After my shower, I went downstairs to the kitchen and met up with the rest of the gang. I was the last one to arrive. As soon as I got there, we left through a door in the kitchen, which led to the side of the house. We walked about twenty-five feet across a stone pathway and into a separate building on the property, to his parents' garage.

"Which one should we take?" Steve asked as he flipped on the lights.

His parents had slightly less expensive taste in cars, but only slightly. There was an M class Mercedes, an S500 Mercedes, and a Lexus IS.

"Any of these convertible?" Dan asked.

"Yeah, this one," he said, as he pointed to the Lexus.

"Alright, let's take this one."

We piled into the charcoal-colored Lexus, popped the top, and hit the road. The cool breeze complemented the warm sun. We were about a block away from the beach before we could smell the fresh ocean. The atmosphere was definitely consistent of summer. There were people everywhere, girls in bikinis, people walking in droves in the direction of the beach, people in shorts eating ice cream, people walking their dogs. The anticipation was painful. I just wanted to be out of this sticky leather seat and start having some fun.

We pulled up to a red light and a carload of attractive women pulled up beside us. I smiled at the driver and she smiled back.

"Excuse me..." I said to her "... can you please tell us how to get to your place?"

"Yeah, take my number," she replied.

I quickly stored her number in my phone. The light turned green and she took off in her little four-cylinder Honda. It was at this point that it occurred to me I had forgotten to ask for her name.

"Dude, I can't believe that worked!" Dan said in disbelief.

"Me neither, I was just joking around. I didn't think she would actually give me her number."

"Well, what are you waiting for, call her up," Steve said. "Ask them if they want to come to the beach with us."

"I just got her number five seconds ago! What about the three day rule?"

"Are you being serious right now?" Jeremy asked, as he leaned in from the back seat. "If you don't call her, I will. Give me the phone," he reached his arm between the front and passenger seat and held his hand out. I slapped his hand to give him a high-five.

"Okay okay, hold your horses. I'll give her a call," I took out my cell phone and scrolled through the directory. The first name in the list was 'Ashley'. I thought about calling her, but then I figured there wasn't much point in that. She had probably moved on by now and I didn't want to be a creepy ex-boyfriend. I eventually found the number I was looking for and called it.

"Hello?" a sexy female voice said.

"Hey, it's me."

"Who is this?"

"We just met five seconds ago, have you forgotten about me already?"

After a brief conversation, I hung up the phone.

"So are they going to meet us, or what?" Jeremy asked.

"Yeah, I told them I would give them a call once we found parking, then we can all meet up."

"Did you get a name this time, genius?" Steve asked.

"Yeah, her name is Sam."

***

Our new-found friends turned out to be really nice. We spent a couple of hours with them at the beach flirting and splashing around in the ocean. The four of us then went downtown to get some lunch. The girls decided to stay at the beach, but made arrangements to meet up with us later that night for a pool party at Steve's house.

"Yo, Steve, can we drink your parents' alcohol?"

"Yeah, whatever is there, just take it."

"Trevor, what time are the girls coming over?"

"They should be here in a couple hours."

"Alright, my stylist is coming over to cut my hair. Who else needs a fresh cut for tonight?" Steve asked.

"I need one," I said.

"Alright, you're in for a haircut, anyone else need one?"

***

A melodic chime resonated throughout the house. "Can someone please get that?" Steve yelled out from upstairs.

I opened the door and saw four attractive young women standing there with the same looks on their faces we had when we first showed up at Steve's house. "Hello ladies," I said, as I greeted them. "Sam, Angela, Maria, and I don't believe we've met."

"My name is Sandy."

"Hi Sandy, I'm Trevor, it's a pleasure to meet you. Come on in."

"Do we take our shoes off?"

"Uh… yeah, it's better if you take them off."

"So who wants a drink?" Jeremy asked, as he led everybody into the kitchen.

Chapter Forty-Three

One foot hit the floor, then the other. I rubbed my eyes and looked over at the other side of the bed. It was empty. Was last night just a dream? I searched for clues. Exhibit A: One long strand of chestnut brown hair on pillow. Exhibit B: lingering aroma of tropical passion conditioner mixed with the pungent smell of chlorine. Exhibit C: Medium sized drinking glass with soft pink lipstick stain around the rim. Exhibit D: A pair of sapphire earrings on the nightstand. I swiveled back around and picked up my phone to view the time. It was 8:15 a.m. I stood up, stretched my arms, and walked over to the bathroom, which was located inside my room. On the way over, I stepped on exhibit E, the last shred of evidence to convince me what happened last night was definitely not a dream.

"Good morning," I said, as I strolled into the kitchen.

"Hey, champ. Good times last night?"

"Yeah. What time did the girls end up leaving?"

"They left about fifteen minutes ago."

"Here, let me help you with that," I said, as I grabbed a large garbage bag and helped Dan clean up.

"You ready?" Steve asked, as he walked into the kitchen.

"Yeah, let's do it."

Steve and I went downstairs and into the gym for a workout. We finished a little over an hour later, but when we went back upstairs, everyone was still sleeping.

"Do you want to go for lunch?" Steve asked.

"Sure," I replied.

"Do you want to drive?" he asked.

"Okay. Which car should we take?"

"Your pick. Hey, that sounds familiar."

"Let's take the Lexus again," I said

"When are you going to buy your own car and give me back my Ferrari?"

"I still have another year left."

"You said you get it until the end of law school, and you just finished a few weeks ago."

"Yes, but I still have ten months of articling, which is technically a part of law school."

We drove downtown and found parking a few blocks away from the restaurant, Andre's Seafood Restaurant. It had been a while since I had been back there after leaving the note for my old roommate. I had never actually stepped more than a few feet into the restaurant before. It was one of downtown's prominent high-end restaurants, so naturally I could not have afforded it when I lived in Vancouver.

We walked in and were greeted by a lovely hostess. Upon request, she escorted us to a booth by a window. The restaurant was probably at least 30 years old. I'm sure it was once considered very high-end, and to some extent, it still was. However, the place was in desperate need of a renovation. I looked around and instinctually started to imagine what I would do differently.

"Have you been here before?" Steve asked.

"Technically I have, but I didn't eat here."

"What do you mean?"

"It's a long story. How about you, have you eaten here before?"

"Yeah, I used to come here all the time. I know the owner, he's somewhat of a family friend."

"Hey, Stevie! Long time no see," a portly man said energetically.

"Hey, Andre, how's it going? You look good, man."

"You too."

"This is my friend, Trevor."

"Hi, nice to meet you."

"I was in the back and I thought 'hey, I recognize that face'. So where did you disappear to? I haven't seen you in, what has it been, over four years?"

"Yeah, I go to school out in Ontario. I'm just back visiting for a few days with some friends."

"That's good to hear. It is so wonderful to see you again. I hope it's not another four years until the next time I see you."

"Yeah, I'm thinking about moving back here actually."

"That's terrific."

After chatting with Steve for a bit, Andre shuffled off to glad-hand some other regulars.

"He seems nice," I said.

"Yeah, he is a really great guy."

"How do you know him?"

"I only know him through here. My dad and I used to come here a lot. He actually offered to sell this place to us at one point. He had a bit of a gambling addiction and needed some money."

"What happened with that?"

"My dad said he wasn't interested in owning a restaurant so he just gave him a loan instead."

"Really? How much?"

"I recall it being somewhere in the neighbourhood of a hundred grand."

"Did he ever pay it back?"

"I don't think so, that's why my dad stopped coming here."

"You know, we could do a lot with this place," I said, as I looked around.

"Like what?"

"First off, this place needs a renovation, but that's stating the obvious. I'm not a fan of the worn out floors and peeling paint look. I would also relocate the bar to the far end of the restaurant. It's taking up way too much space in the centre."

"Okay, what else?"

"I don't know, maybe hire some better looking waitresses."

"Would you change the menu at all?"

"I would change the look of it, and maybe change some things, but I think the food is why people keep coming back here."

"That and its location."

"Yeah, this place is right downtown, the rent must be crazy expensive."

"Actually, Andre owns the property as well. He's had this place for over forty years."

"I wonder if he is still interested in selling," I said casually, still looking around.

"You want to buy this place?" Steve asked.

"Maybe. What do you think?"

"I think we would need to put in at least a couple hundred grand into renovating the place."

"Yeah, but then we would have the hottest restaurant in town."

"Too bad we can't afford it," Steve said.

I paused for a moment then said, "You know what, maybe we can. He still owes your dad, right? What if we use that debt to leverage a deal?"

"Sort of like a discount?"

"Exactly like a discount. Then we would just need to come up with the difference."

"How much do you think the difference would be? The property alone is probably worth ten million dollars."

"We're not interested in the property, just the restaurant," I paused to let it sink in. "So we buy him out and we can probably negotiate a sweet deal on the rent as well. Like you said, he's a family friend."

"Okay, but what do we know about running a restaurant?"

"Nothing, we don't need to know anything. We would keep all the same staff. The place will practically run itself. We do some renos, make a few adjustments, and we are looking good."

"I like it. Here he comes now, follow my lead."

"Hey, Andre, it was really good to see you, man. How're you holding up?"

"The older I get, the fatter I get and the more hair I lose."

"How's business?"

"Business is good."

"You look a little burnt out. When was the last time you took a vacation?"

"I can't remember, but I definitely need one."

"You know, my family has a place in Cabo. Let me know when you want to go, and the place is yours."

"I don't think that would be such a good idea. I haven't seen your dad in a while."

"I know you and my dad have had some issues in the past, but I'm not my dad, okay?"

"Thanks, that means a lot."

"I don't know how you do it Andre. This restaurant is going to be the death of you one day. The long hours, all the hassle, you need a break. How long have you had this place?"

"Over forty years."

"Wow, forty years, you hear that, Trevor?"

"That's a long time," I said.

"Yeah, you should be on a beach somewhere sipping pineapple daiquiris. Instead, you're in here all day, slaving away, bussing tables, and shining windows. You've been so busy serving others, maybe it's time for others to be serving you."

"This restaurant has been a part of me for so long, it's all I know."

"There's a whole other world out there, Andre, and it's passing you by. Enjoy it while you still can," I said.

"Yeah, maybe you guys are right."

"You know, Andre, it just occurred to me that you offered to sell this place at one time, right?"

"Yeah, I was going to sell it, but decided not to."

"Perhaps the timing wasn't right then. Maybe now would be a good time to get out, while you still have your health."

"Then I would have to find a buyer and go through all kinds of hassle. I don't need that right now."

"Perhaps we could buy it from you... hassle free. In fact, Trevor here can draw up the contract, he's a lawyer."

Andre looked at me and I gave him a quick reassuring nod. I could tell he was thinking about it.

"I'll tell you what, Andre," Steve continued. "I'm in town for a few more days, why don't you think it over and give me a call?"

"Okay, I'll consider it."

"Do you have my new number?" Steve asked.

"No, let me go get a pen and piece of paper from one of the servers, I'll be right back."

As Andre walked away, I leaned in closer to Steve and whispered in his ear, "Close him now." Steve looked at me and nodded in agreement. Andre returned with the paper and pen and handed it to Steve.

"So what would be a fair price for this place, Andre?"

"Oh, I don't know."

"What figure did you come up with when you were going to sell it before?"

"I wanted one point two for it."

"Well, you could probably get that if you put it on the market for a few months, or maybe a year, and have buyers constantly coming and going, inspecting everything."

"Sounds like a big hassle," I added.

"Do me a favor, Andre, we go back a long way, and I think my dad even helped you out at one point, didn't he?"

"Yes, and I'll never forget that."

"From what I understand, there was some money involved, and still to this day there remains some unpaid debt."

"It shames me to admit it, but yes, I still owe your father."

"I'll tell you what. How about this, the three of us enter into an equal-stake partnership. We will take over operations, and you can relax on a beach somewhere."

"When you said that you could never forget what my dad did for you, you weren't just saying that were you? You're an honest man, I can tell. The fact you haven't paid him back probably troubles you, right?"

"Yes, I feel horrible."

"You don't have to carry that around anymore, Andre. You don't need that on your conscience. I know you planned on paying him back, but you just got an unlucky bounce."

"Believe me, I know all about unlucky bounces," I said sincerely.

"And now an opportunity has quite literally landed on your doorstep."

Andre didn't say anything. There was a long pause, but not long enough that it became awkward.

"So what do you say, Andre?" I asked.

He looked at both of us for a moment, thought about it for a while, and said, "Sure, let's do it."

"Good. I'm so glad to hear that. Trevor can draft up a contract right away."

"Yes, sir, I will have it ready by the end of the week."

We both shook Andre's hand and made our exit, this time as the proud new owners of Andre's Seafood Restaurant.

"Well played, sir," I said, as we walked back to the car.

"Thank you."

"Really, that was impressive. I can't believe you just talked that guy into selling you his restaurant."

"I know! I set him up first, then knocked him down."

"You did it like a pro. Where'd you learn to sell like that?" I asked.

"I don't know, I guess I'm a natural."

***

"Hey, what took you guys so long?" Dan asked.

"Oh you know, we went to the gym, got something to eat, bought a restaurant, then came home."

"What do you mean, 'bought a restaurant'?"

"Trevor and I bought Andre's Seafood Restaurant."

"How did you guys buy it?"

"Steve knows the owner and made him an offer that he couldn't refuse."

"Well actually, I kind of conned him into it."

"You conned some restaurateur out of his beloved restaurant. He's probably had that place for thirty years."

"Actually, it's more like forty!" I remarked.

"Unbelievable."

"So now what?" Dan asked.

"Hey, what's going on?" Jeremy said, as he entered the room for the first time.

"Steve and Trevor bought a restaurant."

"What? Where? When? Am I still dreaming?"

"Steve, we need to sit down and discuss some business matters."

Over the next couple of days, Dan and I drafted the contract for a limited-liability partnership of the restaurant. We agreed on an equal-stake partnership - a 33.33 percent share each; however, I would have full decision-making authority. I was reluctant to enter into another partnership agreement, so I insisted on this clause. It was a precautionary measure to avoid any ego clashes. I was surprised Steve didn't even fight me with that at all. At first, I thought this clause was much more advantageous for me, but maybe Steve knew what he was doing all along. He was not actually interested in running a restaurant, he was only interested in the profit from it. Now he would get 33.33 percent without the burden of doing any of the work.

Chapter Forty-Four

I stayed in Vancouver a little longer than I had expected. Steve allowed me to continue to stay at his parents' house while he and the others flew back to Ontario. There were still a lot of things I needed to take care of at the restaurant.

I called my old roommate, Chris. Chris was now running a small construction crew that specialized in remodeling high-end homes. I figured since he had worked at Andre's, he could oversee the entire project and input a lot of really great ideas.

"You bought Andre's?" he asked in disbelief.

"Yeah, I'm putting over a million dollars into renovating it."

"How did you afford that?"

"I went in on it with a friend and plan on getting a loan from the bank. If this doesn't work out, I'm screwed. I'm completely tapped out."

"That's crazy, man, good for you."

"So yeah, are you interested in taking on this renovation project?"

"Sure, I'd love to."

A few days later, I met Chris outside the restaurant. We spent the next several hours going through the place inside and out. He had some great ideas on how to improve the functionality as well as the aesthetics of the restaurant. He even went over the current staff list and advised me on some people we should let go.

We developed a clear vision of what the renovations should look like. My next steps after that were to hire an architect to draft up the plans and secure the funding.

***

"Mr. Morrison, welcome. Please have a seat."

"Thank you."

"So what brings you to my office today?"

"I have to say, it was much easier to get an appointment with you this time around."

"I'm not sure I follow."

"You probably don't remember me, but I came in here about seven years ago looking for a job and I ended up working in the credit card division for four years."

"I vaguely recall someone leaving a series of messages on my answering machine."

"Guilty," I said laughing. "I can be very persistent when I want something."

"And what is it that you want today, Mr. Morrison?"

"Mr. Jones, I'm not here today for a job. In fact, my partner and I just purchased a controlling share of Andre's Seafood Restaurant and we are seeking a small business loan to help finance a renovation project."

"Where is your partner?"

"He couldn't make it today; however, I have been fully authorized to discuss these matters on my own."

"Very well then, what do you have for me?"

I opened my briefcase, reached into my brown leather folder, took out a copy of the plans, and handed them to him. I watched his eyes scan the documents. "Mr. Jones, as you may know, Andre's has been serving people for over forty years. I'm just looking to give the place a much-needed modern facelift. The high-end décor will enhance the already popular menu, plus with the prime location, I expect to do quite well."

The branch manager at National Group Bank looked up at me and studied my attire. I wore a classic three-piece Armani suit, courtesy of Steve's dad's closet. A lot of people make judgments based on appearance – even the ones who claim they don't are just not aware they're doing it. That was why it was important for me to look the part of a successful business owner.

"Mr. Morrison, I have to say, I'm quite impressed with these plans, but the restaurant industry is highly risky. Typically, for the bank to grant this type of loan to a person, they would have a considerable amount of experience and collateral. It's just a way for us to reduce our exposure to risk. Now, let me ask you a question, what experience do you have running a restaurant?"

"I have worked in the restaurant industry for several years and have acquired a wealth of knowledge in all aspects of the business. I assure you my ownership will not impede the historical success of the restaurant, it will only enhance it. Please keep in mind this is an established restaurant in a prime location in downtown Vancouver with a successful track record of over forty years. We are keeping a lot of the same staff, management, and the previous owner still has a substantial stake. Therefore, the risk is not the same as starting a new restaurant.

"Mr. Jones, my team has already started construction. I'm just asking for a little loan to help facilitate the cost. I should be able to pay this money back within a couple of years."

Mr. Jones continued to study my proposal.

"Mr. Jones, I came to you first because of my history with you and the bank, but I have several other meetings today. I was hoping we could do a deal today, but obviously you need more time. I don't want to push you into anything, so why don't you get back to me when you've reached your decision?" I snapped the locks on my briefcase shut and stood up. I turned around and began to make my exit. This was the art of the hustle.

"How much were you looking for?" he asked, taking the bait right on cue. I turned around to face him once again.

"I'm just looking at financing a small renovation project, not much, just around one million, perhaps more," I said.

"I think we can do that. Can you come back in an hour? I'll have all the documents drawn up."

"Thank you Mr. Jones, I appreciate it. You've made the right decision," I couldn't resist using my sales techniques on him, one last positive reassurance statement to secure the deal. I don't think he realized what I was doing, but I could not afford to have him change his mind. "I'll see you in one hour."

Now that the funds were in order, I called Chris and gave him the green light. He and his crew got to work right away and started tearing the place apart. With such a major project underway, I decided to stick around Vancouver to monitor the progress and handle any problems that might arise.

Chapter Forty-Five

I stood in the doorway of Steve's parents' garage with a buffet of cars in front of me to choose from. I decided on the Mercedes S500 this time, primarily for its class, but also because it matched my outfit. I wore a dark wash denim pant with a short-cropped leather jacket from Armani. Underneath the jacket I had on a simple white v-neck t-shirt - everything fitted. As soon as I pulled out of the garage, I put on my shades and cruised down to Kitsilano - the neighbourhood where Sam lived.

I texted her right before I arrived. When she came out, she looked stunning. Her dark toned legs stretched out of a smart, but sexy, high-cut summer dress.

"Hey, how's it going?" she said as she stepped in the car. Her fruity fragrance immediately consumed the car, competing with the scent I was wearing.

"You look nice. I like what you did with your hair," I commented.

"Thanks, you look nice too."

The drive downtown was good, there was not as much traffic as I expected. Parking was a problem, as usual. I did a few laps around the block and was lucky to find a spot two blocks away from the restaurant where I made reservations.

"Good evening," an attractive hostess greeted us at the door. "For two?"

"Yes, please."

"Dining room or lounge?"

"Lounge, please."

"Certainly, right this way please."

We followed the hostess through the busy restaurant as she led us to the best seat in the house. We sat down, had a quick glance at the wine menu and ordered two glasses of merlot.

"So tell me about your restaurant," she asked.

"It may be hard to imagine if you haven't been there before, but I'm redoing everything. I'm creating this extravagant bar, which will have a thirty-foot waterfall down the centre of it. There will be LED TVs all across the top of the restaurant. I'm even adding a second level for VIPs only. Trust me, it will be an elite dining experience."

"What do you mean? You're putting in a second floor for VIPs? What's the point of that exactly?"

"It's all about status. The average person will never see the second floor. It's reserved for the elite – politicians, movie stars, athletes, wealthy business owners. Many people will aspire to eat amongst the people on the second floor, but never will. If you make it there, it's prestigious, it means you're important in some way."

"That's ridiculous! And let me guess, that's where you're going to eat?"

"Oh no, of course not… I will be eating on the third floor."

"The third floor?"

"Yes, the majority of the… shall we say, 'second-level patrons' won't even know about the third floor. Membership to the third floor is by invitation only. Each table will be completely private, private entrance, private elevator with a secret access code, private parking, and anything else I can think of that's private. It will of course include state of the art everything and a one of a kind menu offering an array of exotic delicacies. It will be very posh."

"Wow, you're a dreamer."

"No, dreams are for the poor, I'm a realist."

"Okay, is there anything else?"

"Yeah, I'm also replacing all the table cloths," I said with a smile.

"Ha ha, very funny. So are you changing the name too?"

"Yes, the restaurant will be called Ace."

"I find this all very interesting."

"Enough about me, let's talk about you."

"Right now I'm just doing modeling, but I'm also taking acting classes."

"Really? Who do you model for?"

"Do you mean which agency?"

"I was actually interested in the companies you have modeled for, but you can tell me about your agency too if you like."

"I model for all different companies all over the world. I just did a show in Paris and another one in London. I live in New York mostly, but I still come here because this is where I grew up."

"So let me ask you a question," I said.

"Okay?"

"What's it like being so beautiful?"

"Are you being serious?"

"Yes, I'm being serious, I really want to know. I can only begin to imagine what it would be like to have everything handed to you. You get to travel all around the world because of the way you look; designers want you to wear their clothes, people constantly going out of their way to do things for you. It would be like having a superpower. What's it like living in a world like that? What does that do to a person's psychology?"

"To tell you the truth, I don't really think about it. Despite what you think, I'm constantly being critiqued by designers, being told I'm too fat or too skinny or that my forehead is too big. I'm surrounded by other beautiful women all day, which makes me riddled with insecurities about my appearance. Traveling around the world makes it extremely difficult to maintain relationships. Women can get really jealous and vindictive around me, and guys usually only want to sleep with me. Most of them don't even bother to get to know me. So yeah, sometimes it can be overwhelming, but I just try to surround myself with sincere people, and try not to let it get to my head. I guess it would be a lot like being rich, you never know if people want you for you, or for what you have."

"So are you only with me because I'm rich?" I asked bluntly. The reality was I was not rich, but to her, that's precisely what I appeared to be, so I went along with it.

"Are you only with me because I'm beautiful?"

"I admit I was attracted to you when I saw you at first, but it's your personality that made me continue to pursue you. So to answer your question, no, I'm not only with you because you're beautiful."

We sat there for the next couple of hours enjoying each other's company. We decided to leave before the sun went down completely, so I paid for the bill and we left. On the way back to the car, I saw a skinny man with graying hair and loose-fitted clothing standing on the corner with another sketchy guy. At first glance, they were just some homeless guys begging for change on the sidewalk, but one of them looked oddly familiar.

"Hold on a second," I said to Sam.

"What's wrong?"

"I think I know that guy," I walked a little closer and got a good look at the barely recognizable face.

"Who?"

"You see those two sketchy guys standing on the corner? One of them owes me some money."

"You mean those crack heads? Please don't tell me you are mixed up with that stuff."

"No, it's not what you think. We actually used to be friends in high school. He didn't always look like that."

"Darrell!" I called out. The haggard man jumped a little. He stopped whatever he was doing and looked over at me. When our eyes met, he looked like he had seen a ghost. I continued to walk closer. I was able to get a better look at his face. His cheekbones protruded out of his pale face, the face of what appeared to be a much older man. My eyes quickly scanned the rest of him. There were a few scabs and contusions on his arms, the typical signs of a hard life on the streets. I signaled for him to come over. As he got closer, I noticed his eyes were glossy - he was clearly high on drugs.

"Sam, why don't you wait in the car?" I said to her as I deactivated the car alarm. Darrell looked at Sam, then at the car, then back to me. I could tell the very sight of me sickened him.

"What the hell happened to you, Darrell?"

"You know… certain… addictions."

"I hope you can sell enough of those drugs to pay me back."

"What are you talking about?"

"Don't play dumb with me; you know exactly what I'm talking about. You owe me four grand."

Darrell didn't say a thing; he just kept looking around nervously. I wasn't sure if it was the drugs that were making him so paranoid or if it was a life full of screwing people over that had him watching his back every ten seconds. Either way, he obviously did not have any money. Harassing him any further just seemed cruel and unnecessary.

"Take care of yourself, Darrell."

"Yeah, see ya," he mumbled, as he put his head down and walked away.

As he walked away, I continue to watch. I actually felt sorry for him. His spirit was completely broken, swallowed up and consumed by the big city. I couldn't help but think of how divergent our lives were at that point. We started in very similar positions after high school, but apparently, he had made a series of poor decisions. I wondered if that could have been me, or were there fundamental differences between us that kept me on the right path and him destined for skid row?

He met up with his partner, exchanged a few words, and went back to doing what he was doing before –

just hanging around on the street corner. I lost interest and began to walk back to the car. I heard a car horn beep two times, which caught my attention. I turned my head around and saw Darrell hop into the car through the passenger-side door. Curious, I continued to watch. The car drove about a half a block before the red tail lights lit up and the car came to a complete stop. The next thing I saw was Darrell exit the vehicle. There was only one logical explanation I could think of - he was selling drugs.

I took out my cell phone and made a quick phone call to the police. After making the report, I got back in the car.

"What was that all about?" Sam asked.

"Believe it or not, I started a business with that guy a long time ago and he ripped me off."

"Yeah, that sounds about right. What happened?"

"He racked up a bunch of advertising debt and left me with the bill. I sued him and won, but didn't collect a dime from him. He took off and went into hiding. I haven't seen him since, until tonight."

"Look at him now, and look at you. I think your success is the ultimate revenge."

"Yeah, but I still want that money!"

"Seems a bit petty to me."

"Well, it's the principle I guess."

"Don't worry, I have a way to take your mind off of it. Why don't we go back to your house and go for a swim?"

"Did you bring your bathing suit?"

"Nope," she said, as she displayed her perfect smile.

"What a coincidence, neither did I."

Chapter Forty-Six

The construction was coming along nicely. Chris and his men had been working around the clock, trying to get the job completed by the projected deadline. With the expected date of completion just weeks away, I was happy with how everything was turning out so far. The grand opening would take place right on schedule. Soon, I would have one of the most elegant restaurants in the city.

I stopped by Monday morning to go over some final details with Chris. The new sign had finally arrived and he wanted to know where exactly I wanted it positioned.

"Move it higher, and a little to the left," I said, as the massive crane hoisted the sign in the air."

"Hey, Trevor, why did you call your restaurant 'Ace'?" Chris asked.

Before I could answer, two men, dressed in cheap drab suits, approached me. "Trevor Morrison?" a burly man with a thick mustache asked as he flashed his badge.

"Yes."

"Please come with us, sir. You're wanted for questioning in the murder of Darrell Channing."

"What, Darrell's been murdered?" I guess I wasn't surprised, he certainly looked nervous and twitchy when I saw him, but that was not unusual behaviour for a crack head on the street.

I cooperated with the police and got in the back of their unmarked police car. Fortunately, they didn't put me in handcuffs. We took a short drive to the police station on East Hastings Street. I had never been inside a police station before and I did not intend to make a habit of it. I figured I would just answer some questions and be on my way.

"Have a seat," one of the detectives demanded. I took a seat on the cold steel chair. It appeared to be bolted to the floor along with the table. I took a brief moment to get acquainted with my surroundings, but there wasn't much to look at. The pale bluish grey walls looked like they had not been re-painted in over fifty years. Oddly enough, it reminded me of my old elementary school. One wall – the same wall with the only door – had a two-way mirror. There was a good chance there were people on the other side listening to what I was about to say.

Finally, my attention was drawn to the two officers standing in front of me, Detective Riviera and Detective Jensen. One of them had his hands on his hips and the other one had his arms folded. They both had a stern look on their faces to show they were serious. It was clearly an intimidation tactic designed to make me nervous. When a person gets nervous, it tends to affect their ability to lie well. We learned about that in law school - Prosecution Ethics. I thought it was interesting to see it in practice.

"Where were you last Thursday evening around eleven o'clock?" one of the men barked at me.

"I was leaving my restaurant."

"Can anyone verify that?"

"No, I was staying late, working on some final things before we re-open."

"Do you have security cameras?"

"No, we took them down for the renovation."

"Do you typically work that late?"

"No, not usually."

"What time did you leave?"

"I remember checking the time on my phone and it was a little after eleven."

"How do you know Darrell Channing?" the other officer took over.

"I went to high school with him, and we were roommates briefly."

"Isn't it true that Darrell owed you some money?"

"Yes."

"How much did he owe you?"

"Around four thousand dollars."

"That's a lot of money."

"I suppose."

"What do you do for a living, Mr. Morrison?"

"Currently, I'm a law student."

"Where do you go to school?"

"University of Ontario."

"That's a long ways from home. What are you doing in Vancouver?"

"Actually, I consider Vancouver my home. I moved out here after graduating high school."

"Now, you said you were leaving your restaurant on the night in question, is that right?" the first detective chimed back it.

"That's right."

"And you said your restaurant is undergoing renovations, is that correct?"

"Yes, it is."

"That sounds expensive, especially for a student."

"You're right, it is very expensive."

"How long have you owned your restaurant, Mr. Morrison?"

"It's only been a couple of weeks."

"So you have yet to turn a profit?"

"That's correct."

"Tell me, how does a law student from Ontario acquire a premier restaurant in downtown Vancouver?"

"I entered into a partnership with the previous owner and a friend."

"And where did you get the money?"

"The initial investment came from my savings over the past three years. I got into trading stocks around that time and have had some success. As for the renovations, I had to take a loan from the bank."

"So you take your savings and buy a restaurant, then take a loan to cover the renovation costs?"

"Yes."

"It must be stressful having so much tied up in a restaurant that has yet to turn a profit. After all, the juice is running on that bank loan, isn't that correct?"

"Yes, it is."

"So it would be fair to say you could probably use any extra money you can get your hands on, right?"

"I think that is true for most people, is it not?" I retorted.

"You know, you're a young guy, obviously very bright, it must have upset you that Darrell ripped you off. Maybe you felt a little taken advantage of?"

"Yes, I was upset."

"And you wanted some payback right?"

"It depends on what you mean by 'payback'. It would be nice to get the money, but I wasn't looking for it anymore. I had moved on."

"Why did you move on?"

"I didn't know where Darrell was and I didn't want to chase him all around the world for only a couple thousand dollars."

"Until one night, Thursday night, you happened to bump into him."

"Was that a question?"

"When was the last time you saw Darrell Channing?"

I took a moment before I answered. "Last week."

"What's that Mr. Morrison, I didn't catch that?"

"Last week," I said again, loud and clear.

"Oh last week... interesting," one of them said in an accusatory tone.

"What day was that, Mr. Morrison?"

"It was Saturday night."

"So you were downtown on Saturday evening and you saw Darrell. Then what happened?"

"Nothing really. We exchanged a few words, then we went our separate ways."

"But that wasn't enough for you, was it, Mr. Morrison?"

"I'm not sure I know what you mean."

"A call was placed to the Vancouver Police Department from your cell phone that night. Tell us about that."

"I was on a date with a girl who I had met recently. She was a real stunner, you know, perfect body and gorgeous face—"

"We're not interested in the girl at this point," one of the officers scolded.

"After dinner, I took her to my restaurant to show her around. When we were leaving, we saw Darrell. He appeared to be selling drugs on the street corner. I hardly recognized him at first because he had lost a lot of weight and looked a little worn out. There was another sketchy guy with him. They both looked to be under the influence of drugs. So I told my date to wait in the car and I called the police as a concerned citizen."

"Concerned in what way?"

"I didn't want strung out junkies selling drugs near my restaurant, it's bad for business."

"Wasn't the real reason for calling the police to get back at him for what he'd done to you in the past? After all, this guy owed you money."

"Maybe it had a little bit to do with that."

"Trevor, what happened on August 10th a few years ago?" one of the detectives asked me.

"I don't know, what happened on August 10th?" I asked dumfounded.

"Did you, or did you not, assault Darrell Channing that night?"

"No, of course not, you have your facts wrong, he assaulted me. I have a witness who can attest to that."

"We also have a witness who claims otherwise. Says here in this report, and I quote, 'if you ever come near me again, I swear I'll kill you'. You remember saying that, don't you?"

I did not respond. I just stared back at the two clever detectives. They were trying to piece together a story out of a bunch of scraps. It was all quite amusing.

"Give it up, Mr. Morrison, we have you, it's over. You think you're so smart, don't you? Well, let me tell you something, you're not smart enough, okay. You didn't cover all your tracks. Suppose you're on trial and the jury views photographs of both of your faces after the altercation on August 10th. Darrell is all bloodied and bruised, and you don't have a scratch on you. Who do you think they will believe?

"Then, some smart lawyer will bring up the money, and the fact you saw him a few days prior to the murder, and the fact you were downtown on the night of the murder, and to top it all off, you threatened to kill him! Do see where I'm going with this?"

"No, I don't."

"Let me paint you a picture of what I think happened that night. You were at your restaurant one night, feeling a little overwhelmed and stressed out. You think about the mountain of debt piling up and begin to question why you took on such an ambitious project. So you decide to have a few drinks to calm your nerves. After a long and stressful day, you look at your phone at around eleven o'clock and decide to pack up and call it a night.

"Still feeling the effects of the alcohol, you decide to take a little stroll around the block to walk it off before driving home. You were minding your own business, getting some fresh air, then the next thing you know, you see your old friend, Darrell, and it agitates you. By now, the alcohol has had plenty of time to work its effects and it fuels your contempt for him. Your adrenaline starts pumping through your body and you feel invincible.

"You approach him, then you two exchange some unpleasant words back and forth, and you don't particularly care for what he has to say. One thing leads to another, you completely lose your temper, and you attack him. Darrell feels weak and overmatched, so he pleads with you to stop. He has no choice but to run away, so he darts down the nearest alley in an attempt to escape and you chase after him. Once you catch up to him, you tackle him onto the ground, pick up the nearest object which you can find and you stab him several times in the chest."

I sat there listening to the story, parts of it probably were described accurately, but I wasn't the one who chased him down and stabbed him. "You have a wild imagination Detective Jensen, but you also have no idea what you're talking about."

"Okay then, help us out. Tell us what happened that night. If it was an accident, then we'll understand, accidents happen. You didn't mean to kill him, you were in a rage and it just went too far, right?"

"Like I said, I didn't see Darrell that night. You don't have any evidence linking me to the crime - my fingerprints aren't on the murder weapon, there's no DNA, no eyewitnesses, no footprints - nothing. So do us all a favor and let me go. You guys are wasting your time."

"We do have a mountain of evidence on you and it's just a matter of time until we get more. So far, it's not looking good for you, Mr. Morrison. We've established you had the means, the motive, and the opportunity to kill your old nemesis. I suggest you get yourself a good lawyer. Or, if you want to make this easy on yourself, tell us what happened. Maybe we can work out some sort of deal."

"No, forget it, no deal. I'm innocent."

"You know, I have been a detective for a long time, and in my experience, a lot of people who have been in your position now have said the same thing. The smart ones eventually admit to what they did. The dumb ones think they can outsmart the police, but sooner or later, the truth will come out and they really regret not cutting a deal when they had the chance."

"On the night I called the police, I witnessed Darrell get into a car, drive about thirty feet, and then exit the vehicle. I read the license plate out to the dispatch operator. My advice to you guys is to find the owner of that car and chase down that lead. Remember, Darrell was a street junkie. He took advantage of me and I was a good friend of his. Imagine how he treated the people who were not as close with him. He has probably screwed over and ripped off countless people in shady back alley deals, probably done so for years. My guess is he screwed over the wrong person and finally got what was coming to him. He was able to outrun me, but he could not outrun himself. Eventually, people have to reap what they sow.

"Do you have any other questions for me? Because I have a lot to do today."

"No, but we're going to keep an eye on you. Here, take my card. Give me a call if you remember anything else you forgot to tell us."

Even though I was allowed to leave, I knew this ordeal was not over.

Chapter Forty-Seven

It was only meant to be a short trip in the summer, but it turned into a complete lifestyle change. I rented a small apartment along the seawall in downtown Vancouver and furnished it with cheap furniture. I spent half my time in the apartment, and the other half at the restaurant. I had no time for leisure, no time to hang out with any old friends, including Sam. Soon after our date, she landed some big modeling gig in New Zealand and flew out right away. It was probably for the best anyway, I did not see a future with her. She was a pretty girl, but other than that, she had little else to offer.

I did not plan any of this, nor could I have ever planned any of this. Had I sat down on my own and tried to imagine how my life would turn out, there would be no way I could have thought up all the events that led me to be here. Who would have thought a chance encounter with a guy in my building would one day lead to me to buying a restaurant with him on a whim? I guess the universe has a weird way of sorting things out.

I had made a choice to abandon the pursuit of being a lawyer. I was all done with the course work, but I still needed to do my articling and then pass the Bar exam. At twenty-seven years old, I was no longer interested in starting out at the bottom again and trying to fight my way to the top of some law firm. The hours would be grueling and the money would not be worth the stress.

Law school was not a complete waste of time. Over the last three years, I had developed some great friendships, amassed a wealth of knowledge, and managed to save up a decent amount of money. Nevertheless, it was apparent to me I was not put on this planet to be a lawyer. I had not interned at any law firms during my summers like the other students; I couldn't afford to be away from the stock market all day. Whether I liked it or not, my life was now going in a different direction. I was once again back home.

***

I sat at my desk in the back office of the restaurant, opened my laptop, and looked at some files.

"Mr. Morrison, would you like me to bring you something to eat?" one of the servers asked.

"No, thank you, Julia. I'll eat in the restaurant with everyone else. How's the second floor looking?"

"It is really busy up there, but I can reserve a table if you'd like."

"Okay, sounds good. I'll be out there in five minutes; I'm just finishing something up at the moment."

I stepped onto the second floor and did what I always did – scanned the faces in the crowd. I immediately noticed a new face amongst the typical regulars who dined at Ace during their lunch break. I felt compelled to walk over and say hello.

"Mr. Lindberg, it's so good of you to join us for lunch today. My name is Trevor Morrison, I'm one of the owners."

"Oh, this is your restaurant? I like what you've done with the place, it's a vast improvement."

"Thank you so much. How is everything else? Is the food okay? Are they treating you well?"

"Everything is great, thank you."

"I'm really glad you stopped by today. You know, it's funny, when I first moved to Vancouver…" I stopped midsentence. Something caught the corner of my eye. Mr. Lindberg turned around to see what I was looking at, but saw nothing out of the ordinary. "Will you excuse me for one moment, please? I have some business I must attend to."

"By all means, take care of your business," If I was not so distracted, I might have paid more attention to the subtle business advice that the great Allan Lindberg had just passed on to me.

I walked away from Lindberg's table and went over to the hostess. "Mia, who is that man sitting at table five?"

"Umm…" she said, as she scanned her chart. "That's Channing, party of four."

"How the hell did he get up here? This section is strictly for VIPs, that guy is not important."

"He told me he was a local business owner and gave me his card."

"What kind of business does he run?"

"I don't know, here's his card," she dug it out of her folder and handed it to me.

"Mia, this guy runs a hotdog stand. I know this is a new concept for the restaurant, but the second floor is for elite people only. This guy is not elite. Under no circumstances is he allowed to step foot on this property again, okay?"

"Okay. Do you want me to say something to him?"

"No, don't worry about it. I'll take care of it."

I walked toward the table where Jack Channing was sitting. I was about ten feet away before we made eye contact. It was the first time I had seen him since the night he tried to take my head off with a roundhouse kick, but that was not the last time I had heard from him. He had called me a couple of times to harass me about some unpaid debt. I had told him to go to hell and then he made some empty threats. From that moment, Darrell and Jack Channing were my sworn enemies. Now, my enemy was on my territory, which was completely unacceptable. I had to take care of it.

"Good afternoon, Jack, long time no see," I said coldly, making no attempt to sound pleasant. "Could I have a word with you for a moment?"

Jack Channing took a drink of his water and looked at the other people in his party. "Will you excuse me for a moment?" he said, as he stood up and walked over to where I was standing.

"I'm not interested in causing a scene or embarrassing you in front of your friends, especially since you couldn't have known this was my restaurant, but I want you to finish your meal, pay your bill, and never step foot inside this restaurant again."

"Listen to me you little prick, I know you killed my son, and you better believe there will be hell to pay."

"My condolences for your loss, Jack, but blaming me will not bring your son back. And no, I did not kill him."

"You're lucky I'm with clients right now or else I would wring your neck."

"Alright then, enjoy your meal," I said, as I began to walk away. I took a few steps, then stopped and turned around. "Jack, one more thing… have a nice life."

Chapter Forty-Eight

I arrived on the steps of the Lindberg building on Monday morning. Seeing the massive brass sign again brought back memories of my first day in Vancouver. I proceeded through the large glass revolving doors and entered the lobby. Security did not even notice me. I looked like I belonged there. I spent about thirty-five hundred dollars on a wool two-button Euro-cut suit - black with subtle pin stripes. I had on a fitted lavender shirt with an Italian silk tie and handkerchief. To top it all off, I wore gold cufflinks and polished dark-chestnut shoes. My stride matched the attire.

I stepped into the elevator and pressed the button for the top floor. The elevator ascended rapidly, causing my stomach to churn. The fact I was about to have a meeting with one of the most powerful people in the country probably was not helping any. I had managed to get only a moment of Mr. Lindberg's time, so it was imperative that I impress him.

In the time it took for the elevator to rise to the top of the massive skyscraper, I was able to do one final rehearsal of what I was going to say. The elevator came to a stop on the top floor and the doors opened. Using the mirror in the elevator, I looked over my appearance, made some final adjustments to my suit, and then made my exit. I took a deep breath – it was show time.

The first thing I noticed when I approached the reception desk was the spectacular view. The entire city was laid out before me. I felt like I was on top of the world.

"Good morning, sir," a young attractive woman greeted me.

"Good morning. My name is Trevor Morrison and I have an appointment with Allan Lindberg."

"I'll let him know you're here. You can have a seat in our waiting area if you like."

"Thank you."

"Would you like some coffee or water?"

"No, thank you."

I took a seat on the big leather sofa and stared out the window. I could see for miles. Floatplanes were taking off and landing on the water, people hustling around like little worker ants, and the gorgeous mountains on the North shore never looked so serene. I opened up my folder to make sure everything was in order.

"Mr. Morrison, Mr. Lindberg is ready to see you now."

"Thank you."

Although I had never seen the inside of the building before, Mr. Lindberg's office was unmistakable. I walked right over to the two large wooden doors with the large golden 'L' etched in the centre. I pushed one of the heavy doors open and prepared myself for the possibilities that laid on the other side.

"Mr. Morrison, welcome."

"Good morning, Mr. Lindberg. Thank you so much for meeting with me today."

"Please, have a seat."

"Thank you."

"So what can I do for you today?"

"I know your time is valuable so I'll be as brief as possible. Mr. Lindberg, I'm about to revolutionize the way people do commerce and I'm seeking investors to help launch my company," I said, keeping it brief. I reached into my briefcase, took out the prospectus, and handed it to him.

He read the first paragraph, then the next.

"Huh," he grunted. "Is this feasible?" he asked, as he continued to scrutinize every detail.

"I believe it is, sir. I spent the last year and a half working out all the details. I'm the patent holder for the technology, and have several companies already on board to facilitate. All I need is a little funding."

"How much is a little?"

"Ten million."

He did not even bat an eye. "How soon could you become fully operational?"

"I have a multiphase strategy to implement. If everything goes according to plan, I expect to be up and running within a couple of months."

"Why don't you go public with your company or license your idea? I'm sure you would have no problem coming up with the money you need."

"I considered those options; however, I think you of all people can appreciate the satisfaction and freedom of being your own boss."

For the next twenty minutes, Lindberg picked my brain about the company. For every question he had, I had an answer. I was well prepared.

When it appeared I had satisfied his inquiry, he looked at me and said, "I have to say, I get a lot of crazy proposals from people who claim their product or service will be the next big thing. I turn down ninety-nine percent of them in hopes one day someone like you will walk through my doors. There is something different about you."

"Thank you, sir. That means a lot coming from you."

"I'll tell you what. Let me get back to you on this. I like what I see, but I need my team to look it over first."

Although Lindberg seemed impressed by me and my idea, I had no way of knowing if he actually meant any of those praises or if he just said that to everybody. For all I knew, he might throw my proposal in the garbage before the door closed behind me on my way out. I did not want to take that chance. I had to close him now.

The way I saw it, it was a David versus Goliath moment. Here was one of the richest men in the world, wielding a global empire, and I was just a kid with a slingshot. So, I approached it like any other scenario in my life. I was a warrior and this was a battle - me versus him. I had marched right into enemy territory and was staring directly into the eye of the beast. However, this was not a battlefield in the traditional sense; this was business - a war of wits. Who can outsmart whom. If I was going to be successful in taking down this mammoth, I needed a strategy. Luckily, I had one.

Step one: attack with a double-edged sword - the sympathy praise. Make him vulnerable for the attack by lowering his guard with a sympathetic story. "You know, when I first moved to Vancouver, I was just a bright-eyed kid - seventeen years old. I remember coming downtown for the first time and looking up at all the tall buildings. It was like nothing I had ever seen before. One building in particular stood out among the rest - your building. I walked right up to the front of your building, looked up, and felt inspired. I had no idea who you were or what you did, but I wanted to be like you one day. Now, ten years later, sitting in your office is like a dream come true."

Now, for the praise.

"Being here today speaks volumes of your character. I see your name plastered everywhere on this building, inside and out. It marks the sign of a great man - a leader - someone who built an empire because he possessed what others did not have - the courage and intelligence to make his own decisions, to exercise judgment, and to take calculated risks. But above all, you see the value in something when no one else does."

My next move was to make him come to me in the hopes of snaring him in a trap. I had planned every move in my mind and had gone over every detail a hundred times - every variable and every response.

"I was really hoping we could do this deal today, Mr. Lindberg, but obviously you need more time," I said as I snapped the locks on my briefcase shut and stood up.

"That was a good speech, kid."

"Please don't call me 'kid'," I blurted out.

Mr. Lindberg sat back in his chair and evaluated me head to toe. Neither one of us said a word. It was time to up the ante so I turned around and headed for the door. This was a risky play, which could only go one of two ways. Either he would allow me to walk away, or he would fold under the pressure and yield to my will. When you force someone's hand, you never know what the outcome will be.

"Mr. Morrison," he said. I turned around, not knowing what to expect. "You showed a lot of courage in here today, standing up to me like that. Most people have trouble looking me in the eye without wetting their pants. You're going to need courage like that if you want to be successful in this game."

That was it. I had failed. Lindberg was impervious to my pathetic attack. It was as if he just patted me on the head like a little boy and sent me on my way. I bowed my head low in defeat and proceeded to walk out the same way I had come in. Then he said something I had not expected.

"I deliberately called you 'kid'."

I stopped dead in my tracks. This was something I had not prepared for. I turned around to face him. Much to my surprise, he was smiling.

"I needed to know how you would handle being called a kid, and guess what?"

"What's that, sir?"

"You passed," he said, still smiling. "You know, you remind me a lot of myself when I was your age. Please, come back, have a seat."

Game on. I was back in it.

"I appreciate that. Thank you, sir."

"I'll tell you what; I can have the money wired to you this afternoon."

"Under what terms?" I asked.

This was a brand new battle - negotiations. If I won that, I won the war. I was seeking a ten million dollar investment in exchange for a twenty percent stake in my company. A fifty million dollar valuation was hard to justify at that stage in the game, but was still completely reasonable for what I was proposing.

"Since I'm putting up all the money, and therefore all the risk, I think a fifty percent stake in the company is fair."

He had fired the first round at me and now it was my turn to respond. Typically, the person who speaks first in a negotiation loses. He was already at a disadvantage.

"Wow, fifty percent. That's a lot. You know, I really don't think I can do fifty percent." I paused for effect. Waiting makes people anxious, and anxiety leads to desperation. But surely this was not Allan Lindberg's first negotiation. I would need to do a lot more than that in order to persuade him.

Step one: make him feel unnecessary. "Look, Mr. Lindberg, with all due respect, ten million dollars is not a lot of money. I can get that by the end of the week."

Step two: the lowball counteroffer. "How about I give you a ten percent stake, and even that is a lot."

Step three: the hook. "And I'll also give you exclusive access to the third level at Ace."

In order to hook a whale like Lindberg, I needed to use a sizable bait that would attract his attention. I had just dangled the sparkly lure of exclusivity right in front of his face. The only thing left to do was wait for him to chomp down on it.

Lindberg sat back in his chair a moment and studied me. It was as if I had entered his thoughts and was following his chain of reasoning. First, he studied my posture and demeanour. Next he analyzed the inflection in my voice. Then he took notice of the quality and cut of my suit. Finally… the offer.

"There's a third level?" he said, right on cue. That is when I knew I had him. All that was left to do was to wait until he tired, then drag him onboard.

"Yes, but few people know about it, so I would appreciate your discretion."

"Make it ten million for a twenty percent stake and we have a deal."

"Okay, we have a deal."

I was ecstatic. I managed to get the exact deal I wanted. I had just gone toe to toe with the great Allan Lindberg, and won. I nearly exploded with pride. I wanted to open one of the windows and shout at the top of my lungs, but I did not. I kept my composure and remained calm and collected. I confidently walked over and shook his hand to secure the deal.

Now that I had the financing in place, I needed to assemble my team.

Chapter Forty-Nine

The gold embossing on the black cards really achieved the desired effect I was going for. The front of each of them read:

You are cordially invited

I opened one of the letters and read it one last time before I delivered them.

'Dear Mr. Foster,

'It is one of my great regrets in life that I did not get to know you better. I spent several years working under you and have appreciated everything you have done for me. Despite our limited contact, I have determined your character and work ethic are of the highest quality. I would like to think you and I share many common values. In addition, I admire many other qualities you possess. You are a very good person from what I have seen and heard. You are a master negotiator, master networker, and have the drive that will take you very far in life. Because of this, I'm asking you to join me in a highly lucrative business venture.

'I'm in the process of assembling a team of highly motivated and highly competent individuals and it would be a privilege and an honour to have you on board with me. In one of our brief conversations, you disclosed your dissatisfaction with your current working arrangement with the bank. I believe you referred to it as a 'dead end'. I'm providing you an opportunity for advancement without losing your security. The pay will be considerable and you will not lose any of the benefits you currently enjoy.

'If you are interested in hearing more about this opportunity, then please feel free to contact me without any obligation or pressure whatsoever. It would be my pleasure to sit down with you and formally discuss my proposal. Even if you are not interested at this time, I would still like to rendezvous with you sometime in the near future.

'I'm looking forward to hearing from you George.

'Sincerely,

'Trevor Morrison.

'604-555-0565'

I sealed up the letter and put it with the others. As I was leaving the house, my phone rang.

"Hey, McKay, thanks for calling me back."

"No worries, I was surprised when I got your message. What have you been up to since the Banff days?"

"Oh you know, making moves."

"Is that a fact? What kind of moves are you making?"

"Well, I could tell you about it, but you wouldn't believe me. I would like to show you instead. How soon can you get to Vancouver?"

***

Walking up to the front of the National Group Bank where I used to work brought back a lot of memories. I spent over four years of my life there and I never thought I would be back. I met a lot of great people over the years and now it was time to cherry pick those people for my company.

"Hi, I'm here to see Charles Cameron, can you see if he is working today please," I said through the security intercom.

"What's your name?" the voice responded back.

"Trevor Morrison."

"One moment please."

I glanced around and took in the familiar sights. I saw a few people outside smoking cigarettes, but I did not recognize any of them.

"Mr. Morrison, Mr. Cameron is on his way."

"Okay, thank you."

A few moments later, a familiar face emerged from the revolving glass doors. "Trevor, how's it going? Long time no see," Charles said with a huge smile and a handshake.

"I'm doing really well, Charles, it's so good to see you."

"What brings you by?"

"I just wanted to catch up with some people. Are you still managing the old team?"

"Yeah, I'm still managing a few of the old crew. Tami is still there, and Grace… did you ever work with Mark?"

"No, I'm not sure that I did. How about Eduardo, is he still there?" I asked.

"No, he left a few years ago. He was transferred to one of the branches."

"I don't suppose you know which one?"

"I think it was the downtown branch on West Georgia."

"Oh really, that's close to where I live, maybe I'll pop by and say hello."

"How about George Foster, is he still around?"

"Yeah, George is still here."

After we exchanged pleasantries, I revealed the real reason why I was there.

"Charles, let me ask you something. What if an opportunity came your way that allowed you to be a part of something revolutionary, something you could be proud of, would you do it?"

"I don't know, it depends on what it is."

"The truth is Charles, I'm putting together a team for my new company and I want you to be a part of it. I'm offering you the chance of a lifetime to be a part of something special. Of course, I will compensate you appropriately. Would you like to hear more?"

"You know, it sounds tempting, but I'm too old to start changing careers now. Perhaps if you came to me ten years ago, I would consider it. But I'll be retiring next year, so I think I'll just stay put."

"Okay, no problem, I totally understand. Now that I'm back in town, we should stay in touch."

"Yeah, that would be good."

"Hey, do you think you could drop off these letters to Tami and George for me, please?" I handed him two fancy envelopes.

"Sure, no problem."

"And here, take my card."

"Unity Inc.," he read. "What's this?"

"Let's get together for a drink sometime and I'll tell you all about it."

***

A little after noon, I received a call from an unknown number on my cell phone.

"Hello?"

"Trevor, this is George Foster."

"Mr. Foster, I'm so glad you called me back, how are you?"

"I'm doing well. I received your letter and it was very flattering, thank you."

"Well, it's all true."

"Thank you."

"So what else do you think of the letter?"

"I have to say, you obviously put a lot of time and effort into this, and I'm definitely interested in hearing more about this opportunity."

"Wonderful. I'm so glad to hear that. Why don't you come down to Ace Restaurant after work, do you know where that is?"

"Yes I do, I can be there around seven o'clock."

"Okay, great. Just tell the hostess you're meeting with me and she will bring you to my table."

***

George showed up a little after seven and introduced himself to the hostess.

"Right this way, sir," April said, as she escorted Mr. Foster up to the second level.

"Hey, George, you made it, thank you so much for coming," I said, as I stood up to greet my guest with a warm handshake.

"Trevor, how's it going?"

"I'm doing really well, how's everything with you?"

"Things are going well. My wife and I just had our second baby last month, so I'm a little sleep deprived."

"Aren't we all?"

"Yeah, well, it's worth it. We are really excited to welcome the new edition into our family."

"Congratulations. I'm happy to hear things are going well for you."

George looked around and said, "Wow, this is a nice place, huh? Have you eaten here before?"

"Of course, I own it."

"Really? Wow, good for you."

I had two servers scheduled to do nothing but take care of us the entire night. I had them bring us our best wine and had the chefs prepare one-of-a-kind dishes that were not a part of the menu. For the most part, we kept the conversation light during dinner, catching up, small talk - the usual. Then he asked me, "So I'm interested in hearing more about your business."

"Well, I have met a lot of really bright people throughout my life, each possessing their own unique set of talents and attributes. I'm in the process of selecting among those individuals to put together an all-star team, utilizing their natural talents for the success of my company. Your natural talents combined with your knowledge of the banking industry would be a huge asset to our operation. Together, I intend to revolutionize the world of commerce."

"Sounds exciting, I can't wait to hear more."

After a long-winded sales pitch, I had George completely on board. I reached into my briefcase and pulled out a thick folder with my company logo on it.

"I have prepared this specifically for you, George," I said, as I handed him the folder. "Inside, you will find a more in-depth description of what was discussed tonight. It will also outline the job description, the pay and benefits, and a contract. I want you to take this home, read it over carefully, discuss it with you wife, and get back to me by Monday morning with your decision. I know that doesn't give you a lot of time, and this is probably a lot to take in right now, but I can assure you that you will be well taken care of. If you have any questions, please don't hesitate to call anytime, day or night."

"Thank you, I'll look this over as soon as possible and get back to you."

"I want to thank you again for meeting with me tonight, George. I hope I didn't take up too much of your time."

"No not at all, it was my pleasure."

"I hope you enjoyed your meal, which is on the house by the way."

"Thank you so much. The food was excellent."

"You're welcome. It was good to see you, George. I'll look forward to hearing from you on Monday."

Chapter Fifty

The group consisted of friends and family from all parts of my life - college, university, work, and even some people from my restaurant. We all packed in to a small conference room at the Marriott Hotel in downtown Vancouver. In the centre of the room was a large oval table that had enough seats for everyone there. Off to the side was another small rectangular table with an assortment of food and beverages on it. I gave people a moment to come in and get some snacks before I proceeded.

I did one final look at my checklist to make sure everyone was there. As I scanned the faces of the crowd, I felt a great sense of pride. This was my team - or at least, my would-be team. I hand-selected each person based on two principles - trust and merit. I was not sure how many of them would even join me, or how many of them would remain after joining me. I was asking a lot from them. I was asking them to leave behind stable and secure jobs to take a chance on me - a man with relatively no experience. However, if this company was ever to survive, I would need a strong, well-rounded team, and I had to have faith in them as well.

I assessed each player for months before making my final selection. Since I was operating with a tight budget, it made things even more difficult. In this case, it was as if I was a new sports franchise. We were all rookies in this industry and I was certainly not qualified to be the head coach, but that was just on paper. Sometimes in life, there is an indescribable x-factor - a hidden element, which allows a person to garner success where everyone expects failure.

"Ladies and gentlemen, thank you all for being here tonight," I said to my audience. "I have met with many of you over the past couple of weeks and briefly explained to you what my vision for this company is. Others will be hearing this for the first time. Regardless of which category you fall into, I will be giving a more detailed presentation tonight and will be prepared to answer any questions you may have for me."

"First, why don't we go around the room and have everybody introduce themselves to the group. McKay, why don't we start with you? Please tell everybody a little about yourself - education and background, and perhaps how we know each other."

"Okay. Hello, my name is McKay; I'm a University of Calgary graduate. I have a degree in marketing and a masters in finance. I met Trevor almost ten years ago when we lived in Banff together and have kept in touch ever since."

McKay was one of my oldest friends in the room. I had a lot of respect for him as a person, but held an equal respect for his abilities in business. The fact I was able to 'sign' him spoke to the respect he must have had for me and my abilities as well. Coming from him, that meant a lot to me. He was my marketing expert - a person who had a way with people and was a whiz at understanding market needs. I needed McKay to assist me in market acquisition and public relations. He would be someone who I could bounce ideas off and receive honest feedback. Although most of my business team were young and inexperienced, we also had a unique perspective on how modern business should be done. We were not held slave to outdated ideologies and corporate procedures. As such, I believed McKay would complement our team well.

The introductions continued.

"Hi, I'm Steve. I met Trevor a few years ago. We lived in the same building when he was in law school. We graduated the same year, but my degree is in commerce."

Steve was a bit reckless in business and in life, so he would definitely need to be managed. But what Steve lacked in self-control, he made up for it in finding creative ways to make money. He was a visionary and a natural-born leader. Nevertheless, I was not ready to have him be in charge of anything just yet. I determined he would work best under McKay's leadership.

"Hi I'm Dan. Trevor was my neighbour while we were in law school. We were in the same grad class. And I'm a Pisces."

Dan was a lot like me - young, ambitious, and determined. We had similar upbringings and similar educational backgrounds. He would definitely be an asset to me because I could count on him to give me straight answers and objectively challenge any decisions I make. In business, this is often referred to as your second sober thinker.

"Hi, I'm Eduardo, I'm originally from the Philippines. I moved here with my wife six years ago. I met Trevor while working at the National Group Bank. I have a bachelor's degree in economics."

Eduardo was a positive person who would be able to boost morale. My plan for him was to have him be in charge of customer service.

"Hello everyone, my name is Tami. I met Trevor at the Bank. Eduardo and I were on the same team as Trevor. I have a bachelor's degree in English."

With a degree in English, it may not be obvious why I chose to bring Tami onboard. She would be my executive assistant. She was 20 years my senior and was whip-smart. Not only did she have life experience, she had held a variety of jobs in many different kinds of companies over the years. I could really benefit from her wisdom and expertise in how to run the internal business of a company.

"Hello, my name is George Foster. Up until very recently, I was the Senior Director for the Credit Card Division of the National Group Bank of Canada. I held that position for the past eight years. Before that, I was an account manager with the bank for five years. I have a bachelor's degree from University of Toronto in business administration and I have a master's degree in accounting from the University of Saskatchewan."

George would be my CFO. He was the only person in the room with any real experience running a large division of a company. He was my numbers expert and I was truly blessed to have him onboard.

"Hi my name is Will. I have known Trevor since high school. We lived together briefly in Banff, where we had a brief altercation once over a glass of orange juice, but otherwise our relationship has run smoothly. I don't have any degrees, but I have been educated in the streets."

Although Will was not academically accomplished, I brought him on board for one simple reason – he understood people. It would be a mistake to overlook this component when trying to launch a competitive team. People are what drive businesses. He was a kid who went from obscurity to being one of the most popular kids in the entire city. You cannot do that unless you are a master networker and understand the subtle nuances of human psychology. He knew what people wanted and how to deliver it. Will was really a person who could do anything he put his mind to, but to utilize him correctly, I planned to put him on my marketing team, and perhaps later, he could be in charge of human resources.

"My name is Brian, I'm Trevor's brother. I have a degree in mathematics and a degree in computer programming."

My brother was my oldest friend in the room – someone whom I trusted and admired a great deal. We were born only two years apart, but he was vastly wiser than I was. Like me, he was a very systematic and logical thinker. I could always trust in his sound and thorough judgment. I determined the best place for him would be to put him in charge of the company's web development.

We continued to go around the room until all the introductions were complete. Once that was out of the way, it was onto the next order of business - introducing the vision for my company.

Chapter Fifty-One

Everyone in the room seemed extremely eager to hear what I was about to say. I had prepared this night for weeks to make sure everything was perfect. On the table to my right was my briefcase. In it, I had a stack of laminated coil-bound prospectuses to give everyone at the end of the night. For those who wished to join me on this venture, each would receive their own key to the office I was renting.

Earlier that evening, I had pulled Steve aside and asked him to assist me with a little demonstration. Right on cue, I began my presentation.

"Steve, do me a favor. Can you please take out your wallet?"

"Sure."

"Okay, now I want you to take out all the cards in your wallet and read out the types of each."

Steve aptly complied with my request. "Alright, let's see. I have four Visas, an American Express, my gym pass, Air miles, Shoppers Optimum, Safeway, Save-on foods, IGA, my Driver's license, Care Card, Social Insurance card, I have two debit cards, some gift cards…" Steve continued until he had a sizable stack of plastic in front of him.

"Okay, now someone tell me what is wrong with that?"

"It's a lot of plastic," someone called out.

"That's right, and not only that, many of those cards require PIN numbers, and some of those cards are only used once in a while.

"Thank you, Steve. You may put those away now.

"Ladies and Gentlemen, I'm proud to present to you, the solution," I said, as I took out a shiny black card and showed it to everyone. "My plan is to combine all those cards into one card, called the Unity Card."

I had a stack of prototype cards made up and passed them around the room, one for everybody.

"I came up with this idea while working at the bank. I would receive countless calls each day about people forgetting their PIN numbers. The Unity Card solves that problem by combining all your cards into one card, with only one PIN number to remember."

I paused and waited for it to sink in.

"Now, let me assure you, achieving this will be no simple feat. There are a number of problems. First, suppose you are out shopping and you swipe your Unity Card. How are you going to be able to select between your different accounts?"

Nobody volunteered to answer.

"The solution to that problem is to have a new payment terminal installed in every retailer in the world. This new device will have a digital screen that will display all the different card types that the store accepts. The user then inserts their Unity Card and selects their preferred method of payment.

Now, I can see the wheels in your heads turning. Many of you probably foresee a number of problems with this. Don't worry, I have already thought of them. What is one obvious problem with this card?" I asked.

My brother was quick to respond. "People won't leave their house with just one card – what if they need to buy something and the merchant doesn't accept Unity Cards? Since people won't want to take that chance, they will still bring all their cards with them. Thus, the Unity Card will be just another card in their wallet, except it will be redundant and unnecessary."

"You are absolutely right. So what's the solution?" I asked, trying to get some more audience participation. Again, nobody volunteered to answer. "The solution is to make sure every merchant in the country accepts Unity Cards.

As I look around, I can tell some of you already see the catch twenty-two. Merchants have no incentive to update their payment terminals if nobody has the Unity Card, and if merchants don't have the technology, then users have no way of using the Unity Card, so they won't get one. So what's the solution?" I asked.

This time, Steve responded. "We provide every merchant with a new device."

"Correct. Are there any questions?"

As soon as I said that, about a half dozen arms shot up in the air. "Brian, go ahead, I believe I saw your hand raised first."

"Okay, so you somehow create this new device and give it to every merchant..."

"Right."

"How much will that cost?"

"That's a great question. I have collaborated with Trek Micro Systems to update all their devices to enable cardholders to use the Unity Card. They have the knowledge and infrastructure to produce these new devices and get them in the hands of every merchant in North America."

"Wouldn't it be easier to just have an application on your cell phone rather than have a card? In many parts of the world, people pay with their cell phones," Brian said.

"I thought about that; however, merchants would still need the technology to communicate with the cell phone, and not everyone has a cell phone that can do that. Remember, in order for this to work, I need as many people to sign up as possible, so creating a free card is the most efficient way to achieve that. But that's a good idea, maybe we can have a smartphone app version too."

"So how does this generate revenue?" McKay asked.

"Another great question, I'm glad you asked. Unity Card will be free for cardholders, but we will charge the merchants a small user fee, also known as a swipe fee, similar to what the banks charge."

"So, I'm not really sure I understand how this will work," Eduardo said.

"Our cards will have a computer chip in them much like the credit and debit cards have now. The cardholder will insert their Unity Card and enter their PIN the same way. The new devices from Trek Micro will automatically detect the relevant reward points card for that store. There will be a touch screen on the hand-held device that will display 'Credit' or 'Debit'. If the cardholder selects 'Credit', then a list of all the credit cards that store accepts will appear and the user will be able to choose whichever one they want to use."

"But doesn't that create a problem of having all your eggs in one basket? I mean, what if the one card you have to pay for everything gets lost or stolen?" someone from the back of the room shouted out.

"I don't believe it's any more of a problem than placing all of your cards and cash into one wallet. In fact, the Unity Card is better since people will still keep all their cards at home as a backup. If their Unity Card is ever lost or stolen, we can simply place a hold on it, have another card couriered out the next day, and they are up and running again. This is actually much better than losing a wallet since you don't run the risk of losing any cash, you don't have to call dozens of companies, wait or hold, verify your information over and over, and pay for new I.D.s..."

There was some chatter amongst the room, but I silenced it by introducing the final and most important topic.

"I want to address the catch twenty-two problem because solving that problem is really at the heart of this company's success. To combat that, we will need to launch an aggressive advertising campaign to sign up as many cardholders as possible. We will need to have online ads, print ads, billboards, TV and radio commercials, celebrity endorsements, kiosks at every major mall and airport - you name it. We also need to create a website where users can create a profile and update their Unity Card."

There was a buzz in the room; everyone seemed really excited with what I had presented. This time, I simply stood at the front of the room and smiled proudly. I could not believe this moment was actually happening.

Chapter Fifty-Two

I realized very early on that ten million dollars was not going to get us very far, so I brought on some new investors. Everything was really low budget to start off. Our offices were not in the best part of town and a lot of the furniture was either second-hand or rented. For the most part, we had everything we needed.

So far, I was very happy with the team I had assembled. We had all been working very hard to get this company launched over the past few months. I assigned everyone with specific tasks based on their job descriptions and offered everybody a small stake in the company. I wanted to make sure the people who were with me from the grassroots would be taken care of, if and when we made it big.

***

"Hey, Will, how are the numbers looking?"

"So far we have an average of about fifteen hundred new accounts opening per day."

"Which campaign has been the most effective?"

"Our radio and TV ads, but the TV ads cost nearly five times as much. Should we discontinue or cut them back?"

"No, continue with them as long as it is still profitable to do so."

"But we're barely covering our costs."

"I don't care. Keep the ads coming, they're necessary. If we discontinue those ads, we will save money, but we will be losing clients. Part of our success is to make Unity a household name. I anticipated going overboard with advertising in the beginning. Don't worry, it will eventually pay off."

"You're good at this stuff, where did you learn to run a company?" Will asked.

"I have worked for a lot of companies in the past and I have learned how not to run a company. Besides, if you believe in the product and hire the right people, it makes things run a lot smoother."

"It's crazy seeing you now; you're a lot different from the guy I knew in high school."

"Yeah, I have definitely come a long way since then."

"Hey, do you remember almost getting suspended for throwing snowballs?" Will asked.

"Of course, how did you know about that?"

"Because I told Ms. Bennett you were not the one who threw the snowball."

"That was you? Ms. Bennett said someone came forward and cleared my name, but I had no idea that was you. Thanks a lot."

"No worries, that's what friends are for."

"So do you know who threw the snowball?"

"Yeah, it was that punk, Darrell. He was just going to let you go down for something he did. I hated that guy; I'm not sure why you hung out with him."

"It's actually kind of funny learning it was Darrell who threw the snowball after all these years. Even back then, he was only looking out for himself. If only I had known, it would have saved me a lot of grief."

"It's a good thing I had your back."

"I really appreciate you vouching for me. In fact, you have helped me a lot in life, whether you know it or not. Without you, I would not have moved to Banff, and even if I did, I couldn't have afforded to stay there at first. You helped give my life momentum and I'll never forget it. Who knows how my life would have turned out if you were not there to help me all those times, so thanks a lot."

"Thanks, man, but I'm sure you would have been fine without me."

"Do you remember that time in Banff when you said one day we'd be looking back on this moment as a memory?"

Will's head cocked to one side with a puzzled look on his face. "Did I say that? Geez, I must have forgotten."

***

In an effort to multitask, I analyzed some data while soothing 'hold' muzak from Trek Micro flooded through my office from the speaker phone. Just as I was getting into it, a lady picked up.

"Trek Micro Systems, how may I assist you?"

"Yes, hi, may I please speak with someone in your account management department?" I asked.

"Certainly, sir, may I have your name?"

"Yes, my name is Trevor Morrison."

A few moments later a familiar voice came on the line. "Trevor?" she said. As soon as I heard her voice, my stomach knotted up. "Ashley?"

"Oh my god, Trevor, how's it going?"

"Things are going well, how are things with you?"

"I'm doing well. This is so weird, I heard there was a Trevor Morrison on the phone and I thought, no it couldn't be."

"I had no idea you worked for Trek Micro."

"Yeah, I've been here for almost a year. So I take it you're not a lawyer?"

"No, I decided to go in a different direction."

"So what do you do now?"

"I'm back in Vancouver, just working for some company. I would love to get together some time to catch up."

"Sure, what's your number? I'll call you when I'm off work."

I disconnected the phone and exhaled a deep breath. I was so caught off guard that I forgot all about the reason for my call in the first place.

I looked down and felt my hands - they were sweating profusely. Who would have thought a girl I dated so many years ago would still make me feel so nervous. I felt like I did when we first met in Banff. I had no idea my feelings for her were still so strong. I guess I had been suppressing them all this time.

Similarly to when I was seventeen and in Banff, I allowed my mind to wander, once again thinking of all the possible scenarios that could possibly unfold tonight. Would she still be the same person? Had she gotten over me? Was she seeing anyone else? All these questions came to mind. In any event, I was about to find out.

In preparation for our date, I went to the mall and bought a new shirt and some flowers, nothing too fancy, in case she was married. I wanted to send the message I was doing well and still cared about her, but I would allow her to fill in the details of how much. I also went to a car rental agency and rented a mid-sized vehicle for the night. The only decent car they had was a blue Ford Focus. It was not the classiest car, but it would have to do.

I drove back to my place to get ready. After I had a shower, I took my new shirt out of the bag and pulled the tags off. I held it up and looked at it. It still had creases from being folded in the store so I took out my iron and ironed it too. I ironed my pants while I was at it. I wanted everything to be perfect for the evening so no detail was overlooked.

After I was done ironing, I put my pants on and buttoned my new shirt overtop a clean white tee. I did my hair, brushed my teeth, and donned a single spray of her favourite cologne. By the time I was finished, it was 5:30 – time to pick Ashley up from work.

I pulled up to the Trek Micro building and saw Ashley waiting promptly. She looked as gorgeous as ever. Other than her hairstyle, she had not changed a bit.

"Hey, nice car," she said as I got out and opened the passenger-side door for her.

"Oh, it's not mine, it's a rental."

"Still don't own a car yet, huh?"

"No, not yet. So do you want to grab something to eat?"

"Sure, there is this awesome new restaurant I want to try, it's called Ace, have you been there before?" she asked.

"Um, well, why don't we go somewhere else?"

"Don't worry, it's my treat."

"What, no, it's not that, it's just..."

"Have you heard bad reviews or something?"

"No, I was actually just there for lunch and I don't want to go back, it's embarrassing."

"Who cares, weren't you the one always telling me not to care what people think?"

"Okay, fine."

I was a little apprehensive at first taking Ashley to my restaurant; I did not really want her to know too much about my financial situation. I just prayed none of my staff would blow my cover. I had good reasons for keeping Ashley in the dark about certain details of my life, but I also did not want her thinking I was withholding things from her. In order to pull this evening off, I had to spread the word quickly to my staff to treat me like a regular customer. My plan for that was to excuse myself from the table as soon as possible.

When we arrived at the restaurant, I opened the door for her. This actually served a dual purpose. With some luck I could hide behind Ashley and sneak past the hostess - who would undoubtedly greet me by name.

"Good evening Mr. Morrison. Table for two?" the hostess said.

So much for that plan. "Yes, please," I replied, keeping my head down, trying to maintain a low profile.

"Right this way please."

"Wow, they know you by name. You must come here often."

"Yeah, you could say that."

The hostess brought us to our table and stuck around to chat for a bit, the customary glad-handing of the boss. I set my coat down and politely excused myself. I walked right up to the manager and told him to spread the word to the staff I was to be treated like a regular customer tonight. I did not want any special attention. After that was done, I relaxed a little and walked back to our table.

"So tell me about your job," I asked.

"Right now, I'm an account manager for Trek Micro Systems. I've been there for just over two years. The people I work with are nice, but the job itself is a little dull. We actually just landed this big account so it has been really busy lately."

"Tell me about this account."

"The company is called Unity Inc. I'm not sure if you have heard of it, but it's actually kind of cool. With our help, they are launching this service that will allow users to combine all the cards in their wallet into one card."

"Sounds interesting."

"Well, it's a brand new company so we'll see how they do."

"What about you, where are you working?"

"I work for this company called Unity Inc., perhaps you've heard of it."

"No way! Why didn't you stop me, I feel so embarrassed."

"If I told you I worked there, then I might not get honest feedback."

"Oh, so that's why you called Trek today, I get it."

"It's funny because as soon as I hung up with you I realized I had forgotten to ask you about our account."

"Why didn't you just call back?"

"Once you have a date with a girl, you don't call back!"

We both smiled at each other. The chemistry was still there, you could practically cut it with a knife.

"So what do you do at Unity Inc.?" she asked.

"Research and development mostly, nothing I want to bore you with."

"So what happened to wanting to be a lawyer?"

"I decided it wasn't for me. While all my classmates were interning at law firms during the summer, I was inside my apartment all day trading stocks."

"Did you lose all your money?"

"No, of course not."

"So how long have you been in town for?"

"I've been here a few months."

"Why didn't you call? Were you just "busy" like the first time you came to Vancouver and didn't call me?"

"Something like that."

Chapter Fifty-Three

A couple of weeks had passed since I had reconnected with Ashley. It only took a few dates and the discovery that we were both single for things to pick up right where they had left off. I didn't really know what to tell her about what I did for work, so I left that part vague. She didn't ask too many questions, and I didn't volunteer too much information.

"So this is your place, huh?" she asked, as she looked around my modest one bedroom apartment. "It's nice."

"I think you said that same thing when you first came over to my place on West 4th Avenue."

"Did I?"

"Yes, I believe you did, and that place was a dump."

"Oh yeah, I remember. It had the thick orange shag carpet," she laughed. "And remember the owner busting in at three in the morning?"

"Yeah, those were some crazy times."

"Yeah, I miss those times," she said, as our eyes locked for a moment.

There was a brief silence as we studied each other. It was the perfect moment for a kiss and we both felt it. I leaned in closer, and then my phone rang.

"Steve, what's up, man?"

"Hey, sorry, did I catch you at a bad time?"

"No, not at all, what's up?"

"What are you doing right now?"

"I'm with Ashley, we're just hanging out."

"Do you guys want to come car shopping with me?"

"You're buying a new car?"

"Yeah, I need something for the mountains out here."

"What's wrong with your Hummer?"

"I got rid of it; it was bad for the environment."

"And the Lexus?"

"I got rid of that too. I got rid of all my cars when I moved out here, I thought I told you."

"Alright, let me ask Ashley."

I put the phone down by my waist and covered the receiver.

"Hey, do you want to go car shopping with my friend, Steve?"

"Sure."

"Alright, we're in. Can you come pick us up?"

Steve was a little bit late, but I expected it. He picked us up in his parents' Mercedes S500. I remembered the last time I was in this car, I had had a good time. It was probably best to keep those details to myself.

We cruised down to the car dealership on Burrard Street. I really enjoyed watching Steve do his thing, he was a really good negotiator.

"Do you have the V10 in stock … fully loaded?" Steve asked.

"Yes we do, right this way, sir."

We followed the peppy sales associate around the lot. There was no shortage of fine automobiles, but Steve knew exactly which one he wanted.

"Okay here it is," the man said, as he proudly presented the Range Rover Sport. I could tell he worked on commission; you could almost smell it on him.

"This is one of our most popular models, it has a supercharger in it and..."

"It's orange," Steve interrupted him.

"Well, it's a burnt orange – it's a very popular color right now."

Feeling his commission slipping away he quickly shifted gears on his pitch. "This is our last one in stock and I can give you a fantastic price."

"Sir, I appreciate it, but I can't drive an orange truck."

"Yes... well, it's burnt orange and like I said, it's a very hot color right now. You will notice more and more vehicles are painted in earth tones."

"You said something about a fantastic price?"

"Hey, Trevor," Ashley said, as she pulled me aside. "You need a car right, you should get this one," she said, pointing to a cherry red Ferrari 599 GTO.

"Yeah, I've already had that one, it hurt my back."

"Ha ha, very funny."

Chapter Fifty-Four

When I returned to my office, I began to respond to some phone calls and emails. I placed my routine call to the manager of Ace Restaurant. I allowed him the freedom to run the business, but I still liked to check in every few days. When we spoke, he apologized to me because the restaurant was so busy and he had to go. I informed him there was no need to apologize; it was exactly what I wanted to hear. Business at Ace was doing so well that it allowed me to focus most of my attention on Unity Inc.

I continued to get through as many emails and phone calls as possible before my meeting with the city's largest marketing firm. We were finalizing some details on Unity's new marketing campaign. It was a massive effort to push the product name into as many homes in North America as possible, and it was not cheap.

"Trevor, there's a 'McAfee' on line one, shall I put him through?" Tami asked.

"Yes, please, you can put him through."

"Trevor Morrison speaking, how may I help you?"

"Hello, Mr. Morrison, my name is Arthur McAfee, President of the National Group Bank of Canada. How are you today?"

"I'm really busy, what can I do for you, Mr. McAfee?"

"Mr. Morrison, I don't want to take up too much of your time, so let me be brief. The National Group Bank has a great interest in acquiring Unity Inc. We are prepared to offer you a substantial figure for your business. In addition to that, we are willing to allow you and your team to remain in your current positions. How does that sound?"

"I appreciate the call, but unfortunately we are not for sale."

"Mr. Morrison, we are willing to go as high as ten."

I chuckled a little bit. "Ten million? That's funny. Listen, thank you so much for calling, but I have a lot of work to do, have a good day," I said, as I hung up the phone.

"What did Mr. McAfee want, Trevor?"

"He offered to buy us out for ten million dollars."

"I think we should consider the offer, we are struggling to stay afloat here and that's a lot of money."

"Honestly, I don't really care about the money, that's not what drives me. All I care about is running a business the way I see fit and not having to take orders from people. For the longest time, I have been jerked around and held back by people who were in a higher position than I was. Now that I have my own company, that problem no longer exists for me."

"Yeah, but perhaps you could work out a deal where you still have full autonomy."

"Nope, it doesn't exist. There's no such thing. He actually did say that we could keep our entire staff, but if you think National Group is just going to give us ten million dollars and leave us alone, then you're very naïve. You see, the problem with many corporations is that they are run by old egomaniacal white men who have been living in the upper echelon for so long that they are out of touch with reality. They look down on people like me and you and treat them as second-class citizens. They think they know what is best and want things done their way. They also want to protect their position in life so they have no problems lying, cheating, and stealing to maintain it. That's where I'm different. I come from the bottom and I vow that if I ever make it to the top, I will treat people fairly."

"I can see this is a very sensitive issue for you."

"I don't dwell on it, it is what it is, but if he calls back, tell him I'm in a meeting."

Chapter Fifty-Five

The New Year had arrived, marking another successful year. This year, I flew the entire company, over fifty employees, down to Cabo San Lucas, Mexico. I did not have the extra cash to pay for the trip so I put it all on my Amex. It was important to me that I treat my staff well, despite the lack of funding to do so. They had all worked incredibly hard for me and I wanted to express my gratitude. I had faith business would boom and I would eventually pay back all of my debts.

Upon our return, we all felt rested and ready to go. It was nice coming back to work. The new offices were definitely an upgrade. Thanks to my good friend Allan, I was able to negotiate a good deal and relocate our operations to the Lindberg Building.

"Good morning, Trevor."

"Good morning, Tami. Did you enjoy your time in Mexico?"

"Yes, it was a lot of fun having everyone down there, thank you so much."

"It was my pleasure. Give me some ideas on where we can all go next year."

I walked into my office and did my usual morning routine. I checked the stock market, replied to some emails, and read the news.

"Trevor," George said, as he barged into my office holding a copy of the day's newspaper. "Did you read the article about National Group Bank announcing they are discontinuing their partnership with us?"

"Yes, I read that," I replied calmly.

"And...?"

"And, I don't care."

"What do you mean you don't care? This is bad, Trevor."

"You're right, it's bad for National Group Bank. I'm not the least bit worried about us."

"Aren't you concerned other companies will start to pull out, and then our card will become useless."

"That's backwards thinking, George. National pulled out because they make bad business decisions, you know that. I believe in our product and I think our clients do too. If anything, it will just get people to cancel with National Group and switch to another bank."

"Do you want to issue a statement to the paper?"

"No, I think that would be a mistake at this time."

"Why's that?"

"Because George, we're leaders, pioneers, the forgers of new territory. As such, we don't pay attention to what others are doing. They are behind us – they watch us, we don't watch them. We take action, rather than whimsically react to every little thing others are doing."

"So what's our next course of action, what new territory are we forging?"

"Let me answer that question with a question."

"Alright."

"Do you believe in signs?"

"Do I believe in signs?" he repeated. "What do you mean?"

"I think the universe is trying to tell us something, George."

"What's it saying?"

"It's saying we should put National Group out of business."

"Put National Group out of business? They're one of the biggest companies in the world."

"Not for long they're not."

"Okay, so how do you suggest we put National out of business?"

"It's a multiple step process. Hold on a sec, George," I said as I saw Tami at my door.

"Trevor, Bill Simpson from the sign company is here, he wants to know where you want the sign."

"See, George, it's all about signs! Thanks, Tami, tell him to put it above our front door."

"What sign did you order?"

"I wanted to have a banner in our office that says, 'NEW IDEAS WELCOME'. It's to promote innovative thinking."

"Speaking of which, you were saying how you plan to take down National Group."

"Right. Like I was saying, it's a multiple step process. The first step is to get Unity Card into as many wallets in North America as possible. If we can achieve something close to that, then our card will become synonymous with 'payment'. The second logical step – once people have swapped out all their credit cards and replaced them with their Unity Card – is to start lending people money. So instead of replacing a credit card, we become one."

"Yes, but people still like to have multiple credit cards. I don't see how this will put National out of business."

"Right, I was just getting to that. This is where step three comes in. People won't be using their other credit cards because our card will do what no other credit card can do. Suppose by using your Unity Card, you received a discount on everything you bought. Imagine going to a store and receiving a five or ten percent discount off your purchase, everywhere, just by using your Unity Card. Tell me, who in their right mind is going to use any other method of payment?

"Since our competitors can't do what we can do, soon there will be no other competitors. We will have more revenue than we will know what to do with, and that's when we hit National Group right where it hurts."

"So if I'm following you correctly, you're saying you want to become a bank?"

"Correct. You see, George, unlike the major banks, profit is not my sole motivation for existence. Also, unlike the major banks, I don't have to answer to shareholders. That puts me in a unique position to provide a service unlike any major bank. I will run my company the way a customer would – no exorbitant fees, no hidden clauses or fine print, no high interest rates. We will treat our customers and our employees fairly and not let the money corrupt us. If we can achieve that, then we will be one of the largest companies in the world, thus bringing down National Group Bank."

George paused for a moment and looked at me with a smile. "Then what?"

I could not help but laugh. "That's what I like about you, George. If I were to tell ten people what I just told you now, eight of them would tell me it can't be done, one person would be perfectly content with that plan alone, and the final person would wonder what else is possible."

"So, what else is possible?"

"If we take it a step further, the way I see it, Unity Card will essentially eliminate the need for cash. When credit and debit cards were introduced, it nearly wiped cheques off the map. People still used cash, but not as much. It's a lot of hassle carrying around large sums of money."

"Not to mention you constantly have to go to the bank to get more of it when you run out."

"Exactly, then the banks ding you for fees for withdrawing your own money, it's criminal."

"So if Unity Card does what it is designed to do, then who's going to use cash when they can use our card and save money off their purchases?"

"Do you realize the implications of what you're saying?"

"I believe I do. If cash becomes obsolete, then we could create our own e-currency - call it the Unit. Since it can't be printed like traditional money, in theory there will be no risk of inflation. If that's true, then other countries are likely to adopt the Unit. Furthermore, since e-currency is fully traceable, then black market transactions could not occur discreetly. If people no longer feel comfortable operating under the guise of anonymity, then crime and corruption will plummet. Following that, markets will stabilize, the standard of living will improve for all, and the world will prosper. If that happens, Unity Inc. will be heralded as the greatest company in the history of the universe."

George chuckled at my exuberance. "Is that what this is all about, you want to create the greatest company in the history of the universe?"

"Of course, that's what drives me," I said jokingly. "I just want to make a difference in this world, I want to be successful - not necessarily rich - but successful. I'm absolutely terrified of being a loser."

"First of all, you're not a loser. Second, if what you're saying comes true, you will revolutionize the way commerce is done."

"I know, that's what I keep telling people! I'm not deluded about it; I realize that a series of highly unlikely events need to go right in order to achieve even a fraction of this. We probably won't even see this come to fruition in our lifetime, but perhaps our kids or grandkids will, and they can take the reins on it after we pass."

Chapter Fifty-Six

Unity Card was a success, but the victory was not nearly as sweet without having someone to share it with. Ashley still had no idea what exactly it was I did for a living. I told her I was in research and development at Unity, which although was not a complete lie, it was definitely not the whole truth. I did not like lying to her and it was becoming ever more difficult to keep it up. I had done several interviews for national media groups that somehow slipped under her radar. I had to leave the house in disguise whenever I was with her just to avoid being recognized, and my phone kept ringing at all hours of the night. For all she knew, I had a really demanding boss. The worst part about it was that I finally had enough money to live a lavish lifestyle with her, but I was living in a crumby one-bedroom apartment. I still had my one bedroom on the second floor, but that was not my primary residence. I only hung out there when I was with Ashley, but that was about to change.

"Ashley," I said, as we sat down on my cheap sofa, "I feel like I'm at a point in my life where I'm finally happy. There's just one thing that's missing."

"What's missing?"

"I'm not exactly sure, but I was hoping you can help. Here, I have something for you."

I pulled out an envelope and handed it to her.

"What's this?"

I did not say anything, I just sat there and watched her open it. "Is this the card that I gave you in Banff? I can't believe you saved this."

"Just open it."

'Dear Ashley,

We were just kids when you came into my life and gave me this card. I had no idea how my life would turn out or how important that meeting between us was. Now that we are both adults, I'm glad you are still a major part of my life. It would be a great honour if you would continue to be a part of my life until we grow old together. Will you marry me?'

"OH MY GOD YES!" she screamed out.

"It's a little cheesy I know, but…" Before I could finish my sentence, she threw her arms around me and planted a kiss on my lips.

"Don't you want to see the ring first? You might change your mind?"

"Nothing will make me change my mind. I love you," she said as tears of joy rolled down her face. I took out a small box from my pocket and presented her with a beautiful solitaire diamond engagement ring. She was speechless.

She immediately slid the ring on her finger and looked at it.

"Perfect fit," she said, still crying.

"You know, I couldn't afford the real Cubic Zirconia, so I went with this instead," I said jokingly as I winked at her.

"Shut up. This is gorgeous. I hope you didn't spend too much on it, I don't need anything fancy."

"Oh really? That's too bad actually because something tells me your life is going to get a whole lot fancier," I said with a mischievous grin.

"What are you talking about?"

"I'm not exactly sure how to tell you this, but... well, maybe it would be easier if I just showed you."

"Showed me what?"

"Come with me, I want to show you something."

"Another surprise? What are you up to?"

"Just follow me please."

We went into the elevator. I scanned my key fob against a sensor and pressed 16.

"What's on the sixteenth floor?"

"You'll see, it's a surprise."

As we came to a stop, the elevator doors opened. There was a large open space with a couch on one side, a large tinted mirror on the other, and a door in the centre. I led her to the door and inserted my key into the lock.

"Are you ready?" I asked.

"Ready for what? What's going on?"

"Ashley, before I reveal what is behind this door, I just want to tell you I haven't been completely honest with you... but I hope you understand."

I swung the door open to reveal my posh 6300 square foot penthouse suite.

"Ashley, welcome to my real lifestyle."

Ashley did not say anything at first; she just stood there in complete shock.

"Come in, take a look around. Of course, we can get new furniture if you feel it's too 'bachelor paddy'."

"So, you live here?" she finally said.

"Yes... when I'm not hanging out with you."

"How... wait, why... no wait, how...?" she stuttered. Perhaps two big surprises in less than ten minutes were too much for her to process. She was dumbfounded, but not upset, which was good. I gave her a minute to gather her thoughts. She walked around the apartment in awe. She walked over to the large floor to ceiling windows and checked out the magnificent view. When she was ready, she spun around and delivered her questions more succinctly. "Trevor, why do you have two apartments?"

"When I moved back into town, I was renting the apartment downstairs. Then after a while, this place became available so I bought it."

"So you pay rent on one apartment and own another, in the same building, and you live in both of them?"

"Sort of, I actually own that apartment too."

"How do you afford to own two apartments?"

"Actually, I own the whole building."

"What? How?"

"You know the company I work for?"

"Yeah."

"I actually own it. I started it when I first moved into town."

"You own it? Is that why you didn't call me?"

"I told you I was busy."

"I don't know what to say..."

"Are you upset?"
"No, I mean, I'm sure you had your reasons. So what else do I need to know about you?"
"Um, well, let's see... you know that restaurant we went to when we just started hanging out again?"
"Let me guess, you own that too?"
"A fraction of it."
"So why did you lie about it all?"
"I needed to know you'd still be with me if you thought I was broke."
"Of course I would, I met you when you were poor."
"Yes, but money changes people. I needed to know if your feelings for me were still pure and this is the only way I knew how to do it."
"I guess I'm not one to talk, I did the same thing to you," she said with a smile.
"Yes, exactly, Ms. Brand-new-BMW-X5!"
Her eyes scanned the room, then eventually ended up on the ring on her finger.
"Oh, and don't lose that, that cost me a fortune."
"So this is where we're going to live?"
"It's up to you. I don't mind living downstairs in the one bedroom if that makes you more comfortable."
"No, that's okay, I think I could get used to this place."
"Don't get too cozy, I plan on building us a house. Well, I won't be building it of course, but I'll hire someone to build it."
"I don't know what to say, this all seems surreal."
"I'm really sorry I had to keep this from you. And don't worry about calling your parents and telling them the good news, they already know."

"They already know what?"

"I asked your father for permission to marry you and I assume he told your mother."

"Really, when did you talk to my dad?"

"A couple days ago. His firm actually represents Unity Inc. He couldn't tell you of course, you know, attorney-client privilege."

Ashley looked around again, this time something caught her eye. I spun around to see what she was looking at. It was a copy of Force Magazine, which was lying on my coffee table.

"Is that you on the cover?"

"Yes, it's not the best picture I know, but they were able to edit out a lot of my imperfections."

She read the title article aloud, "The Richest Under 30. Did you make the list?" she asked.

"Yes, but I'm not number one. They put me on the cover because of my recent and rapid success. In fact, I have to go to New York tomorrow for an interview with the American News Network. I'm going to appear on their program, In the World of Finance. Do you want to come with me?"

Epilogue

"Welcome back, everybody. I'm Mikayla Martens for In the World of Finance. If you are just joining us now, I'm speaking with the president, CEO, and founder of Unity Inc., Mr. Trevor Morrison. Before the break, I asked Mr. Morrison when all of his success began. So tell us, how did you go from rags to riches?

"Right, well, if you want to know when it began, then I would have to say it all started when I was born. That was probably not the answer you were looking for, but it's the truth. The amalgamation of my life experiences has led me to be where I am today. Even the terrible moments in my life contributed to the collective whole. I credit those times for building character, strength, and wisdom. I needed those moments just as much as the happy times. Without each piece of the puzzle, my life would have been drastically different. I would have made other choices, met different people, had different opportunities, and ultimately would have gone down a different path.

In terms of how I went from rags to riches, I think it came from my hustle – that is, my determination, my work ethic, and my ambition. But hustle is like an art, you can't simply plough through life with hard work and a dream, there are many subtleties that need to be enacted along the way."

"I'm sure there is a lot more to be said on that point. I guess we'll have to wait until you write a book about the art of the hustle."

"That's a good idea, maybe I'll do that."

"So, for someone who wants to follow in your footsteps, what advice would you give them in order to avoid some of the pitfalls you've experienced in your life?"

"Looking back at my journey now, I recognize one common thread. The worst times in my life resulted from when my options were limited. I made some wrong choices that led me to being in those types of positions. So, my advice is to avoid making decisions that don't leave you with many outs."

"Is this another poker analogy?"

"Sort of. This ties into what I was saying earlier about the art of the hustle - life is like a game and needs to be played as such. If you want to be successful, you must think several steps in advance. By doing so, not only will you be able to avoid certain pitfalls, but also you can act instead of react. You never want to be backed into a corner with limited options."

"Did you ever imagine your life would turn out to be like this?"

"No, not at all. Some ancient philosophers believed that things that are alike are attracted to each other. For instance, water flows toward the ocean, fire goes upward toward the sun, rocks on a beach are arranged according to size, and so on. Much like these things, I was always seeking my natural place. Ever since I was young, I felt a little different from the other kids – I didn't quite fit in. However, after many years of shuffling and sorting, I eventually found my place, among the elite few. Some people end up here by chance, but don't quite belong. For them, the universe continues to sort, and they eventually get shuffled out. But I feel this is my natural place."

"You make it sound like it was destiny."

"Yeah, I think about that a lot actually. As I mentioned to you earlier, everything in my life has played some role in getting me to where I am today. The decision to become a lawyer seemed very organic, in that I came up with the idea on my own. However, thinking back on it, it appears as if it was not just one decision, but rather a series of choices in a much larger process. It was as if there were a number of external forces that guided me along the way, pushing me in that direction. In the end, what choice did I really have?"

"So if you could travel back in time, what would you tell the eighteen year old you?"

"I wouldn't say a thing; I wouldn't want to change how my life has turned out."

"Can you describe the contrast between when you weren't so well off and your life now?"

"I'm the younger of two children so I would get a lot of hand-me-downs. The four of us were constantly moving around, living in tiny basement suites that always had huge spiders crawling around everything. We didn't own, we always rented, we didn't own a car, never went on vacation, cut coupons, and did just about every other money saving thing in the world just to scrape by. Today, I still live pretty minimally; in fact, I don't even own a car."

"So does money buy happiness?"

"You always hear rich people say money does not buy happiness, and to some extent that is true. However, money allows you to live a little more comfortably - you can go on vacation, eat well, and you don't have to worry about bills and so on. But I realized what is important in life. The most important things in the world are having meaningful relationships with people, setting and achieving your goals, and being healthy."

"What about having a lot of free time?"

"Time is only good if you have those other things I mentioned. Time to a starving man in the desert is torturous."

"I guess you're right. My next question is one I always ask my guests. I find the different answers fascinating so I will ask you the same thing - who do you admire?"

I chuckled a bit before I answered the question, but finally confessed. "The person whom I admire most and try to model my life around is Clark Kent."

"Superman?"

"Yes."

"That's interesting; I've never heard that one before."

"I don't mean for this to come across the wrong way, but I can relate to Superman in a lot of ways. The people around me didn't seem to understand me or didn't recognize my abilities. Clark Kent is unassuming, he fumbles around, and is constantly underestimated by the people around him - nobody expects him to be Superman. We both have issues with our birth parents not supporting us, we both want to find that one true love, and we both ultimately want to do good. Even now, with all the success I have had, I find parallels between us. Being a multi-billionaire is a lot like having super powers. It's something very few people can relate to or even comprehend. But the reason I say Clark Kent, and not Superman, is because he is a model human being. He always does the right thing. That's who I want to be."

"For someone who has achieved so much at such a young age, what's next for you, what are some goals you have set for yourself?"

"I want to have a long and happy marriage, raise wonderful children, and start a foundation that empowers underprivileged children and helps them realize their potential. Despite what I have accomplished, I'm still very young and I have a lot of goals. This is only the beginning."

Edward Mullen is a novelist, blogger, vlogger, and podcaster from Vancouver, Canada.

Born and raised in beautiful British Columbia, Edward developed a love for the wilderness. This love, combined with an innate curiosity about all things, eventually spawned a healthy imagination for storytelling.

Despite spending a lot of his time indoors writing, Edward continues to enjoy the outdoors. He is an avid tennis player, mountain biker, snowboarder, runner, and traveler.

For more information about Edward Mullen, such as his podcast, blog, vlog, or upcoming books, please visit:

www.EdwardMullen.com

The Art of the Hustle 2

The Art of the Hustle 2 is available in both digital and print. Here is the first chapter.

Chapter One

The young couple walked hand in hand through the Granville Island Public Market.

"Do you remember coming down here when we were first dating?"

"Yes of course," Ashley said. "Come on, my memory isn't that bad."

"They say when you get married, you unconsciously assign different compartments of information amongst your spouse. So one person may rely on the other person to remember all the important dates, and the other person might rely on the other for remembering all the phone numbers."

"When did you hear this?" she asked. "It must have been a while ago since nobody remembers phone numbers anymore. I don't know anyone's phone number."

"Yeah, me neither. I'm not sure when I heard about it. Probably a while ago. The article was about people getting divorced and suddenly half of all the stuff they know is gone because they were so reliant on that other person."

"I know we've only been married a year, but I don't think we rely on each other to remember things."

"Perhaps we live in a different era and that study no longer applies," Trevor said.

"Probably."

"My memory is so bad, that's why I post so much on social media. It's a way for me to catalogue my life."

"You do post a lot," she teased.

Located underneath the Granville Bridge, on the south side, The Public Market hosted an array of vendors selling everything from butchered meats, fresh seafood, fruit and vegetables, desserts, baked goods, and unique homemade products. Naturally, it was a popular destination for locals and tourists alike.

Music filled the air as street performers and buskers dazzled audiences who gathered to enjoy all that the Public Market had to offer. Trevor pulled out his phone and recorded a short video for his various social media accounts. Ashley kept moving, hoping Trevor would put his phone away and enjoy living in the moment with her.

"Don't let the deal of the decade pass you by. I got Gucci, Louis, Fendi, Prada. Get the brands you like for the prices you love…"

A small crowd gathered around a young kid as he appeared to be moving units. The entire time he kept flapping his lips, talking a mile a minute.

"Come on folks, get your authentic designer handbags for pennies on the dollar."

Trevor and Ashley stopped by to watch, but they remained at a distance.

"You looking to buy a stolen handbag for a discount?" Ashley asked. "I think you can afford the real thing."

"I know, I just wanted to listen to this kid's sales pitch. I used to be in sales, you know," Trevor said.

"Yes, that I remember! That's around the time when I met you."

"It wasn't that long ago when I was a little punk like this," Trevor paused. "He kind of reminds me of myself when I was his age."

"Did you ever sell stolen merchandize?"

"I sure did, but I'm not proud of those days. I did what I had to do to survive."

"You make it sound like you grew up in some ghetto. It's not like you were mining blood diamonds in Sierra Leone."

"I know, but we all have our adversities I suppose. Some more than others."

After spending some time at the market, checking out various shops, Trevor and Ashley sat on a bench overlooking the ocean. On the other side of the water was the large steel and glass high rises and the harbour, which had an impressive collection of yachts.

Just east of that was Yaletown, where Trevor and Ashley lived in their marina-side penthouse.

"You ever think about buying a yacht?" Ashley asked.

"Not really. For all the times we'll be on a boat, we may as well just rent one."

"Some things don't change, huh?" Ashley said.

"What do you mean?"

"You're a multi-billionaire and you're worried about money."

"It's not like I have a billion dollars in my bank account. I'm more asset rich. I also read this thing once which said, 'the second best day of a rich person's life is when they buy a yacht'."

"Okay, so what's the best day?"

"The day they sell it."

The couple continued to walk at an idle-like pace, soaking in the sun, sounds, and sights. Although Trevor was the public face of a global company, he didn't get recognized all that often. Still, he usually wore a hat and sunglasses to hang on to his anonymity.

"Excuse me, sir," a familiar voice said.

Trevor and Ashley turned around and saw the same kid who was selling fake handbags.

"I couldn't help but notice your lady's fine LV bag. Perhaps I could interest you in a matching wallet to go with it."

"No thanks," Trevor said.

"Okay-okay, handbags and wallets are not your thing. How about jewellery? I got Tiffany, Pomellato... this one is a custom piece," the kid said, handing Ashley an elegant necklace. "It's real, check it out."

Ashley didn't dismiss it right away. She accepted the necklace and started checking it out.

"Ashley, what are you doing?" Trevor asked.

"I don't know, I kind of like this," she said, checking it out. She held it up to her neck and modeled it for her man.

"That's a real nice piece," the kid said, sensing a sale. "But it won't last. Some other lady was eyeing it earlier. Said she would be back any minute to pick it up. One of a kind. Never find another one like that."

Trevor whispered in her ear, "He's using one of Cialdini's six principles of persuasion — scarcity. Don't fall for this psychologic trick."

"But I like it."

"Ashley, give that back. We can't be supporting criminal activity."

"There's no criminal activity going on here, sir," the kid said.

"Oh really, and where did you get the necklace and all these expensive handbags?"

"I cannot reveal my sources, but I assure you they were all acquired through purely legitimate means."

"Oh sure," Trevor said skeptically.

"How much do you want for the necklace?" Ashley asked.

"You look like nice people. I can give you a very special price today — one hundred dollars."

"Ashley, I can get you any necklace you want."

"Great. You can get me this one," she said in a loving tone.

"So a hundred bucks?"

"I'll give you twenty," Ashley said.

"Fifty."

"Deal."

Ashley pulled out three twenties from her wallet and handed it to the kid. "You know what, just keep the change."

"Pleasure doing business with you, ma'am. I don't suppose you want some earrings to match?"

"Okay, you made a sale, you happy?" Trevor said. "Now go away."

"Trevor!" Ashley said.

"What?"

"Be nice."

The kid looked no more than fifteen years old. A part of Trevor felt bad for him. "Look, I'm sorry for being rude to you. Perhaps there are better ways for you to make a living."

"Oh yeah, like what?"

"You're persistent, you talk a good game, you have hustle. That can take you far in this life. If you become a legitimate sales person you could make a lot more money than what you're doing now."

"Nah, I ain't about that life yo. If you're lucky you make, what... fifteen bucks an hour, and that's before tax. I can make twice that much doing this."

"Thirty dollars an hour. Wow. Good for you," Trevor said in a patronizing tone. "Tell me, what happens when you take a day off? How much money do you make then?"

The kid thought for a moment as if it were a trick question, but then finally answered, "Nothing."

"Exactly. If you sell your labour, then there's a limit to how much you can make in a day. But if you create something of value that people will want to buy, then the sky is the limit."

"Yo, thanks for the free advice."

Trevor and Ashley walked away and the kid went in the other direction.

"See, that was nice. You don't always have to be so mean. You were a punk kid once too. Imagine some snooty billionaire talking to you that way. How would that make you feel?"

"You think I'm snooty?"

"Maybe a little snooty, but you're my snooty."

Ashley pulled Trevor in for a hug and a kiss. They held each other tenderly for a moment before continuing on, holding hands. Ashley had a smile on her face as she was thoroughly enjoying the sunny weekend stroll with her husband.

"I didn't mean to be snooty," Trevor said. "I guess I just have an adverse reaction to being hustled."

"Didn't you invent the art of the hustle?"

"I guess so."

Ashley put on her new necklace. "Look, baby," she said, showing off her necklace. "Fifty dollars for a one of a kind Pomellato necklace."

"Sixty."

"Either way, it's a good deal. This would probably cost at least $5,000 in any store you're lucky enough to find it in. I think we hustled him."

"The kid probably didn't even know what he had."

Printed in Great Britain
by Amazon

16532966R00221